ROLLING THUNDER

A NOVEL

MARK MYNHEIR

Multnomah® Publishers *Sisters, Oregon*

ROLLING THUNDER
published by Multnomah Publishers, Inc.

© 2005 by Mark Mynheir

Cover image © Nonstock

Scripture quotations are from:
The Holy Bible, New International Version (NIV) © 1973, 1984
by International Bible Society,
used by permission of Zondervan Publishing House

Multnomah is a trademark of Multnomah Publishers, Inc.,
and is registered in the U.S. Patent and Trademark Office.
The colophon is a trademark of Multnomah Publishers, Inc.

Printed in the United States of America

ISBN: 0-7394-5522-2

Printed in the USA.

To the Lord Jesus Christ, who rescued me from my pit,
and to my wonderful wife, who teaches me daily
the true meaning of love and devotion.
Forever, my love.

I'd like to thank my agent, Les Stobbe, as well as Don Jacobson and the tremendous staff at Multnomah Publishers—especially my editor, Julee Schwarzburg, whose skilled eye and careful instruction made this project possible.

And to my mom, dad, and stepfather, who have been the best parents anyone could ask for. Thanks for all the encouragement and support.

1

It breaks my heart when a killer goes free." The corrections officer adjusted his gun belt around his plump waist. A buzzer echoed through the thick, overly painted walls of the hallway, and the huge brown door slid open on the railings, like a rock being rolled away from a tomb.

Frank Moore shuffled through the entrance into the administrative portion of the prison, a place he hadn't seen in thirty-three years. Stooped slightly at the waist and walking with a cane, Frank quickened his pace to the window that read "Property & Evidence." His new state-bought clothes barely clung to his emaciated body.

"You seem to be in a hurry, Frank." The officer chuckled with the two other guards who were escorting him. "Like you got someplace to go."

Frank pulled his inmate ID from his pocket, ignoring the pesky minder standing uncomfortably close behind him. A woman approached the window and took his ID and paperwork. With a quick scan of his processing forms and a raised eyebrow, she walked toward the back of the office without saying a word.

"What are you gonna do with yourself now that you've finally made it outta here?" the officer said loudly enough for everyone around to hear. "Maybe look for gainful employment?"

Frank tilted his head slightly, eyeing the man. "I got unfinished business."

"What kinda business could you have, old-timer?" The guard fiddled with his gun belt, which seemed to have a difficult time staying in place around his super-sized figure.

Frank turned and faced his heckler. Leaning toward him, he said, "The *unfinished* kind." His eyes burned with passion and fury, locked in a stare with the portly officer, who let out a nervous chuckle then looked toward the floor. Although Frank's once strong body was wrecked and weak, his spirit was vibrant and alive with anticipation.

The clerk returned to the window. She handed him a paper bag that contained everything he brought to prison with him— a black leather wallet; a pack of Wrigley's chewing gum, spearmint; and a baseball cap, the Mets.

She handed Frank a check from the state of Florida for eighteen hundred dollars—a paltry sum for thirty-three years, but it would be enough to get him where he needed to go and to finish what he needed to do. If everything went well, it wouldn't take that long anyway.

"Have you seen the warden?" She adjusted her glasses to read his checklist.

Frank nodded while tapping his gnarled fingers on the counter. As he waited for her review, he opened his wallet, exposing his driver's license, which had expired in 1971. His chipped and faded picture could still be made out. His coal-black hair from so many decades ago had now been replaced by gray wisps sparsely covering his head. His once rugged facial features had softened and drooped.

He closed his wallet and placed it in the small bag he carried. He knocked the dust off his Mets cap. Pushing back his errant strips of hair, he cinched the cap on his head, adjusting it for a snug fit.

"It looks like everything is in order, Mr. Moore." The clerk handed him his paperwork. "Good luck on the outside."

Frank snatched up his belongings and steadied himself with his cane.

"Well, old-timer, you ready?"

"Let's go," Frank said, already marching toward the only door standing between him and the world outside. The guard signaled the man in the control booth, and with one more sharp buzz, he pushed the stiff metal door open, holding it for Frank, who stopped just short of the threshold.

The midafternoon sun pierced the doorway, illuminating the darkened corridor, and a slight breeze wrapped around Frank. He bathed in it. The wind swirled around his creased, leather-worn face like soft, gentle fingers drawing him toward the world that awaited him. He had forgotten what wind felt like.

Breezes didn't blow inside the walls of Union, not even in the yard. But as rare as a breeze was, rarer still was a condemned man walking through that door. Home of Florida's death row, Union didn't give up its murderers easily. The likes of Ted Bundy, Gerald Stano, and countless other infamous killers were all carted out of Union feet first. Now Frank Moore was poised to do what few other murderers sentenced there had ever done.

With a deep breath and all the strength he could muster, the seventy-three-year-old man leaned forward and plunged into freedom.

"Good luck, old-timer," the guard said as the door slammed behind him. "You're gonna need it."

The free-flowing wind and unabated sunlight overwhelmed Frank, who rocked back in awe, lifting his hand over his eyes to see. The cascading sunshine on the dense swampland of Raiford replaced the gray cement walls and barbed wire that had served as Frank's horizon for more than three decades. Palm trees and saw grass were within reach, and a flock of egrets sailed just over the tree line. The low rumble of thunder in the distance signaled the coming of the afternoon rains that dominated Florida's summers.

He felt good, for the first time in a long time. But he didn't care about feeling good. If getting out of prison were his only goal, it would have been a great day. But that was just the first step. More urgent matters needed tending to if his plan was to work. There wasn't time to waste worrying about feeling good. He hurried toward a taxi already waiting in the parking lot.

The driver opened the door, and Frank didn't slow down as he slid onto the backseat.

"Where to?" the driver said as he jumped in the front and put the cab into gear.

"The bus station." Frank rested against the seat and closed his eyes. "Hurry." His jaw muscles wrenched back and forth as he groaned and clenched the small of his back, the pain throbbing rhythmically with every heartbeat. A crack of lightning forced his eyes open—a long-awaited expectancy filled him. Nothing short of death was going to stop him.

Maybe not even death.

2

THE GOVERNOR'S OFFICE, TALLAHASSEE

Satellite trucks and a horde of reporters were camped outside the governor's office as his motorcade rounded the corner. Once they saw him coming, the multitude flowed from the front lawn into the street, blocking two lanes of traffic. Three police motorcycles sliced their way through the reporters and led the governor's Lincoln toward the curb. The press enveloped the car before it even stopped.

"This isn't going to be fun," Governor Ronald "Mac" Maclartey said to his driver. A little over two years before, "Mac" had plowed into the governorship of Florida like a Mack truck. He promised sweeping reforms in all of the state agencies. He promised leaner, smarter government, and for the most part, he made good on those promises—until yesterday. That's when a reporter for the *Orlando Sentinel* broke the story that could put the brakes on any aspirations he had of being a two-term governor.

Dylan Jacobs. It was a name that in twenty-four short hours had become synonymous with bloated, ineffective—if not corrupt—government.

Dylan had been placed in foster care about six years before, and his tragic story was like so many others in state custody. His mother was a drug-addicted prostitute, and no one really knew who his father was. She couldn't attend to her own needs, much less those of a four-year-old boy, so Dylan was removed and placed into foster care. She died of an overdose not long after he was taken. Dylan had disappeared, lost in a sea of helpless, wounded children.

Mac had called for a grand jury investigation, but that would take time. The public wanted answers now. *He* wanted answers now. How could a four-year-old vanish from the state system without anyone noticing?

The former judge turned governor now had to face a problem he didn't create but was most certainly going to be held accountable for.

The media smothered his car, already barking questions before the governor could open the door. Three massive state troopers shoved their way through the mob, forcing the reporters back enough to open the car door.

The siege began. "Where is Dylan?... Who's responsible?... What are you going to do about it?"

Mac exited his Lincoln and held his hands up, hoping to silence the crowd. The state troopers held the hysterical mass of reporters back. Boom microphones dangled over the governor's head, and reporters pushed their tape recorders around and in between the troopers like weeds growing through a picket fence.

"Please...please move back," the governor pleaded, jostled a bit by the crowd. "I will give a formal statement as soon as I know all the facts. But until then, I'm just asking for a little patience."

"How long has Dylan been missing from foster care?" a reporter yelled as the others chimed in. "Do you think he's still alive?"

"I'll have a formal statement for you as soon as possible." He forced his trademark smile. "Thank you."

The officers formed a hedge around the governor and whisked him through the crowd, cutting a wake through the sea of reporters up the steps and into his office, where George Anez and David Lyman were waiting.

"Both of you, my office, now!" Mac stormed past his secretary, who was waving a fistful of messages. "Hold my calls. All of them."

George and David glanced at each other and shook their heads. David went in first; George followed with his head down, like a scolded puppy.

As a former prosecutor in Mac's courtroom, George had been a close friend of the governor for years. When Mac took over, the Department of Family Services was in shambles, and George was selected as director to lead that division, not because of their friendship, but because Mac knew he was a tenacious, get-it-done kind of guy. But more important, George had integrity. This newest dilemma piled onto the embarrassment of the already demoralized agency shrouded the director in shame like a burial cloth, from head to toe.

"How did this happen, George?" Mac marched behind his large, well-polished walnut desk; a lone laptop and a single lamp adorned the top.

David pulled a chair away from the wall and placed it on the Florida State seal embroidered on the rug covering nearly the entire center of the room.

George pulled a chair in front of the desk.

"Don't bother sitting down. You're not going to be here that long." Mac stood to the side of the window and stared at the media spectacle below. "How long? How long has he been missing?"

The question lingered without answer for enough time to give the governor opportunity to release a displeasing hiss. George finally said, "We don't know...we're not sure...yet."

Mac regarded the ceiling, then turned to George. "That's not the answer I'm looking for. We've got an Amber Alert issued, and every law enforcement agency in the state, if not the nation, is looking for him. We better know a lot more. And we better know soon."

"Yes, Governor." George stood in front of his desk like a schoolboy being chastised by the principal. "I understand how important this is."

"I truly hope so." Mac's gaze locked onto George. "Because this could mean both of our careers. I think you know what I'm talking about."

George nodded and then swallowed hard, as if choking down a shot glass full of sand.

"As you've already guessed, I'm turning the investigation over to FDLE," Mac said, shifting his attention back to David.

"With all due respect, Governor, my people can handle this. Give us a little more time. We'll uncover what happened and find this kid."

"Sorry, George." Mac closed his eyes and held his hand up. "It's gone way too far for that. FDLE has statewide law enforcement powers, and they're the only ones equipped to take on this kind of investigation. Besides, you'll be too busy cleaning up that mess of a department. And I want you and your people to give full access to David's team—all of the people and documents involved in this thing. I want complete cooperation. Do we understand each other?"

"Yes sir," he said, sweat beading on his forehead as he adjusted his glasses.

"That's all, George." Mac leaned forward with both hands on his desktop. "Now get it done."

George Anez vanished from the office in a flurry of purposed footsteps. Mac had been hard on him. Dylan's disappearance wasn't George's fault, but now wasn't the time or place to be cordial. They had spent enough time together that he knew George wouldn't take it personally.

David Lyman sat stoically in his chair, sliding back slightly as the governor turned his focus to him. Straightening his red power tie and crossing his legs, David exuded a quiet confidence that George lacked.

As the former chief of police for Miami PD, David was well accustomed to the treacherous political waters, although it was becoming increasingly clear that the pressure was certainly going to be turned up on him now. His salt-and-pepper hair was neatly combed, and he looked more like a TV anchorman than a seasoned police chief.

"This makes me sick," Mac said. "I want your top agents on this. I want every lead tracked down, every rock overturned. Plain and simple, I want this kid found—dead or alive. I want answers, David, and I want them now."

"I understand, sir. It'll be done today," he said, trying not to look upset about having this load dropped in his lap.

"That's all." Mac massaged his forehead. "You can go."

David, too, wasted no time leaving the office.

"One more thing," the governor called.

David poked his head back around the corner.

"Don't make us look bad. Everybody's watching on this."

"Yes sir." Then he was gone.

Mac plopped onto his chair and let out a deep sigh. These were the days he questioned his sanity for running for governor. His wife had pleaded with him for weeks not to even consider it. He'd spent enough years in service on the bench, making the kinds of life-or-death decisions that kept invading his sleep. She'd hoped for a peaceful retirement. Some travel. Maybe some quiet time alone with her husband. But he felt drawn to the position.

This case was more than just political expediency for him. The pictures of Dylan that had been on the news since the story broke haunted him. One picture in particular struck a nerve: Dylan was wearing a red-and-white-striped shirt and a giant smile. He bore a scar from his cleft lip, but other than that, he resembled Mac's own grandson, Nelson. The similarity disturbed him.

How could a small boy who looked so happy in his picture have met with some awful demise and nobody noticed? He felt sick to his stomach.

It was painfully obvious that Dylan Jacobs was not going away anytime soon—personally or professionally. He must have answers, if for no other reason than to be able to look at his grandson again with a clear conscience.

3

A police car and two unmarked units pulled up to a dilapidated house in an older section of Melbourne. Most of the homes along the street were built in the late fifties, early sixties, and were in varying stages of decay. This house was the worst on the block. Bottles and papers overflowed from trash cans spilling onto the driveway. The unmowed lawn crept well beyond its barriers, growing up through a faded plastic slide in the front yard like a malevolent spider engulfing its prey.

Two agents with the Florida Department of Law Enforcement exited the first unmarked car and were careful not to slam the doors. Being noticed too soon could be a bad thing.

Agent John Russell slipped his coat on and clipped a badge to his belt next to his holstered Glock 9mm. Reaching his arms above his head, he stretched his tall, muscular frame to chase the morning creaks from his bones. The forty-year-old investigator walked to the curb and scanned the house. He checked his clipboard, making sure his paperwork was in order, and brushed back his dark brown hair that was just sprouting some flecks of gray.

John's partner, Tim Porter, paused before getting out of the car.

"Need some help?" John offered his hand.

"Nah, I got it." With one hand on the roof and the other on the doorjamb, Tim hoisted his bulky body from the car. A little shorter than John, the black former Marine groaned and clutched his side, rubbing his hand along his protruding midsection. He met John on the sidewalk.

John felt odd about "training" his new partner. Over twenty years of police work behind him, most of that as a homicide detective, honed Tim's instincts; he could "read" a person before they ever spoke a word. After working a couple of cases with him, John wondered who was really training whom.

Two and a half years ago, a bank robber's bullet tore through Tim's abdomen, nearly ending his career. After being shot, Tim finished out his remaining two years and then retired from the Orlando police department. But retirement almost drove him crazy. Tim wasn't ready to give up on law enforcement yet, so he brought his skills to the FDLE. With a couple of deep gulps of air, he slid his paddle holster for his pistol inside his waistband and tugged it twice to make sure it was locked in.

John, too, understood the strange attraction of law enforcement. Since he was young, John felt God's pull in his life for some kind of service. Thinking God wanted him to go into the ministry, he went to seminary and earned his degree in theology with a minor in counseling.

But as he graduated and was ordained, something wasn't

quite right. He dismissed it as the jitters about receiving a call from his first congregation. Then he saw the job posting for a detective with the Florida Department of Law Enforcement. He knew then he would never be a pastor. Something deep in his spirit told him that this was his true calling. He was to be a cop. That was fifteen years ago.

John, Tim, and two officers from Melbourne PD huddled on the sidewalk. Jessica Tarrant from the Department of Family Services exited her car and carried a satchel full of paperwork to them. Wearing a suit and with her brunette hair pulled back in a tight bun, the twenty-something woman looked out of place for an early morning visit such as this. But she didn't have to do the rough stuff. Her only responsibility was to look after the children. She was already sweating, and the sun hadn't even cleared the trees.

"Thanks for your help." John shook her hand. After a few hasty introductions to the officers and Tim, John laid out the plan—Stacie Morris was coming with them, one way or another.

Once John was sure everyone understood, they snaked their way up the cluttered path toward the front door. The two officers took up the rear behind Tim, John, and Jessica.

"I hate this part of the job." John crept onto the porch, moving just off center of the door, one of the little habits he'd picked up through the years. Standing in front of a door—or "the fatal funnel"—was always a bad idea, especially if someone decided to shoot through it. "It's a shame. She's the best informant I've ever had."

"It's gotta be done." Tim peeked into the front window then jerked his head back. Jessica stayed at the bottom of the steps; the officers stood back from her, spread out on either side so they could cover the windows and corners of the house.

John knocked on the door. He could hear movement in the house, but no one came to the door. Standing on tiptoe, he glanced into the window at the top of the door but couldn't see through the grime. He shrugged at Tim and knocked again.

The door flung open, and a bony young woman greeted them. Her face instantly crinkled in confusion. Pasty white with dark circles under her eyes, she appeared to have just woken up. Her brown hair was stringy, matted, protruding in several different directions like a cat caught in the rain.

"Detective Russell." She scratched her head. "What's going on? Who are these people?"

"We've got to talk, Stacie. We're gonna need to come in."

"Excuse us, ma'am." Tim pushed the door wide open so everyone could enter without a problem.

John crossed the threshold and nearly retreated as the overpowering stench of soiled diapers and refuse assaulted his nostrils. The inside of the house made the outside look manicured. Papers, diapers, and fast-food wrappers littered the floor and couch. Dishes were heaped in the sink, mold dotting some of the plates like fat, furry caterpillars. He couldn't believe she was living like this, even worse, raising her children in this. His stomach churned and threatened to eject his breakfast on the already nasty floor.

"What's...what's happening, Mr. Russell?" She wiped her face with her hand as if it were numb. "I did everything the court said. I've been doin' real good."

"Your drug test came back. You tested positive for co-caine...again."

"That's not possible." She clamped her hands on the sides of her head, as if to keep it from exploding. "I haven't used in a long time, at least six months. The test has to be wrong."

She picked up her toddler, who was crawling through the

assorted debris on the floor and was in dire need of a diaper change; a three-year-old boy peered around the corner from a back bedroom, too frightened by the commotion to come out.

"Tests don't lie. Besides, I can take one look at you and tell you're using again."

"All right. All right. I used a couple of times last week." She turned her back to John and picked some papers off of the couch in a vain attempt to clean. "But I have it under control. I'm not using nearly as much as I used to. I can still take care of my babies."

"You knew the rules." John walked closer and looked her straight in the eyes. "The only reason we were able to keep you out of prison the first time was your promise to stay clean and to take care of your children. You're not doing either." The calm tone in his voice belied the anger brewing just under the surface. How could she do this to her own children? He would never understand child neglect and abuse. It made this part of his job much more difficult. He let his comments sink in, and it gave him time to compose himself.

"I testified and gave you everything you wanted. Why are you doing this to me?"

"I'm not doing anything to you. Look around, Stacie. You can't take care of yourself right now, much less your children." John was not in the mood for any more of her denials. Her drug habit was destroying both her and her children.

"I went to the judge for you, again, and pleaded with him to give you another chance. Thankfully, he agreed. You have two choices—come with us and go to rehab, or come with us and go to jail for violating your probation. Either way, you're coming with us. Only you can decide how. We have placement for your children in foster care until you get out—that is, if you choose rehab."

"No! No! You're not takin' my babies." She shook her head wildly and clenched her youngest to her breast. "You're not takin' them. I'm not going anywhere with you. This isn't fair."

One of the officers grabbed her arm to pry the baby away. "Give him to me, ma'am," he said, grunting. "Make it easy for everyone."

"No!" She backed into the corner of the room, squeezing her child tight.

The officer pushed a chair out of the way and went for her again.

John took hold of his arm. "It's okay. Give me a minute."

Reluctantly, the young cop relented as Stacie's wails pierced John's eardrums and his spirit.

"I love my babies," she said, hunching over. "You're not takin' em. I can handle this. I have everything under control."

The older child sprinted from the room and grabbed his mother's leg. Tim stood between the front door and her, blocking any idea of escape. The two officers backed off some and let John talk with her.

"I know you love your children," John said. "That's why you've got to let us help you."

He didn't want to do anything to make the situation worse. Even though she was drug-addicted and overwhelmed, she was still their mother. And no mother gives up her children easily. If she got violent, the four men in the room could certainly subdue her and wrench her children away from her, but at too high a cost for John. The children had already been through enough; they didn't need to witness that.

In the months leading up to this, he'd developed a good rapport with Stacie, trying his best to keep her off the drugs. He'd always been fair and understanding. He prayed she would remember that.

"This isn't the kind of life you want for your children. Or for yourself, either. But you've got to get back on your feet before you can be any good to your kids. You won't be any good to them in prison or on the streets...or worse."

She stood quietly, surrounded and backed into a corner, trembling.

"I've already got you a room at rehab," he said in a soft, soothing voice, his hands up. "I pulled a lot of strings for you. Now I'm going to help you through this. I promise. I've never lied to you, and you know that. I give you my word. When you're released from rehab, I'll help you restore your family and get back on your feet."

Her shoulders relaxed some.

"I know you want to do the right thing for your children," John said, praying that he was getting through to her. "Don't fight us on this, and I'll keep my word."

"I wanna do the right thing, but I'm scared. I don't want to lose them. I couldn't handle that."

"I know, Stacie. You're just gonna have to trust me."

John reached out and lifted the toddler away from his mother. He passed the boy to Tim, who hurried out of the kitchen toward the front door.

Stacie wiped the hair from her face and picked up the three-year-old. "Mama loves you," she said, trying to stay composed. "You're gonna stay with these nice people for a while, but I'm gonna be back real soon. I love you, baby."

She kissed the boy and handed him to John, who passed him to Jessica. As she left with the boy, Stacie darted after them.

John stepped in front of her, putting his hands on her shoulders. "Don't do it. They'll arrest you, and our whole plan will be shot. If you want to get your children back, you'll have to listen to me. Trust me. Let them go."

"I don't want to lose my babies, Mr. Russell." She let loose with a guttural cry that only a broken, defeated mother could give. She wrapped her arms around John and wept.

Shocked at first, he didn't know how to react. Then he lowered his hands slowly and held her for several minutes as she vented the agony of her shattered life.

One of the officers sighed and checked his watch. John ignored him and took his time, making sure she was ready to go with them. He gave her last-minute instructions and promised to meet up with her at the rehab center to check her progress and give her updates on her children. She hugged him again.

Calmed and more composed, Stacie went with the officer. She waved at John and Tim from the patrol car as she went by.

"You did a good thing back there." Tim slid into the driver's seat and buckled himself in. "I don't know if I would have had that kind of patience. Twenty years on the streets will ruin a man like that."

"I just try to help people. That's all." John took his coat off and loosened his tie. The whole ordeal drained him, and it was still early. He didn't know if he had anything left to tackle the rest of the day. "That's why I took this job, and it's the only reason I stay—to help people like her. She's a broken spirit. The drugs are only a symptom of that."

Tim pulled away from the curb and did a U-turn in the street, glancing back at Stacie's house. "You're not gonna get all Christian on me again, are you?"

"I might." John chuckled. "I just might."

"Well, at the risk of sounding like a heathen, I can't agree with you about her." Tim shook his head. "I don't buy that whole 'victim' thing. Bad decisions lead to bad consequences. It's that simple. The reality is, we can't help these people because most of them don't want to be helped. We try to do the right things and protect the kids, but that's all we can do. It's up to them to help themselves—and most don't or won't."

"We can help some people." John closed his eyes for a moment, thanking God for a peaceful end. "Maybe not all, but some. I like to think everyone we come in contact with is a little bit better off because of it—even if they don't realize it."

"I think I finally have you pegged, Russell." Tim smirked. "You're an idealist; that's what you are. John, the idealist."

"You say that like it's a bad thing."

"Not a bad thing," he said, shaking his head. "Only a misguided thing."

Frank jerked violently as the bus driver's voice boomed throughout the Greyhound. "We're pulling into the Melbourne station for those getting off here. For everyone else, we'll be leaving in twenty minutes. So take some time to freshen up if you need to."

He didn't know how long he'd been asleep, but it didn't really matter. He was where he needed to be. Frank snatched his bag from underneath his seat and stood, trying to force himself into the line getting off the bus. Everyone was moving a bit too slow for his liking.

He saw an opening and shuffled into the aisle. Cane in one hand and his bag in the other, he hobbled down the steps.

Still dazed from sleep, he balanced himself against a cement pillar outside the station. He never imagined a day when just sitting would take such a toll on him. He massaged the small of his back and groaned.

Reaching into his shirt pocket, he pulled out a small pill bottle. *Two should do.* He popped the pills into his mouth.

Many years had passed since he'd been to Melbourne. Back in the early sixties, he worked with a construction crew that traveled the state building houses. While working in Melbourne, he spent a couple nights in the county jail, courtesy of a drunken disorderly charge. A lot had changed since then. Had he not been told where he was, he would've never recognized the place.

Leaning against the pillar, he pulled a manila folder from his bag and scanned the various clippings and reports compiled through the years. It took twelve years and three different private investigators to find who he was looking for. Now did he have the strength to carry out his plan? At this point, he didn't have any other choice. He looked at the name on his report again—John Russell, 1443 Staten Place, Melbourne, Florida.

After a couple minutes of rest, he hobbled toward three cabs parked at the curb. Too much time, too much energy, and too much planning had gone into this to stop now.

Strength or no strength, pain or no pain, it was time to finish what he'd started.

4

L et's go, Brandon," John called from the dugout, clapping
his hands while panning the bench, trying to encourage
the rest of the players. "You can do it. Take your time."

He gave a thumbs-up to his son, who was pitching. The
eleven-year-old was sweating profusely under the torturous
Florida sun. Behind him, a ring of dark, pregnant clouds in the
distance rumbled toward the field like an elephant stampede in
the heavens.

John alternated his attention between the impending storm
and his son on the mound. He wiped his damp hands on the
sides of his shorts and checked his watch. *Please, God, just let us
finish this game and get outta here. I don't need this right now.* His
pulse quickened.

John focused as best he could on the game. Nine innings
of hard-fought baseball had come down to this: the best hitter
in the league at bat, one runner on second with two outs, and
winning by one run.

Brandon shook his right arm several times and gazed

toward his father for direction. John knew he was tired, but just a couple more pitches and this game could be over. He wasn't sure if coaching his son's team was the smartest thing to do. John worried that he might be too hard, or worse, too lenient on Brandon, who showed real talent but lacked confidence.

His wife, Marie, convinced him that coaching would be a good distraction from all the stress of work and give him more time to spend with Brandon. Once John started coaching, he was hooked.

Baseball had been a part of his life for as long as he could remember. He went to college on a baseball scholarship, and just when it looked like he was heading for a possible pro career, a rotator cuff injury put an end to ideas he entertained about the majors. He played a few years in the minors and then hung up his bat and glove for good, except for the occasional trip to the batting cages to blow off steam.

"Give'm the heat, Brandon!" Marie waved her arms up and down from the bleachers. Their youngest, Joshua, sat next to her with his mitt in hand. Marie was the team mother, in more ways than one. She not only made sure everyone knew when practices were, she also led the crowd in any number of cheers and waves throughout the games. "Whooo…go honey!"

John glanced back and smirked, breaking his tension for a moment. She'd promised she would try to tone it down. Since spraining her ankle in what she called a "slight tumble" down the bleachers, John encouraged her to remain seated and dial the volume down a couple of decibels—for her safety, if for no other reason. He bet her lunch she couldn't do it. If she kept this up, he would soon be dining at his favorite Chinese buffet.

Brandon settled back on the mound. Pulling the ball close to his chest, he eyed the blond batter, who'd already blasted a double and one home run on him. Bigger than most of the kids on both teams, Ryan Bennett, every pitcher in the league's nightmare, was poised and focused.

Winding up slow, Brandon let the pitch fly. The batter connected, launching the ball over John's dugout and into the parking lot. A throng of children chased the ball as it skipped through the lot, bouncing from car to car.

John looked back at Marie, then wiped the sweat from his brow, glad the kid didn't connect solid.

"Time out." John made a *T* with his hands as he walked toward the mound. Brandon's head sank as John approached.

"Boo, Coach, don't take him out," Marie yelled, her short black hair bouncing from side to side. "Boo."

"Dad, I can get this guy out," he said, not able to look his father in the eye.

"You've pitched a good game, son." John placed his hand on top of Brandon's head, forcing him to look up. "Your arm is tired. It's okay to let someone else finish up. There's no harm in that."

"I can do this, Dad. I know I can get him out."

John sized up the batter, who stood outside the batter's box working his swing. "You think you have something left?"

"Yeah, I think so."

"Don't try a fastball. Give him an inside curve."

"Thanks," Brandon said, beaming.

John took a couple steps off the mound, then turned and walked back. He placed his large hand on Brandon's shoulder. "I believe in you, son. No matter what."

Brandon nodded, smiled, then took the ball from his glove. He rotated his arm around again to loosen up.

"Good call, Coach." Marie applauded. "Good call. And might I say you're looking mighty fine today. Mighty fine!"

The crowd giggled with Marie, and John shook his head. It would definitely be Chinese.

Brandon pulled the ball close to his chest. The runner on second took a short lead. Brandon glanced back at him, then quickly turned forward toward the batter and let the pitch fly.

The batter dug in, then swung.

When he heard the *thwack,* John knew the game was over. The ball sailed carelessly over the fence with the gentle grace of a dove gliding onto a field.

Brandon slammed his glove to the ground and crossed his arms as Ryan jogged the bases and was greeted by his hysterical teammates at home plate.

John met Brandon on the mound and gave him a hug. "You pitched a good game. We'll get 'em in the play-offs."

Head down and shoulders slumped, Brandon walked with his father and the rest of the team to the dugout. John watched the menacing squall line that growled its sinister intent rolling toward the field. As he corralled the team into the dugout, he stretched his shirt collar away from the baseball-sized lump forming in his throat. *Lord, help me keep it together at least long enough to get everyone out of here.*

"Lift your heads up, boys, and keep 'em up," John ordered, clipboard in hand, taking purposeful breaths. "You played a great game today, and you should be very proud of yourselves...I am. The Braves are a good team, but we're going to get a second chance at them—"

Lightning cracked several hundred yards away. Leaping back, John dropped his clipboard and trembled. He ducked into the dugout.

"Coach Russell is afraid of the lightning!" The team catcher pointed at John. The other players laughed as John stood in the corner of the dugout, his eyes wide and wild.

Brandon reached over two of the players and thumped Matt Ferger on the side of the head. "Don't make fun of my dad.

He's not afraid of the lightning. He just doesn't like it, that's all."

Matt stroked his head, still smarting from Brandon's thump. "Okay, okay. I was just kidding."

"I'm not." Brandon's eyes narrowed at him.

"It's all right, boys," John said, regaining his composure but still scanning the distance. "Settle down. We'd probably better get going, before we all get drenched. See you at practice on Monday. Remember, hold your heads high. You played a great game."

John picked up his clipboard. He and Brandon met Marie and Joshua just outside the dugout. Joshua was dressed in the same uniform his brother wore, even the same number. He would do anything to emulate Brandon.

Lightning fractured the air again. John seized up, this time clenching his clipboard so hard he almost snapped it in two.

"It's all right, hon." Marie stroked his arm. "Get in the car. The boys and I will grab the equipment."

John could only nod. Jogging toward the van, he looked over his shoulder at the encroaching assault on his sanity. He jumped into the passenger seat.

Marie, Brandon, and Joshua picked up the rest of the bats and gloves as a curtain of drizzle covered the field. John leaned back in the seat, the hair on the back of his neck bristling. He closed his eyes, trying to relax, deliberately breathing slowly through his nose.

Lord, why did that have to happen in front of the kids? As if fighting this isn't hard enough already.

He paused and gnashed his teeth. "Forgive me, Lord." A twinge of guilt halted his complaints. He'd never blamed the Lord in the past for his condition, and he wouldn't start now. "Please help me get through this." As was his custom, he began reciting Psalm 23: "The Lord is my shepherd—"

The next salvo of thunder collided with his psyche, pummeling his meager defenses. John dug his nails into the armrest. His heart raced and sweat rolled unchallenged from his forehead. His breaths were short and sharp, his body rigid; the juggernaut of irrational fear and tortured emotions had seized control. The anxiety attack was in full swing.

"I hate this time of year," he whispered through clenched teeth.

"Tim, John, I need to see you both in here, pronto." Alan Cohen held his office door open. The special agent supervisor of the Melbourne office didn't have a cheerful tone.

Tim and John were preparing their morning coffee in the lounge area, just down the hall from their cubicle. John always thought that it would be nice to have a full office instead of side-by-side cubicles. But the setup was functional. He had any number of detectives right at his disposal, and it made for interesting conversation during the day.

"What did you do?" Tim dumped a load of sugar in his cup. "It sounds like you did something to get us both in trouble."

"Wasn't me." John shrugged. "I haven't made anyone mad recently."

"Suppose we better go see what he wants." Tim stirred his coffee. "He definitely doesn't sound happy."

Alan poked his head out the door. "I heard that. And for your information, I'm not happy. I've got the governor breathing down my neck. He's already called me twice today. That fails to make me happy." Alan popped back into his office like a prairie dog scurrying into its hole.

"The governor?" Tim grimaced at John and mimicked

Alan's facial expression, capturing the essence quite well. John tried not to laugh as they walked toward Alan's office. They took their seats in front of his desk.

Alan had a good build for his nearly fifty-year-old frame and worked out regularly to keep age and stress at bay. Most of his hair was a patchwork of gray and black and had retreated to the sides and back of his head. A thin, well-groomed beard of the same color along with wire-framed glasses gave him the distinguished appearance of a college professor.

In his twenty-five years with FDLE, he'd seen the good times and the bad. He was one of the lead investigators on the Gainesville student homicide case and was one of two detectives who interviewed and finally cracked the prime suspect—Danny Rolling. He received countless awards and accolades for that case, as well as an ulcer and a divorce.

Alan pulled a case file from his drawer. "Did either of you watch the news last night?"

John and Tim shrugged as they looked at each other; neither seemed quite sure where he was going.

"Dylan Jacobs." Alan tossed the file to the other side of his desk. "He's missing from the Department of Family Services foster care, and the governor took a real beating for it by the press. It's turning ugly quick."

John grabbed the thick file and opened to the first page, which contained a picture of a smiling four-year-old blond boy with a large scar on his lip. His face was jovial and bright, belying his circumstances.

"That's an old photo," Alan said. "Maybe six years old, as best as anyone can tell."

"How long has he been gone?" Tim asked.

"No one knows for sure. That's just one of the problems. Not only are we not sure how long he's been missing, we're not even sure which foster home he's missing from. The last records DFS has date back some six years ago when he was first placed with a foster family in the Fort Lauderdale area. After that, nothing."

"How's that possible?" John asked, still fixated on the boy's picture. "Don't they have records or a case agent who knows something about him? He can't just drop off the face of the planet."

"Well, that's why I'm talking with you two." Alan tipped his chair back and folded his hands over his stomach. "This has gone past the possibility of a records glitch or a misplaced file. The Fort Lauderdale regional DFS director, Cindy Sampson, thinks something criminal might have happened to Dylan. I spoke with her this morning, and she wants to meet with you two as soon as possible to turn over what she's uncovered. It doesn't look good. We might have a child homicide case on our hands."

"I was afraid you were going there," John said, his insides twisting at the thought.

"The governor has made this a priority. And make no bones about it, Mac really wants this thing solved quickly. You can put all of your other cases on hold until this one is finished. Whatever you need to make this work—overtime, travel pay, extra investigators—it's been approved."

It was a good time to catch this case. The baseball season was winding down, and John carried a pretty light caseload— a couple of bank frauds, a money laundering case that was going nowhere, and an officer-involved shooting from one of the local municipalities, for which he was just waiting on lab work results before he closed it out.

As he studied Dylan's picture, a peculiar feeling overtook him, as if the eyes of this small child called out to his spirit for help. Child cases of any kind were the hardest for John—and most other detectives—to work. He found it difficult to separate his feelings from his work, instinctively imagining his own children in whatever predicament he investigated. No matter how intriguing the case might be, these kinds of situations troubled his sleep. But that was a small price to pay if they could bring closure to the victims and families.

"John, you've been with the agency for fifteen years now, and there's no one here I respect more than you. If anyone can ferret out the truth, I know you can." Alan stood, retrieved a bottle of Maalox from a drawer, and sat on the edge of his desk. "That's why the governor and I have chosen you to lead this investigation. Tim will be your backup. The case is going to be on TV every night until we get some answers. A child missing from state care will draw national attention, so I'm going to need both of you at your best."

"We can get this done," Tim said, a confident smile crossing his broad, pronounced cheeks.

"We'll start right away." John glanced again at Dylan's picture. He truly looked like a normal, happy boy. The possibilities already whirled through his head. "We'll clear this thing up."

"I hope so." Alan slugged down a shot of Maalox straight from the bottle and wiped his mouth with his sleeve. "Or it could be a long, hot summer for all of us."

5

When John walked through the door, he knew something was up. The aroma of burning candles and an enticing meal permeated the house, and there was a peculiar silence that was foreign to his home.

Their two-story house vibrated with excitement when the boys were here. John usually walked into chaos. Joshua would often be storming a castle or doing battle with any number of foes, but he would always take time out to kiss his father, then resume the skirmish. Always smiling, happy, and full of energy, Joshua was a free spirit, much like Marie. He bore her dark hair and even smiled like her.

Brandon, the more sedate of the two, took more after John, prone to bouts of seriousness and intensity. John would often find him in the driveway smacking baseballs into the yard—at least most went into the yard. Two front windows fell victim to wayward Russell foul balls in the last year.

Sometimes Brandon could convince Joshua to fetch them for him, but Joshua would lose interest quickly and chase any number of insects on their three-acre property. Despite their opposite personalities, the boys were close and cared for each other.

John set his briefcase next to the front door and looked out a side window into the yard. Still no sign of the boys.

He drew in a deep, cleansing breath and appreciated the comfort that his home provided. Inheriting it from his parents when they passed away, John considered the house and property his oasis from the craziness of his work and the rest of the world. It was close enough to downtown Melbourne to be convenient to stores and his work, yet the surrounding woods gave the house the feeling of being far away from everything. He and the boys often walked the property and would fish in the small pond behind the house.

He heard a commotion in the kitchen, then Marie breezed into the living room.

"Honey," she said, startled. She adjusted her dress, as if she was modeling it for him. "I'm sorry. I didn't hear you come in."

"Where are the boys?" he said, finally noticing her black formal dress, which accentuated her slim, athletic figure. Something was definitely up. "What's going on?"

"You don't remember, do you?" She pouted, arms crossed.

His expression froze as his mind raced. His next response would be critical. She was dressed to go out. The children were gone. And he had no idea what she was talking about. He feigned a smile.

He was in big trouble.

"You don't remember." She stamped her foot slightly, looking at him as if he should know exactly what she was talking about.

He was in dangerous territory and didn't dare try to guess or, even worse, lie. He chose his only reasonable option—silence.

After an extended, uncomfortable delay, she said, "It's our anniversary."

Horror overtook him as if the angel of death just landed in his living room. As he struggled for answers, heat radiated off his face. How could he have forgotten? How could he have been so foolish? "Hey, wait a minute. Our anniversary is on November 19, not May 12."

"Gotcha." She laughed and clapped her hands. "You should have seen your face."

"That's not funny." He chased her around the dinner table. "Not funny at all. You nearly gave me a heart attack."

She squealed and kept the table between them as they did one lap around.

"Well, it's our anniversary of sorts." She placed her hands on the table. "It was sixteen years ago today that we met."

John did the math in his head. "Okay. So do we call a truce or what?"

"Truce, my handsome husband." She slid cautiously over and kissed him. "You've been working so much lately I just thought we needed a night together—alone." She wrapped her arms around him.

"So where are the boys?"

"They're staying with Kevin and Cheri." She grinned. "That means just you and me for dinner."

"So they're gone for the *entire* evening?"

"The entire evening."

"My day is beginning to look up," John said, eyebrows raised. "By the way, I forgive you for the dastardly trick you just pulled. That could be considered husband abuse. And I know a cop."

Marie kissed him again, still giggling about her charade. She showed John to his chair and then brought in the dinner—

grilled red snapper and homemade egg rolls, a Chinese concession for her rowdy game-day behavior yesterday.

They enjoyed their dinner and their time alone, which didn't happen as much as either wanted. John made it a point to spend quality time cultivating his marriage. He'd seen too many marriages crumble under the brutal stress and long hours of the job. Shouldering other peoples' problems and delving into the darkest areas of the human condition all day could take a toll on a person and certainly a marriage. He did his best to guard against it.

Even though they were spending a night away from the boys, their conversations always seemed to drift back to them. Talk of baseball and summer schedules filled the room.

After they finished eating, Marie took John by the hand, and they walked into the living room, where the huge stone fireplace's inviting warmth drew them close to it. Pictures of their family lined the wooden mantel. John took down the picture of his mother and father, who were in their eighties when the picture was taken. They were holding hands, obviously very much in love.

John dusted the picture with the corner of his shirt.

"I wish I could have met them." Marie slipped her arms around John from behind.

"You would have loved them. Everyone did."

"They had to be special." Marie squeezed him tight. "Any couple who would adopt a baby at their age had to be something. Our boys wear me out, and I'm not even forty yet. I can't imagine adopting a baby if we were in our sixties. They were some kinda brave."

"Yeah. Not a day goes by that I don't think about them. Dad was the godliest man I ever knew. Everything I know about Jesus and the Bible, he taught me. He lived the faith. I really miss them."

He set the picture back on the mantel, making sure it was positioned just right.

"When I was young and couldn't sleep, Mom would sit up with me and rub my forehead with a washcloth and sing hymns to me until I drifted off. Since they weren't able to have children of their own, when I came along, she spoiled me rotten. I could do no wrong in her eyes."

"Do you ever wonder about your biological parents?"

"Nope." John turned to face his wife.

The flicker of the fireplace danced in Marie's eyes, and he took notice of the subtle, sensual sway of her hips that called him even closer. She'd tried so hard to make this night special—and it was. The Lord had blessed him more than he deserved when He brought Marie into John's life.

He pulled her tight, brushed her hair back, and kissed her like they were newlyweds. She took his hand and led him to their bedroom, where they celebrated sixteen years of blessings.

6

DEPARTMENT OF FAMILY SERVICES,
FORT LAUDERDALE

"Thanks for coming," Cindy Sampson said as she shook hands with Tim, then John. "I know the Melbourne office is a bit of a drive." In her mid-fifties, the diminutive director of DFS would have been lucky to crest five feet tall. "Follow me." The intensity of her blazing red hair matched her fiery, determined pace as she turned and scooted down the hallway. Even with his long legs, John had a hard time keeping up with her. Tim didn't even try as he straggled behind.

She unlocked her office door and held it open. "I don't want to discuss all of this on the floor. It's difficult enough as it is."

"We understand," John said, checking out her office, which was well-kept and professional. The walls were covered with various degrees and training certificates. She held a master's degree in public administration from Rollins College. Two pictures of her with former Florida governors held prominent positions on the wall behind her desk. "We appreciate your meeting with us, Cindy. We'll need to ask some questions about what's happened."

"I'll tell you everything I know." She pulled a packet from her desk and handed it to John. "Unfortunately, it's not as much as I'd like."

John opened the small manila folder and started reading the page-long narrative as she sat behind her desk.

"It seems that Dylan Jacobs was placed in foster care after his mother, a known prostitute among other things, was arrested on a burglary and grand theft charge." Cindy folded her hands on her desk. "Dylan was living, if you can call it that, in a one-room apartment with her. She would take off for hours, sometimes days at a time, and leave him there alone to fend for himself. Some neighbors finally called it in. Dylan was removed and placed in foster care. We know that much for sure."

John checked the signature at the bottom of the report. "Who is this Ernie Chambers?"

"He was Dylan's first caseworker. As you can see, he documented his activity quite well and did a good job monitoring him. Ernie left the agency about six years ago to do consulting work. I was sad to see him go. He was a good caseworker and had a real heart for kids. After that, Dylan was reassigned to a new caseworker, one of the people out of our office here—Janet Parks. Ernie was back in town last week and came to visit me. He asked whatever happened to Dylan. I checked, and that's when all this started to come to light."

"What have you done up to this point?" John said, still scanning the file.

"I've sent two caseworkers to investigate Dylan's whereabouts and what might have happened. They have since come up empty. There's virtually no trace of him in our system or with any of our foster families. It's like he just vanished six years ago. We knew then it was a law enforcement matter. I contacted Director Anez and got the ball rolling. Somehow the *Orlando Sentinel* discovered what was going on. Now we have a first-class crisis."

"Is it possible that Dylan could have been returned to his mother, and it just wasn't documented?" Tim asked.

"Not likely. His mother died of an overdose shortly after Dylan was placed in foster care." Cindy leaned back and steepled her hands in front of her face. "I added a copy of the Fort Lauderdale police report of her death to your file. Dylan didn't have any other relatives…none that we could find anyway."

"Tragic. As if he didn't have enough problems as it is," John said. "Have you spoken with Janet Parks? Was she able to shed any light on this?"

Cindy was quiet for a moment, pressing her index fingers against her lips. "She called me yesterday out of the blue and told me she quit."

"She quit?" Tim said.

"Strange, isn't it?" A trace of sarcasm laced her voice. "I sat down a couple of days ago and asked her about Dylan's case. She gave me some very strange, inconsistent answers, finally saying she didn't remember anything about Dylan at all. Later that same night, the story appears on the news, and now she's gone. If I had a suspicious nature, I would think she had something to hide. Then she had the gall to ask me to box up her things, and she would call me with the address to send them to later."

"What did you tell her?" Tim asked.

"I told her to come and get her own stuff. I'm not about to send anything to her." She smirked. "Something's going on here, and I won't help her leave town."

"Smart move." John nodded. "Is all her stuff still here?"

"Absolutely. We haven't touched a thing. We knew you'd be coming."

"Excellent." John handed Tim Dylan's file. "Is there anything else you can think of?"

"Unfortunately, several things," she said, clicking into a different screen on her computer. "For starters, Dylan's case is nowhere in our system. That just doesn't happen. I've been the director of the Fort Lauderdale office for over eight years now, and we just don't lose things out of our computer. We have safeguards against that. I wouldn't even have a copy of Ernie's narrative if he hadn't faxed it to me yesterday. By some miracle, he kept copies of all his records. We have backups upon backups here, and I can't find Ernie's reports or Dylan's records in our system anywhere—except one area." She raised a sly eyebrow and tilted her head toward them.

"Where's that?" John asked.

"In Finance, of all places." She motioned for John and Tim to join her to view the computer. She rolled her chair out of the way, so they could see clearly. "Each child is issued a controlling number so we can coordinate everything about their care, monitoring, placement, services needed, and such."

"I understand." John leaned forward to read the reports.

"When I run Dylan's number, the only thing that comes up is a hit in the financial area, which is where the checks are made out for the foster-care families."

"What does that mean?" Tim asked.

"It means two things," she said, typing again. "First, someone got into our system and deleted all Dylan's information other than this. I'm not quite sure how that happened, because only supervisors are supposed to have access."

"And the second?" John asked.

"Someone is still cashing the checks for Dylan's care. The last one just over a week ago."

"That's interesting," Tim said. "Who are those checks made out to?"

"Jesse Lee and Linda Morgan. I've printed out the addresses listed on the checks for your file."

"Are they part of your foster family program?" John asked.

"Not at all. I don't know who these people are, and they're not in any of our case files."

"You should have been a detective," Tim said. "You're good. Real good."

"This is *my* office, Agent Porter. Everything that goes on here is my responsibility. I'm disgusted by this. It's going to be another black eye to the agency. We do good work here. We help people. And then something like this happens, and we're all painted as foolish and ineffective...if not criminal. If Janet had something to do with Dylan's disappearance or has been monkeying around with our system, I want her fried, skewered, and hung out to dry. I don't care what happens to me or how embarrassing this is. We need to find this child, and that's the only thing that matters."

"That's why we're here," John said. "Can we look at Janet's office, her files and such? Something there might be able to give us a start."

"It would be my pleasure." She shuffled around them and led John and Tim out the door and down the hall to a small set of cubicles.

Janet's name was on a placard pinned to the outside wall of her workspace. The entrance had no door. Her desk ran along three sides of her office with a computer in the center and various sticky notes pasted on it like a disastrous modern art collage. Manila file folders were piled all along the desktop, and a picture of Janet holding up a kitten was poised on her desk. If disarray was the office look she was going for, she nailed it.

"Wow," Tim said as they filed into her workspace. "I thought I was bad."

"Yeah," Cindy said. "I had to stay on her to keep her station organized, among other things."

"How was she as an employee?" John said.

"Marginal at best. She'd do just enough to get by but never pushed herself to go above and beyond. She was one I had to watch about cutting corners and not being thorough. But she never messed up enough to get in real trouble. It was like she was always walking that fine line. Truth be known, whatever the outcome, I'm really not sad to see her go."

"We'd like to go through some of her stuff here if that's okay?" John said.

"No problem. The case files, computer, and disks are all DFS property, so whatever you need to search is fine by me. I hope this can somehow help. I'll be in my office if you need anything else. I've got quite a bit to do myself." She hurried back down the hall.

John attempted to open a file drawer underneath the desk. It was stuck, stuffed full of files and papers. He tugged twice and the drawer rolled open. He thumbed through the case tabs, searching for any paperwork tied to the Dylan Jacobs case. Tim reviewed some of the folders on the desk. They worked for several minutes in silence.

"I don't get it."

"Get what, Tim?" John said while keeping his attention on the file he was reading.

"How does someone go to seminary and then become a cop? The two don't seem compatible; they're almost at odds.

Like, do you arrest a suspect and then go home and read the Bible in the original Hebrew and Greek? I mean, how does that work?"

John shifted his attention to Tim, surprised that he knew the original languages of the Bible. Many Christians didn't know that, much less professed unbelievers. "Restraining evil is certainly biblical. And at the risk of getting all 'Christian' again, it's just a matter of calling and service. It's hard to explain, but I feel that God has called me to serve in this way, to uphold justice and help whomever I come in contact with. He is a God of justice, you know."

"Maybe." Tim put one file down and picked up another. He paused for several moments, appearing to chew on the answer, and then peered at John out of the corner of his eye. "My father used to say the same thing. He was a Methodist minister."

"Really." John swung his chair around to face Tim. "I didn't know that."

"Oh yeah. My sister and I probably knew the Greek alphabet before we learned the English one."

"But you don't share your father's faith?"

"Nope. Not like he did anyway. The man was stalwart, a giant in his faith, and he stayed that way until the very end. He died with Scripture on his lips. I never really understood it. Too much wickedness and evil in this world for me. We never saw eye to eye on that, but I always loved and respected my pop. He was good to us, too."

"Sounds like your dad was a great man." John stacked the files into a neat pile. "He and my father, my adoptive father, would have probably gotten along real well. Dad was a missionary. I suppose that was one of the reasons I went to seminary. It just seemed natural and right. And the education has come in handy. I think my dad would have been proud to see me as a cop. He was like that. He would have just wanted me to follow God's will…wherever it led."

"I can't much imagine my pop out there enforcing the law. Now don't get me wrong, he could get excited and sometimes downright blistering in the pulpit. But I couldn't see him snatching someone up and tossing him in jail. When he laid hands on people, they got healed. When I lay hands on people, they get broken."

"The context *is* a little different, I suppose." John chuckled and scanned mountains of potential evidence. No way would they be able to get through it all today. "Well, with Mrs. Sampson's information, at least we have somewhere to start. We should box up this mess and take it back to our office."

"This case is starting to get a foul smell to it," Tim said.

"And that smell seems to be emanating from one Ms. Janet Parks."

7

Marie hoped she could outrun the storm. John sat in the passenger seat with his eyes closed, and Brandon and Joshua were in the back. Brandon just won his first midweek play-off game, pitching a two-hitter. Play by play, he and Joshua were reliving the game.

The storm battered the van back and forth. John was having a tough go of it. With each new round of thunder, he would twitch slightly in his seat. After the last strike, sweat pooled on his face.

Marie could tell when John's anxiety attacks were at their worst. If someone didn't know him, he or she would think John was just trying to sleep or get some rest. Marie, on the other hand, knew he was fighting to keep it together against a whirlwind of panic and stress, all colliding in his mind like a twister through a trailer park. She researched anxiety attacks and tried to encourage John to seek counseling, not something that sat well with him.

He told her that it was just his cross to bear, and he had learned through the years how to deal with them. John didn't need a counselor to tell him anything he didn't already know. He also didn't like anyone making a big deal about it, especially in front of the boys.

It sickened her that she couldn't be more help, couldn't provide him more relief than just driving when necessary or praying for him when the attacks were at their worst. Marie often wondered if it could be genetic, but since John was adopted, there was no way to know. But in the end, it didn't really matter. She loved him with all her heart, and he had etched out a beautiful life for them. It was just an oddity in the man she loved.

"We're home now, hon." She rubbed his shoulder. A wind gust rocked the van as they pulled into the driveway. Brandon and Josh bolted toward the house. John hurried to the back of the van and grabbed the bag of bats and gloves and slung it over his shoulder, just as lightning struck nearby.

John jumped, almost hitting his head on the open rear door.

A cab pulled up to John's house, and the brakes squeaked so loudly, they could be heard even through the storm. An old man opened the door and struggled to get his wallet out of his pocket.

"Wait for me here." He handed the cabbie an extra ten. "I might be back quickly."

"No problem." The cabbie took the money and crumpled it in his hand. "It's a slow day anyway. Take your time, Pops."

He put on his Mets cap and with a cane hobbled toward John and Marie, still in the driveway. A vicious storm cloud rolled in behind him.

Marie took John's arm and pointed to the man coming down the drive. "Can I help you?"

The man lifted his head and made eye contact with John, not saying a word. He walked a little closer, squinting, straining, as he sized up John from head to toe. He glanced down at a piece of paper he was carrying, then back up at John.

"Sir," John looked past the stranger to the impending storm, "can I help you?"

He shuffled closer and leaned toward John. "Frankie?" he said in a gruff, hollow voice that seemed to echo.

"I'm sorry." Marie tried desperately to get her umbrella open. "You must have the wrong address. There's no Frankie here."

The man checked his paper again and then drew his attention back to John. He stepped even closer, staring at John as if hypnotized by his face.

John shrugged at Marie. "Sir, I think you have the wrong house. Who are you looking for?"

He continued to search deep into John's blue eyes. He pointed at John, nearly touching John's nose with the tip of his finger. "Frankie," he said again, this time more confidently.

John perked up and dropped the bat bag. The voice and the name unlocked something deep in his spirit, something so deep, so terrible that he refused to believe it could be true. He cocked his head and gazed back at the man. Then realization beaned him like a line drive. It was the eyes—the cold-blue, sadistic, murderous eyes.

"No…it can't be." John staggered back, colliding with the van. His legs wobbled, searching for strength. "It can't be you. It's not possible…what? Nooo!"

"What's wrong?" Marie tried to grab John's arm as he slid across the back of the van.

"No." John snatched an aluminum bat from the bag. "You leave here now." John pointed the bat at Frank's head. "I want you off of my property!"

Marie grabbed John's shirt as he marched toward Frank, who backpedaled as fast as his tired legs could take him.

Stumbling over a root, Frank fell backward, hitting the ground hard on his back, knocking the wind out of him.

John sidestepped Marie and continued toward Frank, who covered his face with both arms to protect himself from the blow he thought was surely coming.

"Stop, John! For goodness sakes, don't!"

Frank lay helpless, his hands still protecting his face, his eyes wide open as he struggled for air.

With the rain hammering down, John hovered over the ex-con. A battle raged in his spirit as he struggled to regain his composure and not do to this man what every inch of John's flesh screamed for him to do. This man, this evil incarnate who had caused him more grief and agony than anyone alive, now lay at his feet, well within reach of his bat.

Fury bubbled up from a part of John's soul he thought he'd buried decades before. With his body quaking, he squeezed the bat so hard he thought he'd break it. He looked around at Marie and the boys, who were sprinting from the house toward the mêlée. He slowly lowered the bat to his side and took several steps back.

Marie, her mouth agape, stepped between the two. John glared at Frank, who gasped as the color returned to his face.

The taxi driver ran toward them from his cab. "I'm calling the police, you psycho." He lifted Frank off the ground. Placing Frank's arm over his shoulder, the cabbie put his arm around Frank's waist, supporting nearly all of his weight. "What kinda maniac attacks an old man? They're gonna lock you up, mister."

"I didn't hit him." John shook his head. "He fell down. Now get him off of my property!"

"Yeah. Yeah. Tell it to the cops when they get here, buddy."

"I don't want the police involved," Frank said, gasping and staggering, the cabbie holding firm. "I don't want the police involved at all. I need to speak with you, Frankie. There's not much time. We *must* talk."

John pointed the bat at him again. "Don't ever call me that." Marie put her hands on his chest, keeping distance between the two. "Don't ever call me that name from hell again."

The cabbie and Frank tottered together back toward the cab. "Come on. I'll get you away from this nutcase."

"I'm staying at the Riverside Motel." Frank leaned heavily on the cabbie as his legs were giving way. "I must see you. There's not much time."

"I will never meet with you! Never talk with you." John's body went taut as his eyes pierced the old man. "If you ever come here again, I'll kill you. Understand?"

"John!" Marie screamed. "Have you lost your mind? What are you doing?"

The cabbie eased Frank into the cab, then handed him his cane. He peeked over the top of the cab. "You need help, fella. If it were up to me, I'd have you put in jail for that. You're a lunatic."

"Who was that? What just happened?" Marie rattled off, her hands still on John's chest, which pounded like an out-of-control war drum.

Brandon and Joshua were crying, horrified looks covering their faces. "Dad, what did he do?" Brandon said. "What happened?"

John fell back against the van, his arms limp at his sides, and the bat tumbled to the ground. He stared off into the distance, under the spell of some distant, tormenting memory.

He jogged toward the house, then picked up speed as he got closer to the door. By the time he opened it, he was at a full sprint up the stairs.

"John, talk to me." Marie followed him up the steps into their home. "What's happening?"

He ran to their bedroom and slammed the door. Right on his heels, Marie opened the door and met him in the middle of their room.

"I'm scared. The boys are terrified," she said, panting, trying to regain her composure. "Who was that man?"

Thunder exploded and the sky lit up as their home quaked. John shrieked and clenched the sides of his head. "Lord, it can't be him. This has to be a nightmare. It *cannot* be him. God, how could You let him come back?"

Marie reached for his arm. He jerked away. Pacing toward the window, he looked out as the rain now covered everything outside. He trembled so violently it felt as if he were being electrocuted, and his shirt was ripped from where Marie had pulled him away.

"John, talk to me, please." Tears flowed freely down her face. "Who was that man? Why did he call you Frankie?"

John scanned the front yard like a scared rabbit, then turned to Marie. "He's…he's…my father." He convulsed at the words and doubled over as if he'd been impaled by a dull sword.

"Your father? But that's impossible. How would he know? How would you?"

Another clap of thunder rattled their home, and John shuddered uncontrollably. As he clenched his chest with both hands, his face turned hot, then cold. Struggling for air, he wobbled back against their nightstand, knocking it over. His knees gave way, and Marie caught him just before he hit the floor.

"Oh no, please, Lord, no." Marie held John's head off the floor. "Brandon, call 911. Hurry!"

"Jesus help us." She prayed with John's head in her hands. "Please help us."

8

John breezed by Tim, who'd just come out of the break room with a fragrant cup of coffee pressed against his lips. The honeycomb of cubicles and work spaces around them were buzzing with computers firing up and detectives scurrying about, toting files, and making appointments.

"Morning," Tim said, automatically. He twisted back around, spilling the coffee on his hands and the carpet, narrowly missing his shirt. "I mean, what are you doing here? You're supposed to be home, resting." He licked the coffee from his fingers.

"We've got work to do." John picked up his coffee cup from his desk and hurried past Tim, not looking him in the eyes. The case wouldn't wait for him, and he really felt…okay, anyway. At least well enough to get through the day with the aid of a quickly induced caffeine boost. "Besides, I'm feeling fine." He flashed a synthetic, I'm-trying-to-convince-you smile to Tim.

"Well, partner, you don't look so fine. As a matter of fact you look like, well…" Tim scanned John from head to toe, then shook his head. "Let's just say, you don't look good."

John's clothes were wrinkled, and his hair looked as if it had been combed with a rake. But it was his face that showed the wear of the previous night. Drawn and pale, it was obvious that sleep had eluded him. Why did he even attempt pleasantries with another cop? Tim saw right through him. What would John tell them? How much did they already know? He just wanted to move on, get through the day, and not think about the night before. If he could accomplish that, his day would be successful.

Alan Cohen walked around the corner. "What are you doing here, Russell? You look terrible."

John sighed and threw up his hands. "It was just…it was nothing. The test showed nothing. Other than four wasted hours in the emergency room, I'll survive."

"Glad to hear it." Alan tilted his head and regarded John. He didn't fool his boss either. Some days he hated working with other cops. "You're sure everything's all right?"

Gloria Davis strolled into the room carrying a stack of freshly printed reports. In her early sixties with gray-and-black-streaked hair and a figure that betrayed her age, she brought some desperately needed elegance to the office. The mother-henish secretary watched over the agents, demanding they check in and out on the whiteboard that listed their exact locations and that they carry their radios with them at all times.

She was responsible for the décor as well. Several agents complained to Alan that the office had more floral arrangements than the rain forest. Alan was wise enough to dismiss the complaints and let Gloria tend to her business.

"Marie left a message that you wouldn't be in today. You look terrible." She straightened his collar and adjusted his tie.

"So I've heard." John peered at his coworkers over his cup

as he raised the brew to his lips. "That seems to be the prevailing theme around here this morning."

"John Russell, you need to get yourself home and let your wife pamper you until you're feeling better." Gloria stared at him straight in the eye. "Don't let me catch you back here until you're fit to work. Do you understand me?"

"We've got a missing boy to find, and I don't have to look good to do that."

"Yeah, but it sure helps." Tim smirked as he sipped his brew. With his free hand, he dug in his pocket and pulled out a small message slip. "This should put some pep in your step." Tim held it up for John to read.

"What's that?"

"Only the current address and phone number of one Janet Parks, suspect extraordinaire." Tim's smirk transitioned into a full grin. "And I think she needs a visit."

"How'd you find her so fast? Last info we had, she dropped off the face of the planet."

"Let's just say I have low friends in high places," Tim said. "Are you ready to go?"

"This is it right here." The brakes on Tim's mid-'90s unmarked car squealed as they pulled up to the apartment complex. The car was unmarked only inasmuch as it didn't have a light bar on top and a police logo on the sides. But the retired Florida highway patrol car still screamed of "cop." In some neighborhoods, it was cause to run when they drove around the corner.

But this wasn't one of those neighborhoods. The mostly middle-class family apartment complex bustled with activity. Several children still too young for school swung on a swing set between the buildings while two mothers kept watch nearby. Cars passed to and fro through the parking lot toward the main highway as the complex bloomed in the early morning sun.

They parked in a spot just in front of Janet's building. The two-story complex was new, part of the massive building around the new mall in Fort Pierce. There was nothing outstanding about the location or area—a perfect place to blend in and hide.

"Let me see the file." John eyed the second-story apartment and made a hurried plan for their approach. "Janet Parks. White female, thirty-four years of age. Bachelor's degree in business. No criminal history."

"You know, the chances of her talking to us are slim." Tim slid his holster underneath his belt, securely strapping his 9mm to his hip.

"I know, but we don't have much choice. She could have been the last person to see Dylan." John thumbed through several sheets while shaking his head. "It doesn't make any sense. If she didn't have anything to hide, why did she up and quit? And where's all the missing paperwork? Dylan's file and such? The whole thing is weird."

"Maybe she's simply incompetent, got scared, and took off." Tim slipped his radio into the front pocket of his jacket.

"Possibly. That could be a good angle to use with her." John closed the file. "Since we don't have anything to do with her job, she might be willing to talk with us…if her only crime is incompetence. We have a lot of questions, and only one person who can answer them."

"And she's right up there." Tim pointed to her apartment.

Both men climbed out of the car and checked the parking lot. They slung their coats on. As they walked toward the stairs,

Tim wrote down several car tag numbers from the parking lot. Tiptoeing up the steps, they were soon at her door. Tim stood on the left side, John on the right.

Tim pressed his ear to the door. After a few moments, he looked at John and shrugged, indicating that he couldn't hear anything.

Tim raised his hand to knock when the door swung open. The woman standing in the doorway screamed. Tim screamed. She slammed the door.

"FDLE," John blurted out, holding his badge up to the peephole. "Janet, we're with the Florida Department of Law Enforcement. We just need to speak with you for a moment."

"I'm calling the police."

"We are the police. We didn't mean to scare you. We just need a moment of your time."

John's request was met with silence. Then finally, "Show me your badge again. I want to see both your badges."

Tim held his up as well, and the two stood in the hallway with their arms extended.

"Are you sure you aren't reporters?"

"Well, we weren't when we left the office this morning." Tim chuckled. "We're agents with FDLE, Janet, and we need to talk with you."

She unlocked the door and cracked it open, exposing a less-startled expression than the one that greeted them earlier. "What do you want?"

"We'd like to talk, ma'am." John could still read the apprehension on the slice of her face that was visible. He waited a couple of seconds to let it sink in. "Can we come in for a moment? We won't be long."

She hesitated and scowled, then opened the door. "I only have a minute."

"We've come to talk about Dylan," John said as he crossed the threshold.

"I figured that much." Janet wore a knee-length navy blue dress; her strawberry blond hair hung just above her shoulders. She was a slender woman, and her features were sharp, hard, and cold, like an ice sculpture. "I've seen the coverage on the news. I thought you might be reporters. By the way, how did you find me so quickly? I've only been here a couple of days."

"We're detectives, ma'am." Tim studied the room, not even looking her way. "We detect."

John noticed her earrings and necklace were small and ordinary. She was wearing high heels. It was too early in the morning for a date; her look was wrong for that anyway, much too bland. She looked more professional than personal. Her briefcase was next to the door. He figured she had a job interview.

"Got someplace to go this morning?" John surveyed the tiny, cluttered apartment. Unopened boxes lined the walls, stacked nearly to the windows. A pile of clothes still on hangers dominated the center of the living room, and dishes with wrapping paper on them were stacked on the counter in the small kitchen area.

"Yes." Crossing her arms and pursing her lips, she sighed and kept time with her foot to an angry, impatient rhythm.

"I know you didn't have much to say to your supervisor," John said. "But we don't have anything to do with your job or what procedures were or weren't followed. We don't care about that. Anything you can do to help would be appreciated. All we want to do is find Dylan."

Janet stood, seemingly frozen in her position like a store mannequin modeling the latest in frumpy women's wear. An awkward silence filled the room as both Tim and John expected her to respond. She didn't.

"Look, if you point us in the right direction, maybe we could help you with your troubles." John grinned and worked for a friendly, caring look. She was making it tough.

Janet's expression changed slightly from tight-lipped to a wry Cheshire-cat smirk. "I'm sure that's *all* you're concerned about. But like I told my boss, their investigators, and now you, I have nothing to say. And I want my attorney. That's my right. I'm sure you know that because you're *detectives*." She glared at Tim. "Why don't you go out, detect, and find that boy—like you found me."

"*That boy* has a name." John pulled a picture from his file and held it so close to her face that he was sure she could smell the ink. "His name is Dylan Jacobs. Remember him? Dylan was your responsibility, and now he's missing. Doesn't that bother you in the least?"

"You bother me, Detective," she hissed, pointing to the front door with her chin. "Both of you need to leave right now, or I'm calling my attorney." She darted into the kitchen and seized her cell phone. With a sneer, she held it up as if it were a sword and put her thumb on the keypad, ready to dial.

"We're going to find him with or without your help." John's pulse rose with each syllable. "And when we do, we're going to see where you shake out in all this."

"You think I had something to do with that boy's disappearance?"

"I think you had something to do with *Dylan's* disappearance."

"Prove it!"

"You can bet on that," John said as he and Tim walked toward the door.

"Tell your attorney we said hello." Tim smirked as he passed her. "And we'll see you both real soon."

As they got into the car, Tim slammed the door extra hard. "Oh, that lady makes me mad. And I use the term *lady* loosely. I hope we get to lock her up." Tim started the car and jammed it into reverse. "Promise me one thing."

"What's that?"

"When we get to arrest her, I wanna be the one to put the cuffs on."

"Don't let her get under your skin, Porter. Besides, we learned a lot talking with her."

"She didn't say anything."

"Yeah, but it's what she didn't say that's important." John smiled. "She never denied any involvement. She never claimed her innocence. That tells us we could be on the right track."

"True," Tim said. "But it would be nice to have a little more to go on."

"We will most definitely determine what happened, find Dylan, and if she had anything to do with it, lock her up. I can guarantee that."

"How can you be so sure?" Tim asked, still stewing.

"Because the most committed wins."

Tim nodded and glanced at John from the corner of his eye. "By the way, you're not going to tell anyone about my little scream back there, are you? Janet did surprise me, you know."

"No." John shook his head. "I won't tell anyone you screamed like a little girl when she flung the door open."

"You're a good egg," Tim said.

"But...I can't guarantee it won't end up on department e-mail before lunch."

"That's not right, man." Tim crossed his arms and scowled at his partner. "That's just not right."

9

Marie watched the lights from John's car pass across the front of their house as he turned from the main highway onto their driveway. The crunch of the rocks underneath the tires resonated through the night like the roar of the ocean during a storm, breaking the unusual silence of their home.

Perched on the couch with her legs curled tightly beneath her, Marie clutched a pillow close to her breast as she lingered in the dark corner of the room. John's keys danced at the door, announcing his arrival. He skulked in and eased the door shut without a sound.

"Why did you sneak out this morning?"

John stepped back against the wall. "Oh...you scared me." With his coat folded over his arm, John did not attempt to move any closer. "I didn't see you over there."

"Why did you sneak out?" she asked again, still coiled into herself. "I woke up, and you were gone."

"I didn't want to disturb you." He folded his arms across his stomach. "It was early, and you needed your sleep. Are the boys awake?"

"It's eleven o'clock. You know they're asleep. Why didn't you answer your phone or pages? I've been outta my mind all day."

"It's been a long day, hon." John exhaled loud and long. "I really don't want to get into this now."

Marie rested her feet on the floor. She clasped the pillow snug in her lap and leaned forward, squeezing the life out of it. "So now we're just going to pretend yesterday never happened, right? Pretend you weren't going to kill that man last night? That you didn't spend the whole evening in the emergency room with us thinking you were going to die?" She tried to control the anguish in her trembling voice. "And we'll pretend that you haven't lied to me for our entire marriage."

John rocked back. She knew her last comment stung in a way that only well-placed truth can. Her stomach churned as she struggled to control the sea of emotions ebbing and flowing inside her. She wanted to let loose with a tirade of angry jabs and a hundred whys. She also wanted to run and hold him, never letting go. But most of all, she wanted to know the truth—good, bad, whatever. She wanted to know, to understand.

But the image of John's pale, overwhelmed face in her hands the night before haunted her like an oppressive, recurring nightmare. She knew how John acted when pushed. He wouldn't fight and get it out in the open like she wanted. When he was upset, he withdrew, pulling into himself, unwilling to discuss anything. He'd close her off until he was ready, in his own time, to talk about it.

This wasn't the usual argument about disciplining the boys, or how to spend their money, or mildly hurt feelings. This struck at the core of their relationship—who they were, or who she thought they were.

The only thing she knew about the man who came to their home was that he was John's father. When she questioned him further, John had another anxiety attack and couldn't, or wouldn't, answer. For him to lash out with such rage, there had to be much more to the story.

Although she wanted to know everything, she would have to wait and be patient—not one of her strongest attributes. She'd hoped that, after his hospital stay, they could calmly talk about what happened and why John led her to believe all those years that he never knew his biological parents. None of it made sense. *Lord, help me to know what to say...please.*

They faced each other in the dark, waiting for someone to break the excruciating stillness. Marie could see only the outline of her husband along the white wall he stood against. She couldn't make out his face or read his expressions. Only the dim, vaguely familiar sketch of the man she loved.

"So you were named Frankie?" Marie asked, calmer, less accusing.

"Don't ever say that name in this house again." John stepped out from the shadows. "My name is *John Russell.* I took the name of my *real* father, the man who loved me and raised me as his own. That other man, that monster whose name I won't even speak, means nothing to me. He's as evil as they come, and he has no part in our lives. The rest is the past— dead and buried, never to be dug up again. And that's the way it's going to stay. Besides, this has nothing to do with you or the boys. This is my problem."

"Nothing to do with us?" She rose and walked closer to him. "How can you say that? Whether you like it or not, this man has come to *our* home, disrupted *our* lives, and obviously hurt you. That has everything to do with us."

"Not anymore. I'm fine. I'll talk with the boys. They'll understand. And he's never coming back here."

"Why are you so angry with him?" Her voice shuddered. "John, I'm really trying here, but you have to help me understand because I'm lost in all this."

Marie's questions were greeted with silence. For the first time, she was glad the room was still dark. John squirmed, shuffled, and twisted his head in a manner that told her it pained him to consider each question—something she wouldn't enjoy seeing clearly.

"What does he want from you…from us? Why has he been out of your life for so long? Did he abandon you? What did he do to make you hate him so?"

John tugged at his tie and pulled it over his head. He fought with his top button and pinched at it, working it back and forth, finally opening it wide. He forced back his shirt and drew glutinous gulps of air. "He's been in prison."

"Prison? I…I…" Marie didn't know what to say. The last day was turning into a bizarre dream, a nightmarish vision of someone else's life, not hers and John's. "What did he do?"

John wobbled at the question like a boxer who didn't see the last punch. He took hold of the railing at the bottom of the stairs to steady himself. Marie prayed she hadn't pushed too much, but she needed to know.

"It doesn't matter now. It was a long time ago." He tossed his jacket over the railing, with no concern for its position, and piled his tie on top of it. "I thought he was dead. I hoped and prayed that he was. And as far as I'm concerned, he is dead."

"He said he needed to talk with you." Marie dropped her arms and dangled the pillow at her side. "What if he does come back? What then?"

After taking a deep breath, John's body stiffened, as if the anger had inflated inside him like some tight, seething balloon. "I can't promise what will happen. I don't know if I could control myself. You better pray he doesn't."

"I've prayed a lot today. That's practically all I've done."

Staying quiet, he exhaled and propped himself against the wall, his head lowered a tad.

"He didn't seem like he was here to cause trouble." She shrugged. "He looked too frail for that anyway."

"Drop it, Marie." John pushed off the wall and stood erect again. "He's unspeakably evil. He's not welcome on this property. And there's to be no more talk of him. I told you, he's dead to me."

"I just don't know why he's come to see you after all these years, that's all. It didn't look like he was trying to hurt you."

"He's already hurt me, and everyone else he's ever known, more than you could ever imagine. Now there's nothing more to talk about."

John turned and ascended the stairs toward their bedroom. Marie's arms were wide open at the bottom of the steps. "What was he in prison for? At least tell me that."

John halted on the stairs but refused to face her. The light from the hallway cast an elongated and distorted shadow of John down the stairs to where Marie stood.

"He murdered my mother."

10

Marie jogged to answer the doorbell for her expected guest. She swung the door open and threw her arms around her friend.

"I came as soon as I could." Cheri Phillips squeezed Marie long and hard. Cheri's husband, Kevin, served as John and Marie's pastor at United Bible Fellowship. From the moment they met four years before, Cheri and Marie had instantly connected, soon becoming best friends. They felt more like sisters than friends.

Cheri and Kevin had two girls and a boy around Brandon's and Joshua's ages. They would often get together for cookouts and play days.

With boundless energy and an irrepressible smile, Cheri seemed born for the role of a pastor's wife. Her mercy knew no limits, and she had the rare ability to be genuine no matter what the circumstance. John referred to Cheri as a "perpetual hugging machine."

A little shorter and heavier than Marie, Cheri kept her dirty blond hair braided down to the small of her back. Except for

Sundays, she would only be seen in blue jeans and a casual shirt.

"I'm sorry John didn't want to see you and Kevin at the hospital," Marie said. "I think he was more embarrassed than anything else. He's never had an episode that severe. I really thought he was having a heart attack or something."

"It's okay. Neither Kevin nor I took offense. We just wanted you both to know we were there for you."

"I appreciate that more than you know."

"How'd it go yesterday? Is John doing all right now?"

"*All right* is a relative term." Marie shrugged. "He finally came home around eleven last night. I can't believe he didn't call. He's never done anything like that before."

"I'm sorry, Marie. Did he tell you about his father or whoever that was?"

Marie lowered her head as the two walked toward the kitchen. "Yeah. Maybe more than I wanted to know. It's worse than I thought."

"How so?"

"You might want to sit," Marie said. "Do you want some coffee?"

"Sure. Cream and sugar. The usual."

Marie rose to her tiptoes to reach the sugar from a shelf in the pantry. Cheri took her seat at the counter that separated the kitchen from the dining nook. After preparing the coffee, Marie slid a cup over to Cheri then took a seat next to her.

"John finally told me a little more last night. It wasn't painless, of course. I swear, sometimes I think it would be easier to extract information from a terrorist than to get my husband to talk about what's going on inside him."

"I'm with you there." Cheri passed the cup underneath her nose several times, savoring the French vanilla aroma. "Kevin's idea of opening up emotionally is getting teary eyed when the national anthem is played at the Daytona 500."

They shared a much-needed laugh. Marie sipped her brew and placed it gently back on the counter, contemplating how to deliver the news. The direct way was best. "His father has been in prison all this time." Marie checked Cheri's reaction. Just speaking the words made her squirm.

"No wonder he didn't tell you anything."

"It gets better…I mean worse," Marie said.

"It can get worse?"

"Much. He was in prison for murdering John's mother."

Cheri's mouth fell open and her eyes widened at the revelation. She clasped Marie's hand. "Oh, girl, y'all need some prayer."

"We really do. I have to admit, I'm floundering here. I can't imagine what John must have gone through, the pain of dealing with all of this as a child. I'm trying to understand and reconcile that. But what I can't understand is, what is so wrong with our relationship that he couldn't trust me with that part of his life? Why did he work so hard to hide this from me? What did he think I would do or say? I love him. Nothing is going to change that."

"I know. Maybe he just needs some time."

Marie nodded. "We really do need the prayer."

Cheri pulled closer to Marie and held her as they appealed to the Lord together. As she said Amen, Marie opened her eyes with a refreshed sense of purpose. For the first time in several days, she knew what she had to do.

11

"How do you want to approach this, John?" Tim asked as they turned onto the dirt road that would take them into the most rural area of Broward County. The morning sun flickered and winked off of the trailers strewn along the bumpy, ill-kept road that led to the newest residence of Jesse Lee and Linda Morgan.

"Let's start off slow and see what they have to say. If it all goes well, whatever they say will work in our favor. Just follow my lead."

"Sounds like a plan."

John examined the face of Jesse Lee Morgan from a booking photo at the front of the case file. He knew all too well that sometimes a person's looks could surprise you. That wasn't the case with Jesse. *Felon* radiated from him as sure as if it were stamped on his forehead. Mostly bald, the forty-two-year-old multi-offender had a hateful sneer that was minus two front teeth—one lower, one upper. Judging from the scar on his lips, John figured the missing teeth were courtesy of a well-placed punch instead of poor dental care, although he couldn't rule out that possibility either.

Dark, deep, and depraved looking, Jesse's eyes told his story every bit as well as the printout of his criminal history. Even the copy of his driver's license photo bore the same scowl that his booking photo held. Jesse had been arrested so many times that he must reflexively grimace every time his picture is taken.

Rubbing his eyes, John had a more difficult time than usual keeping everything straight. His mind drifted between his family, the drama of the last few days, and the case. Images of Dylan, Marie, Joshua, Brandon—and Frank—flashed before him with maddening frequency. He pushed his thoughts away and tried to focus on the task, but they were always under the surface, like a dangerous rip current in the surf, ready to pull him under at any moment. He couldn't work like this. *Lord, please settle my mind so I can get this done. I'll deal with the other things later.*

Tim parked the car two trailers down from the Morgans' address. As they approached the trailer, they stopped at a fence around the Morgans' property. A dog was tethered to a metal stake in the middle of the yard, which was more of a trampled-down dirt pit. The beast was large and muscular like a pit bull, but it had bald patches interspersed with long clumps of mud-colored hair, as if it had been exposed to some unknown radiological experiment gone terribly wrong. The beefy mongrel stretched its lead to the limit, snarling at the would-be intruders to his territory.

"I believe that's the ugliest dog I've ever seen," Tim said, awestruck by the mutant animal before them.

"Settle down there, Cujo," Jesse Lee called from the porch.

"Cujo?" Tim whispered. "Nice."

"Who you looking for?" Jesse said.

"We're agents with the Florida Department of Law Enforcement. We're looking for Jesse Morgan." John knew he was talking with Jesse, but he wanted to play ignorant. It would be best if the man underestimated them.

"What do you want with me?" He moved off a shaded area of his front porch into the light. Jesse had porked out since his last arrest. His jowls sagged, and his paunch was well nourished, bubbling over his waistband like forty pounds of oatmeal poured into a thirty-pound sack.

"We'd like to talk about the foster-care program you and your wife participated in several years ago," John said.

Jesse tilted his head, as if considering his options. "Come on up. He won't bother you none." Jesse pointed at the hound from hell. "He's just a pup. Walk along the fence there."

"Just a pup?" Tim said.

John opened the gate, and he and Tim hugged the fence up to the walkway to the home. Cujo sprinted toward them and was jerked backward by his chain, casting rabid saliva their way.

"If that dog breaks out," John said, "you have my permission to shoot it."

"Will do." Tim didn't take his eyes off the animal, his hand riding up on his holster.

They eased underneath the aluminum awning that served as the porch. The front half of the home was a trailer attached to an older wooden house in the back.

"What did you say you were here for?" Jesse's attention alternated between John and Tim.

"Something's come up about the foster-care program that you and your wife, what's her name?" John opened the file and shuffled a couple of papers, "Linda, that's it, Linda, participated in a few years back."

Jesse opened the door and let them in. "Wait here." He hurried to the back of the house and called for Linda, his determined footsteps rocking the trailer. The toxic aroma of animal waste watered John's eyes; he tried to fan the smell off. It wasn't going to happen.

The living room was tiny and jumbled, dirty laundry and empty beer cans vying for positions on the floor and coffee table. A picture of Linda with her arms around a gaggle of children of various ages rested on top of the television. Although numerous toys were around the room, John couldn't hear any children in the house. That would make things easier.

Jesse and Linda talked in the back bedroom. Although he couldn't make out the particulars, the conversation seemed animated and took an extravagant amount of time. Eventually, they emerged. Linda followed Jesse into the room. Her body was slumped forward, and her shoulders drooped with her arms wrapped around her stomach. She looked unsure of herself, lacking the cocky, arrogant strut of her husband.

Even though she was only in her early forties, the years had not been kind to her. Her greasy salt-and-pepper hair was pulled back, with a few belligerent strands hanging in her face. Her face was dotted with numerous pockmarks, and her teeth lacked even the basic dental hygiene. She wasn't pretty, and she carried herself like she knew it all too well.

"Linda, I'm Agent Russell and this is Agent Porter. We're with FDLE."

"That's what Jesse said." She shook both their hands, brushed the locks of hair from her face, then looked at the floor.

"Do you know what I'm here about?"

"Yes, we remember—"

"She took care of most of that," Jesse interrupted. "She just loves kids. I really didn't have anything to do with it at all."

John found it interesting that Jesse was already putting everything off on Linda. He pulled a picture of Dylan from his file and handed it to her. "Does this boy look familiar?"

She turned the photo for Jesse to see. His artificial smile turned down. "I think he stayed with us for a short time. That was so long ago."

"How long ago was it?" John said.

Linda looked at Jesse again, seemingly asking for permission to speak. She was proving to be more obedient than Cujo. Jesse answered for her. "A long time ago. Maybe five, six years ago. He wasn't here that long before he was taken away by someone at the Department of Family Services. We didn't take in any more kids after that. Too much of a hassle."

"I thought you said that she took care of the foster kids." Tim pointed at Linda.

Jesse flashed an indignant glance his way but didn't respond.

"Do you remember who the DFS caseworker was?" John asked.

"No. Like I said, we weren't in the program that long. It was too much on Linda here to keep up with."

"You sure you haven't been part of the program since then? No more foster children or anything?"

"No. We tried it. It didn't work out. We didn't do it again."

"Does this person look familiar?" John handed Jesse a picture of Janet Parks. "Is she the woman who placed Dylan here?"

"That's her," Linda said, catching a cross glare from Jesse. She bit her lip and bowed her head again.

Jesse's body went tense, and he shifted his position, narrowing his eyes at John. "I told you. It was a long time ago. We don't remember anything."

"So you're no longer part of the foster-care program?"

"You already asked me that, and I already answered. No! Now we've got some things to do, if you don't mind."

With the trap baited and set, it was now time to reel in the catch. "If *you* don't mind, I have one more photo to show you."

"Fine. Make it quick."

John handed Jesse another photo. "Does this person look familiar?"

Snatching the photo from John's hand, Jesse glanced at it, then glared at John. Jesse's hands trembled enough to make the photo vibrate. He was holding a picture of himself from a security camera at the Fort Lauderdale Savings and Loan just a week prior.

"That's a picture of you cashing one of the state checks for Dylan's care. It's really quite a nice shot. See how clearly we can make you out?" John pointed out the detail to Jesse. "I have a bunch more of those, as well as six years' worth of receipts from both you and Linda bilking the state out of what will probably amount to tens of thousands of dollars."

John paused, locking eyes with Jesse. "Now we can keep playing games if you'd like. Or we can get to the good stuff, the important stuff—like where's Dylan? What happened to him...really?"

"I want you outta here now!" Jesse barked, his arms falling to his sides. "We don't have anything else to say. Now get out!"

"Oh, we're leaving," Tim said. "But you're coming with us."

"You're under arrest for umpteen million counts of fraud," John said.

Tim grabbed Jesse's wrist with one hand while he pulled his cuffs out from his back pocket with the other. "Put your hands behind your back."

Jesse jerked away and swung a wild punch at Tim, who

ducked and fired an uppercut into Jesse's doughy center. Jesse crumbled forward, eyes bugging, air exploding from his lungs.

Before John could grab his other arm, Tim stepped forward and foot swept Jesse, knocking his legs out from under him. The trailer shook as he crashed flat on his back. Tim buried his knee in Jesse's chest and kept a hand on his throat, squeezing until Jesse's face turned a brilliant submission red. "Still wanna fight?"

"Don't beat him." Linda rushed toward her husband. John scooped her up by the waist and carried her away from the fracas. "Please don't beat him."

"Okay. I quit." Jesse wheezed under the crushing pressure of Tim's grasp. "I give up."

"Get him cuffed," John said. "I'll have the sheriff's department roll a couple of units."

"Don't say nothing!" Jesse screamed to Linda, finally catching his breath. Tim rolled him onto his stomach and finished cuffing him. "Don't say nothing at all. Just keep your mouth shut. They don't have anything. I love you, baby."

John and Tim walked Jesse Lee and Linda out past Cujo, who frothed and snarled his displeasure. Several minutes later, two Broward County sheriff's patrol cars pulled up to the front of the residence. Jesse was placed in the lead car; a tall athletic-looking female officer sat Linda in the backseat of her car.

"Thanks, Sergeant Keller." John shook her hand. "We appreciate the help."

"No problem." She was every bit as tall as John's six feet two inches and could look him in the eye. "We'll meet you at the jail, and you can take it from there." She slammed the door and drove off.

Tim waited until the patrol cars rounded the corner and were well out of sight before he bent over and gasped, clenching the side of this stomach.

"You gonna be okay?" John placed his hand on Tim's back.

"Yeah. It's this stupid old wound. I don't think it's ever gonna heal." With his hands on his knees, he groaned through the pain. "I'll be all right in a minute."

"Take your time. You earned it. Those were some pretty fancy moves."

"They used to be fancy," Tim said, still crouched over. "Now they're just antique...like me."

12

Marie pulled her minivan off U.S. 1 into the parking lot of the Riverside Motel. Facing the Indian River, part of the intracoastal waterway that divided the barrier islands from the shore of Melbourne, the single-floor motel looked like a throwback to old Florida during the tourist invasion of the fifties and sixties.

At one time, the motel might have been a nice place for vacationing families to stay and take in the beach and the natural beauty of the area. But that time had long since passed. Its flamingo-pink paint was chipped and faded, and the Riverside Motel sign now read "R VE S D MO EL." Several derelict cars in the parking lot were rusting into oblivion.

Troubled and anxious, Marie's spirit cried out for her to flee as fast as her van could take her. She didn't come this way often, and she certainly never stopped at this motel. Local news accounts mentioned drug arrests and other seedy activities occurring here.

But it wasn't only the area that made Marie apprehensive. Her reason for being here disturbed her much more than that.

She spent several minutes in the parking lot, van still running, praying quietly and debating if she was doing the right thing. If John knew she was here, he would be extremely upset, to say the least. If she did nothing, though, that man might show up again at their house, and she wasn't going to stand by and allow him to harm her husband and possibly tear her family apart. Something would be done—because she was going to do it.

"Jesus, give me wisdom and strength. I'm gonna need it." She turned off the van and walked toward the office, which was nothing more than a converted motel room. A young man sat behind the desk. His gaunt and bony face had not seen a razor in several days, and his pale, chalky skin rivaled the flaky white paint of the office wall. His mouth appeared frozen open as he gazed hypnotically at a small television.

"Excuse me, is there an older gentleman staying here named Frank?"

"Oldguy is in room seven," he said, still fixated on the television. "Don't know his name. Don't have much need for names. But he's the only old guy here, so I suppose he's the one you're looking for. You're not the police, are you?"

"No." She smirked and shook her head at the prospect. She didn't think being married to a cop qualified. "I just need to see him."

He turned toward her and checked her out from head to toe. "Didn't think so. You don't look like a cop. Manager says if the police come, I'm supposed to call him. It happens about twice a week. No big deal."

"Thank you," she said while taking an extra look at the parking lot. Oh, yeah, *that* really helped her comfort level. She hurried toward room seven, which faced the river.

The breeze off of the water was constant and nasty. The

combination of putrefied fish and algae collected in the tiny harbor just across from the motel, and the rancid aroma routinely hovered around the area. The Melbourne locals often said that everything rotten dead-ends at the Riverside Motel.

Pushing the hair away from her face, she stood outside the door for several minutes, building her courage. The television inside the room was loud enough to be heard from the parking lot. She prepared to go face-to-face with a murderer and child abuser.

She didn't know fear much in her comfortable life, but now she was truly afraid. She prayed quietly for strength to somehow keep this man from hurting her family. *Lord, I hope this is the right thing. Please be with me.*

She took a deep breath and then knocked on the door. There was a rustling inside, the doorknob wiggled and shook, and then the door opened slowly. Frank emerged with his cane keeping him steady.

Marie took two steps off of the sidewalk and into the parking lot, giving her plenty of distance from him. His look was hard and fierce, the cavernous wrinkles of his face looking more like scars from some unknown battle. In spite of his age, she could see the resemblance to John. Her knees buckled slightly, and she struggled not to let him see her quiver.

Frank leaned forward, staring at her. He stood upright and smiled as the flash of recognition crossed his face. An odd, uncomfortable hush followed.

"I'm glad you've come." His dry, raspy voice broke the silence.

"I'm not." Marie crossed her arms and looked toward the office. Could the man see them? And if so, would he call the police if something went wrong? She didn't have a lot of confidence in that.

"Would you like to come in, missy?" He slid to the side to give her enough room to enter.

"No! No, I wouldn't." She shook her head. "I'm not going to be that long."

Frank tilted his head like a confused puppy.

"Stay away from my husband! Don't come near our house or my family again."

"I come a long way to see my son," he said, both hands resting on his cane. "I can't rightly do what you ask. There's something I must do."

"I don't care what you have to do. You *will* stay away from John. He's a detective, and if you come by our house again, he'll have you arrested and put back in prison. You can bet on that."

"Well, missy, what's your name?"

"My name doesn't matter," she said, frustrated at his attempts to be civil. She wasn't going to play into his charade. She knew what he was. "I'm telling you to stay away from my family."

"Afraid I can't do that."

"Don't you think you've done enough to him?" Her face turned warm and her voice crackled. "Haven't you hurt him enough?"

"Didn't come to hurt no one, but I waited too long and fought too hard to turn tail now. I must see Frankie…I mean, John, just one last time. All I want is ten minutes of his time, and I'll be outta his and your life forever."

"Well you might as well leave town now because that's not going to happen." She glowered at him. "I will not let you hurt him again. You will *never* get to talk with him. Can't you understand that?"

"I beg to differ." Frank interrupted her and leaned on his cane. "I got faith that I'll be able to see my son one more time. Somehow, someway it *is* gonna happen."

Marie's face contorted, and she took two steps forward. "I don't know much about you." Her eyes locked with his, not giving an inch. "But I know you're a child abuser and a murderer, and you lost your right to see John. He wants nothing to do with you. So leave him alone. Leave us alone."

"You're right, missy." Frank straightened, standing tall against her charges. His eyes moistened; his voice wobbled. "I'm everything you say I am—and more, much more. I'm a murderer and a child abuser and a thousand things you never dreamed of."

His admission confirmed everything she suspected: He was truly as evil as John described.

Frank swiped his left hand across his face, wiping away the tears. After a short pause, he continued, "And I been washed clean by the blood of the risen Savior. I come to see my son. I come to seek his forgiveness. And I ain't leavin' til I get my chance."

Marie's arms fell to her sides, and she stood silent, stunned by his proclamation. She bit her lip and shuffled her feet back and forth. Frank didn't waver.

Marie scanned Frank up and down for several seconds. "Just because you got some jailhouse religion doesn't mean you can come here and make demands. You will never get to speak with him, and I'm telling you for the last time to stay away from my family. We'll have you arrested. I mean it—*stay away!*"

She backpedaled toward her van, not wanting to take her eyes off of Frank, who stood in the doorway of the motel room, seemingly unmoved by her passionate declarations.

As she backed out of her parking spot, her van crushed an old beer can that was in her path. She jammed the gearshift into drive, and the tires skipped the flattened can across the parking lot toward Frank's room as she drove back to U.S. 1.

Speeding toward home, for the first time in her life, Marie felt cruel. She'd never talked to anyone like that, especially a crippled old man. But she'd never been so afraid in her life either, afraid of the pain and wounds that the feeble old man could inflict on her husband and her family—wounds John wasn't ready to face, much less heal.

She replayed the exchange over and over in her mind. She thought that once she'd warned him and said her piece, it would be finished. Frank looked so determined. She had the eerie, gut-wrenching feeling that it wasn't over as she'd hoped and prayed.

The farther away from the motel she got, the calmer she became. The words *risen Savior* galloped through her mind like the Four Horsemen of the Apocalypse. She couldn't shake the look on his face as he spoke the words. He seemed so sincere when he described her Lord.

She settled back in her seat as she turned onto the interstate. *Just because he claims to be a Christian doesn't mean he is.* After all, she had known people who claimed Christ and then turned around and committed some hideous act. But something about the way he said it, the way he spoke the words tugged at her heart. If he was a phony just using the right religious words to gain favor, he was good—very good.

But she knew she had done the right thing…or had she?

13

Crammed into the bustling downtown area of Fort Lauderdale, the Broward County jail was a twenty-four-hour depot for those who didn't play well with others in south Florida. Municipal police and sheriff's deputies delivered their prisoners here while bond was set or to be held for trial. Concertina wire and layered fences distinguished it from the other brick buildings in the business district. The two patrol cars transporting Jesse Lee and Linda just pulled into the large sally port, and a metal fence rolled down, securing them into the prisoner drop-off area.

The first deputy escorted the disheveled, now limping Jesse Lee from the patrol car into the booking area. Sergeant Keller waited until Jesse was in the detention area before she helped Linda from the backseat of her car.

"How in the world would the likes of Jesse Lee Morgan get approved to be a foster parent?" John shook his head as he reviewed Jesse's criminal history. "It doesn't make any sense. Burglary. Petty theft. Assault and battery. Domestic violence. No way he should have been approved. He couldn't even pass the first basic review. I wouldn't let him watch a hamster, much less a child, especially now that we met him face-to-face. Everything is right here in his history."

"If someone would have bothered to look," Tim said.

"No foster family files on them. Nothing. How could this have happened?"

"A lot of things about this case don't make sense." Tim parked the car in a visitor's spot.

"And there's only two people who can tell us right now," John said. "I don't think Jesse will be in the chatty kind of mood. But Linda's a different story." He pointed to her as she shuffled, handcuffed and shackled, into the back door of the jail. "We might have a real chance with her."

John and Tim gathered their equipment and walked toward the rear entrance. "Sergeant Keller," John called. "We're gonna want to talk with Linda. Is there somewhere we can interview her before she's booked?"

"We can set you up in the educational room just off the booking area. You should have some privacy there. Follow us on in, and I'll get you situated."

Sergeant Keller opened the gate for them, and they followed her and Linda through the first set of doors. She frisked Linda again and confiscated all her property, placing her jewelry and ID in a clear plastic bag.

Sergeant Keller punched a code into the keypad on the wall, and the second door buzzed open. They all entered the booking facility, which was swarming with fresh arrestees and reeked of beer and bare feet. A row of deputies sat at tables processing new prisoners arrested from all around the county. One side of the room had four giant holding cells—one for female prisoners, the other three for male. All of the cells were filled to capacity.

"Do you want me to take her right to the education room or book her first? It's your call," Sergeant Keller said.

"Book her first," John said. "That will give her some time to stew, play with her mind a little. It should work in our favor."

She placed Linda in the woman's holding cell. "Follow me." She waved to Tim and John. They passed through another set of double doors and into the jail facility itself, then down a long corridor to the educational room. Sergeant Keller unlocked the door, and they entered the room, which was large enough to be used as a classroom or worship service area. Bookshelves, mostly filled with religious materials and books, lined the walls. Another door at the opposite end of the room led into the holding area, so the prisoners could be escorted directly into the room without leaving the secured area.

John assessed the spot for its usefulness as an interview room. He moved three chairs away from the tables and placed them in the center of the room, then pulled the tables into one corner. He didn't want anything between Linda and him. He and Tim would sit directly in front of her. If it worked well, she would feel extremely vulnerable, making it much more difficult for her to concentrate on any lies. They could also watch her body movements for signs of deception, no matter how slight.

After a couple more desks were shoved into the corner, John felt comfortable with their impromptu interview room, although he much preferred their specifically designed room at the office, which they referred to as "the box."

Preparing for a good interrogation was like preparing for a boxing match. Every time John conducted an interview, he convinced himself that he would get the confession; he was going to win. He prepared a strategy for each person. He read their criminal histories, pulled any police reports they were involved in, and even checked their credit reports, searching for any piece of information that would help him learn more about the interrogatee.

Information was power. Even seemingly insignificant tidbits could be used to push the suspect toward confessing. John would feed the facts he'd learned back to them during the interview, making that person think he knew everything about them. Many times, the suspects would feel overwhelmed and confess.

Sergeant Keller entered the room. "They just finished booking her. We should have Linda to you in a couple of minutes."

After the little ruckus with Jesse, John and Tim figured that Linda was the weak link. Jesse had been influenced by too many years in prison and was more likely to keep quiet. Linda, on the other hand, lacked fortitude and didn't have any past problems with the law, other than a couple of traffic tickets. Janet Parks had been no help whatsoever.

"What did you arrest her for, if you don't mind my asking?" Sergeant Keller said.

"Fraud…for now, anyway. More important, she might have some information for us about Dylan Jacobs." John held up his file. "We're not sure."

"The little boy on TV?" she said with an eyebrow raised.

John nodded. "Yep, that's him."

"Well, I hope you have good luck. That whole thing is a tragedy. Let me know if you need anything else."

A muffled squawk came over her radio. John could make out enough that Linda Morgan was on her way up.

"Ten-four," she replied into the microphone clipped to her shoulder. "She's leaving booking now. It should be just a minute."

John and Tim stood by the door, watching the bustling jail.

The control center for the interior of the jail was just outside the door. Although no lights were on in the control center, it radiated a surreal blue-green glow from the computer screens and video monitors throughout the secured room. Several guards watched the monitors, scanning the large hall area and three floors of cells.

The sounds of inmates rustling about and guards barking orders reverberated throughout the jail. Mattresses were stacked along the walkways as there wasn't enough space to accommodate the number of prisoners they housed.

John spotted two deputies walking a female prisoner toward their room. Linda was still crying. One of the deputies moved her aside and then motioned for the control center to open the door, followed shortly by the same metallic buzz that had followed them throughout the jail.

Linda shuffled through the door with her arms folded. She passed by them without saying a word.

"Call when you need us." The deputy pointed to the intercom mounted on the wall as he made a swift retreat.

Linda twitched as the slamming door echoed through the room.

"Please, take a seat." Tim pushed the chair closer to her. She hesitated for a moment, then complied.

"Are you holding up okay?" John asked as he eased into his chair. He started the tape recorder.

She shrugged and wiped the tears from her eyes but didn't answer.

John leaned forward. "Linda, do you know why all of this is happening?"

She nodded. "Dylan," she said as if it hurt to speak it.

"That's right." John's heart revved up. It was a good start. "Do you have an attorney yet?"

"No, and it doesn't look like anyone's going out of their way to help me."

"Well, maybe we can change that." John smiled at Tim. He placed the form on the table, and then carefully read her Miranda rights to her, making sure she understood each item.

It was a precarious procedure. If he pushed too hard, she might invoke her rights, and the interview would be over. If he didn't make sure she understood everything he was telling her, in court he could lose any of the information he gained.

"Do you wish to speak with me now—" he pointed with his pen to the line on the form—"without a lawyer present?"

She paused, alternating her gaze from the paper to John then back to the paper. She took the pen from his hand and scribbled her initials next to the box indicating that she would talk with him.

John lined up his questions in his head, all the while trying not to let emotion show on his face. A good interview could be physically, mentally, and emotionally exhausting. John had to remember the questions he wanted to ask, keep the facts of the case in order, watch her body language for clues, and listen to her responses. And if all that wasn't difficult enough, he'd also have to be careful of his responses and body language, so he didn't give away any key information. He once had an interview with a homicide suspect that lasted eight hours. After that, he was wiped out for three days.

Looking down at her feet, Linda picked and brushed imaginary lint off of her orange jumpsuit.

John started with simple questions about her background, what kind of work she did, where she was from. He already knew the answers to most of them. This initial period was to get her comfortable speaking to him. It didn't matter what she was saying, as long as she was saying something.

John acted interested, leaning forward just a little, nodding his head at the appropriate moments. He let her do most of the talking. He asked small follow-up questions. His warm-up time could take anywhere from twenty minutes to an hour, depending on how well Linda responded. Longer was better. If he started in too early, she could shut down and either ask for an attorney or just stop speaking altogether. It was a delicate process.

When John first started speaking to her, Linda's knees were pulled to her chest and her feet rested on the seat of the chair, almost in the fetal position. The longer she talked, the more she opened up, like a flower blooming in the sunshine. She seemed needy for positive attention, which told John volumes about her relationship with Jesse Lee.

Linda stretched her feet back down to the floor, but her arms remained crossed. If he was going to get anywhere, he'd have to watch for her arms to uncross.

"You seem like a hardworking and caring person." John inched his chair forward.

"I try," she said, smiling.

"It's because of people like you that we have a foster-care system at all." He wanted to build her up, bring her along as an ally. "It takes people like you to step up and take on the responsibilities that other people have failed to do."

She said nothing but blushed, and a slight smile crept across her face.

John shifted in his chair, then slid even closer. He mimicked her body position. "You know I'm here to talk about Dylan." John sensed that she was ready to move forward. "So, when did you first take him in as a foster child?"

Linda didn't say anything for a few moments. She was clearly calculating her next move. Her relaxed, comfortable demeanor disappeared, replaced by turmoil that radiated from her as she gnawed on her lower lip. Her face contorted into awkward, almost painful expressions, as if someone stepped on her foot and was grinding her toes into the floor.

Had he moved too quickly? He thought about taking a step back, but he felt he could still move forward.

"Linda, no one thinks you're a bad person." John had to seem nonjudgmental. She had to feel that he liked her as a person. John was always surprised by that characteristic in people, even people who have committed hideous crimes.

"Sometimes good people get themselves into situations they have no control over," John said in a monotone, rhythmic pace. "Sometimes good people make mistakes, have lapses in judgment."

Linda took another deep breath, then nodded. It was the sign John had been looking for, a crack in her armor. He'd found the area he needed to attack. He kept his thoughts together and contained his excitement. With a little more prodding, she would be ready to tell everything.

"You know what happened to Dylan, don't you." It wasn't a question but a statement of fact.

She shook her head and slumped forward. Her hands went to her lap, palms up, a sure indication that she was ready to confess.

"What happened to Dylan, Linda? Help us help you."

"It was Jesse's idea." She glanced out of the corners of her eyes. "I didn't want anything to do with it; I swear."

"I believe you." John edged his chair even closer. "I don't think you would hurt anyone or do anything wrong. I know Jesse's history. I know what he's capable of."

"You have no idea." She perked up for the first time in the interview. "No idea."

"Help me to understand."

Linda sat back and closed her eyes. It looked like she was praying. She opened her eyes. "He—"

A loud, frantic banging echoed through the room. Linda screamed and jumped from her chair. Tim and John swung around to see a man at the door, still pounding away, with Sergeant Keller behind him. She pointed at the man and mouthed *lawyer* to John and Tim.

The man, who was considerably shorter than Sergeant Keller, shrieked something at her and hysterically waved his hands back and forth like he was doing jumping jacks. She reached down with her keys and unlocked the door.

"Step away from my client." The attorney marched into the room. "Step away now."

"Oh no," Tim said in disbelief, "not *him*."

"Richard Cromwell." John glared at him. "What brings you here?"

"It's *Counselor* to you." He stepped between Linda and John, pushed his wire-rimmed glasses up on his nose, and then declared, "I'm representing Mrs. Linda Morgan, and I demand that this interrogation stop immediately."

With his dark blue tailored Armani suit and red power tie, Richard Cromwell was one of the highest-priced lawyers in Florida, maybe in the entire nation. Cromwell made a habit of representing any client who could get him media exposure. His courtroom antics and elitist demeanor had earned him the name "King Richard" to those in the legal system.

"So what brings a high-priced, low-moraled lawyer like you to this case, *Richard?*" Tim said, barely able to contain himself. "How's she able to afford the likes of you?"

"Who hires me and how I work is quite none of your business. And it's Counselor to you too, Detective."

"She told us she didn't have a lawyer," John said. "So, technically, until she says that you're her lawyer, she's still unrepresented. And she waived her Miranda rights."

"I'm her attorney, and that's all there is to it. Now I want you to leave this room, and you are to have no more contact with my client."

"She's not your client yet," John countered. "Linda, this is your call. You were ready to tell me what happened. Don't let this guy get in the way of clearing your conscience. You know this is the right thing to do."

"Stop speaking." Richard wagged his finger in John's face.

Tim lunged forward, his nose nearly touching the lawyer's forehead. "Don't be rude, *Richard*, let the man finish."

"Sergeant, I demand that you get these men out of here and away from my client. And you, Detective, take two steps back before I slap an injunction on you so fast that your feeble head spins." He flicked his hand dismissively at Tim, who clenched his fist and leaned in closer.

"Gentlemen, we all need to calm down," Sergeant Keller said, her hands in front of her. "Detective Porter, can you give this man some space?"

"Come on, Tim." John grabbed his arm, which was flexed and unyielding, and pulled him back two steps. "Back off a little."

Richard smirked. "I need five minutes to confer with my client. Sergeant, can you escort these *gentlemen* into the hallway, so we might have some privacy?"

She looked at Tim and John. She was caught in the middle, and John knew it.

"We'll wait in the hallway...for five minutes," John said. "But that's all you have." He turned to Linda. "You don't have to accept him as your attorney. Just remember that. It's your call, *not* his." John walked to the door, but Tim held back for a moment, glaring at Richard.

"Tim." John gestured with his hand for him to follow. "Five minutes."

Sergeant Keller opened the door, and the three were back in the hallway, although they could still see into the room. Cromwell's hands waved vigorously, and he used dramatic facial expressions, as if he were in the closing arguments of a major trial. Linda stood with her arms crossed, nodding or shaking her head in intervals. Occasionally she looked up at the window, where they were staring back.

Richard glared at the door and then walked almost behind Linda, so she had to turn around to look at him and wasn't able to see the door again.

Tim focused on his watch, timing Richard. And he made sure that Richard could see it, too.

"I'm so sorry about him," Sergeant Keller said. "Her husband made a phone call from booking, and a few minutes later this guy showed up. I did everything I could to slow him down. I fumbled with my keys, I walked slowly, and I even took him to the psych ward by mistake. He wasn't happy about that."

"I bet he wasn't." John laughed at the thought of King Richard being mistakenly locked up in the psych ward for a couple of days. It would probably do everyone a world of good. "It's not your fault. Just our bad luck. She was so close." John held up his thumb and index finger as if pinching a thimble. "So close. Two more minutes and we would have had everything we needed."

"Yep." Still fixated on his watch, Tim counted the seconds.

"I just don't understand why he would be representing Linda," John said. "Where would they get that kind of money? How are they going to pay him?"

"Maybe they aren't paying him." Tim didn't take his eyes off of his watch. "Maybe someone else is picking up the tab. Or maybe he's doing it out of the goodness of his heart...*not*."

"Well, it's certainly worth finding out."

"Time!" Tim yelled loud enough for Richard to hear through the metal door and turn their way. "Get it open quick."

Sergeant Keller had the door open within seconds.

"Time!" Tim screamed again as they rushed into the room. "Your time is up, *Richard*."

He smoothed the front of his suit with a single pass of his hand, and he pushed his glasses forward. "My client will not be concluding her statement today...or any other day, for that matter. She is invoking her right to remain silent, which for the unlearned can be found in the Fifth Amendment of the U.S. Constitution," he said, panning toward the three.

Tim charged at Richard, but John stepped between them.

"Tsk, tsk, Detective. You really should take an anger management course to curb that brutish behavior of yours."

"I'll curb something of yours, *King Richard*." Tim's eyes were riotous with rage.

"Linda, do you really want him to stand in the way of clearing your conscience and our finding Dylan?"

Linda could only move her head up and down as Richard put his arm around her and pushed his chest out, as if he were her great protector.

"Don't you people understand plain English?" Richard flung his hands into the air. "You are to have no contact with my client whatsoever. If you do, I will bring a civil action against both of you and your department, and I'll contact your employer to report your gross violations of the Constitution. Do I make myself clear?"

"You haven't seen the last of us," Tim said. "Not by a long

shot. We'll see you and *your* client in court."

"Don't be so melodramatic, Detective. Do you really think you have that much? Really, a few trivial counts of fraud, is that what my client should be afraid of? She has no criminal history. Do you think she's going to do time for that? I don't think so. You've lost, again." Richard twisted a gaudy diamond ring around his finger and smiled at Tim. "But *you* should be used to that by now."

Tim growled and gritted his teeth, his body quaking.

"Give it a rest, Richard. We're leaving." John picked up his tape recorder and case file. "But we'll see you soon...real soon."

As they walked out and the door was closing, John poked his head back into the room. "If you ever want to talk, Linda, call me anytime."

"Stop speaking, I tell you—"

The boom of the closing door cut him off midsentence. John's stomach churned with the sickening feeling of being so close but still not knowing much more than they did before they came. If he'd moved a little quicker on Linda, would they know everything by now? Would it have been too late for King Richard to interfere?

Tim slumped as he walked, and periodic sighs escaped him like the chug of an old steam engine grinding to a halt. John was surprised at how angry his partner got with Richard. Although Richard could provoke Gandhi into a murderous rampage, John hadn't seen Tim that upset since they started working together.

"Don't let him get to you, Tim. He's just being obnoxious. That's what he does. Cromwell tries to throw you off your game that way."

"I know what his strategy is like. We've gone at it before."

"Really?" John was glad to see Tim's anger waning.

"When I was at Orlando PD, he got a child molester off on a technicality. He attacked some of the evidence collected from one of our new evidence technicians. Cromwell ate her alive on the stand. The guy got off, and then I had to arrest him again two years later for the same thing—with three more new victims. Those kids were destroyed by what that monster did, and Richard Cromwell was the one who got him out."

"I'm sorry to hear that." He could see that time had not diminished the pain for Tim.

"I just want the good guys to win some, John." Tim opened the car door and plopped onto the passenger seat, rocking the car. "Especially against that snake King Richard."

"Don't get too discouraged. We actually did learn something today."

"What's that?"

"That Jesse Lee and Linda are definitely involved, too. Before King Richard interrupted, Linda said that 'It was Jesse's idea.' And we have that on tape." John held the tape recorder up and shook it. "Maybe we have more than we think."

John's hopes of getting home early were crushed when he and Tim drove into the back of the station after their less-than-successful morning in south Florida.

"This doesn't look good," Tim said. Satellite trucks lined the fence of the back parking lot like barnacles lodged to a dock, and reporters in power suits with power strides milled around, checking their gear and primping themselves for the next greatest story. Every news agency in the state seemed to be represented, a veritable potpourri of big hair and great teeth.

Tim and John parked in the farthest space in the lot, then snaked through the obstacle course of reporters and camera crews, hoping they wouldn't start the questioning early.

Alan met them at the back door. "I need you two in my office." He looked at his watch. "And we don't have a lot of time."

Inside the building wasn't much better. Alan, John, and Tim waded through the staff to get to Alan's office, where the governor and Director Lyman rose from their chairs as they entered. Alan closed the door and made the introductions.

"Gentlemen, we've got a press conference in ten minutes on the updates in the case." Governor Mac shook John's and then Tim's hands. He was larger than John thought he would be; his presence seemed to fill the whole room. "Alan said that you made two arrests this morning. What can you tell me before we get going? Have you found Dylan's whereabouts or anything that could lead you to this boy?"

"Well, sir, we arrested a husband and wife who were his foster parents six years ago," John said. "They have been cashing his checks for the whole time. But neither told us where Dylan was or what happened to him. We don't know a lot more now than we knew this morning. Dylan is still missing; that's about the only thing we know for sure."

"Have we narrowed down a time frame for how long he's been missing? We still have the Amber Alert up and running. His picture and information are all over the TV. Can we add more information to it?"

"Sir, I don't think you're going to like this."

"By your tone, Agent Russell, I'm sure I'm not. Give it to me anyway." Governor Mac glanced at his watch. "We've got seven minutes."

"The last confirmation we have of his being alive was six years ago. Even that's sketchy at best."

"Please don't tell me that this boy has been missing from

state care for six years, and no one happened to notice." The governor rubbed his temples and turned in a half circle. "Please do not tell me that kind of incompetence and malfeasance has been running rampant, and we have to explain that to a contemptuous press corps. What about records, reports, visitations, schools, any kind of trail?"

"Next to nothing, sir," John said. The room suddenly felt tiny, suffocating. "And we're not sure why. We have our theories, but nothing solid…yet."

"Theories don't matter. Facts and found children matter." The governor sat on the edge of Alan's desk, which groaned under his weight. "It looks like the sharks outside are gonna get some chum today…in my name, of course. The only way we're going to play this is straight up. We'll tell them the truth and then knock down every wall we can to find this kid. Does everyone here understand that?" Everybody nodded, and every eye bore down on John. "Alan, I want a daily report on this investigation. I won't be blindsided again."

"Yes, sir."

"One state agency is going down in flames on this; let's not make it FDLE, too." The governor regarded Director Lyman, who nodded. "It's time, gentlemen, so let's get out there and take our beating."

14

D ad…Dad." Joshua sprinted through the living room
toward John, just walking into the house. Joshua
leaped into his arms and grabbed him around the neck
in a ferocious hug. Brandon slipped around the corner and
joined his brother.

Marie was putting the finishing touches on dinner. Wiping
her hands with a towel, she watched the boys love on their
father. John glanced up, kissed the boys, and walked tentatively
toward her.

"Hey, hon." He pecked her cheek as his hand skimmed
across her hip and stomach. She caught his hand and held it
tight; he pulled it away quickly and moved into the kitchen.
She hadn't realized how much she missed his touch, even if it
only lasted a second.

"How was your day?"

"Lousy." He displayed a wide, counterfeit smile. "I had a
meeting with the governor and Director Lyman, and then I had
to appear at a press conference with them. It should be on the
evening news."

"That must have been fun. Hobnobbing with the governor and all the bigwigs."

"About as fun as a tax audit. This case isn't going well."

Marie tried to make eye contact with John, but he avoided it altogether. "We'll try to watch the news after dinner to see if they show the press conference."

He opened the oven and peered in. "What's for supper?"

"Chicken Cordon Bleu. It'll be ready in five minutes." She looped the towel back over the handle of the oven. "Wash your hands and get ready for dinner, boys," she called out into the living room.

"How was your day?" he asked while loosening his tie.

"Do you really wanna know?" She leaned against the doorjamb, her arms crossed. "Or should I just fake it?"

John paused, then said, "Fake it, while the boys are around, anyway." He peeked into the living room to make sure they couldn't hear. "We can talk later."

"Really? How much later? The next millennium, maybe?"

John sighed and cocked his head, eyeing her with his I-don't-want-to-get-into-it-now look.

"I can do that if you want, John." She crossed over to the sink and washed her hands. "I can pretend as well as you can. My day was great. Everything is wonderful. Just peachy." A plastic smile adorned her face.

"Please don't patronize me now." He leaned back against the counter, his tie pulled halfway down his shirt. "It's been a long, tough day. I just need some rest."

"We've all had a tough day. And it's not getting any easier." *Real nice. John's been home less than ten minutes, and I've already broken my promise.* She wanted to wait until the time was right, until they could sit and talk sensibly about what was happening to them. She wanted to be loving and supportive, but the frustration of her argument with Frank and John's avoiding her pushed Marie to the edge.

"Fighting about it isn't going to help."

After a deep sigh, she closed her eyes. "I'm sorry, John. Let's just have dinner and see what happens."

John accepted her terms. He did look worn-out, which made her feel even worse about being angry. It was probably better if she left out the part of her day involving Frank. Revealing that certainly wouldn't help.

The wall just behind the kitchen shook as two marauding boys stomped their way down the stairs and into the kitchen. Everyone took their places around the table.

"Who wants to say the prayer?" John asked. Both boys raised their hands. "Josh, you said it last night; let Brandon say it tonight."

Joshua frowned but conceded. Brandon blessed the meal, and the family joined into their supper. Between the passing of the food and the clanking of forks against ceramic, the boys told about their day. Joshua related how one of his friends ate a bug at recess on a dare then later had to go home after complaining about a stomachache. Brandon had done well on a math test and then talked about the upcoming play-off game.

After dinner, Joshua and Brandon raced back upstairs to take their baths and get ready for bed. John rolled up his sleeves and started washing the dishes. Marie turned on a small portable TV just in time to catch the evening news.

John perked up when he saw Alan Cohen giving the press conference from behind a podium that bore the state of Florida seal. John stood in the background but was still clearly visible, along with David Lyman and Governor Mac.

"Looks like we're on." John turned up the volume.

"We're seeking the public's help in finding Dylan Jacobs. Agent

John Russell is heading up this investigation. If you have any
information that could help locate Dylan, please call our office." The
phone number appeared underneath Dylan's picture.

Several computer-generated, age-enhanced pictures of
Dylan appeared on the screen. One depicted him with black
hair, another with brown, still another with his natural blond
hair. The scar on his lip was pronounced and was the one thing
they hoped people would recognize.

"Earlier this morning, Jesse Lee and Linda Morgan were
arrested in Broward County for fraud related to this case. Other
charges against the couple could be pending. Both are still in the
Broward County jail awaiting bond hearings.

"That concludes our statement," Alan said. "I will be happy to
take any of your questions now."

"Have you established when Dylan first disappeared?" a
reporter asked.

Alan hesitated, "It appears that Dylan could have been missing as
long as six years. We haven't narrowed it down any further than that."

"Six years?" the same reporter said. "Dylan Jacobs was lost in
state care six years ago, and it's just now coming to light?"

Alan's face contorted, and he paused. "Yes."

"Do you know if Dylan is alive?" another reporter yelled
above the cacophony of questions.

"We don't have any more information than what we've given
today," Alan said. "That's why we're asking for the public's help."

"Governor Mac...Governor Mac," one reporter called. The
governor stepped to the podium, straightened his tie, and
began to speak.

John turned off the TV as more reporters barked questions
at the governor. "If we don't get a break soon, this case will be
the worst case I've ever had."

"Well, at least you made the news again." Marie rubbed his

back, which was like massaging granite. "And you looked very handsome up there with the governor and all."

"Believe me, it's not as fun as it looks." He arched his back and melted slightly; his shoulders lowered and became more pliable. "Although I have to admit, it wasn't the worst part of my day—that shows you what a rotten day I've had."

"So your trip to Fort Lauderdale wasn't productive?"

"Only in raising my blood pressure. Richard Cromwell showed up just in time to kill a perfectly good interview. Linda Morgan was so close to telling me everything. And then we got back to town just in time for that circus."

"I'm sorry." Marie hugged John from behind. It had been several days since they held each other. Even if she was doing all of the holding, she would take what she could get.

John turned his head toward her. "Did anyone come by today?"

"No," she said, knowing full well who *anybody* was. "No one came by."

While that was technically accurate, it felt like a lie just the same. She wanted to tell him everything about Frank and what happened, but it would spoil the moment. Perhaps sometime later. Perhaps never. She would need time to work out all of the possibilities.

As she held John close, Frank's words flooded her mind. The skirmish in her soul escalated into a full-scale war. She thought she had it all figured out. She could simply keep Frank away and keep her family intact. Now she didn't know what was right anymore—about anything. She didn't know how to help John, she didn't know what to think about Frank, and she didn't know how to deal with her own frustration and anger.

She clung to John, hoping to hold on for the ride—wherever it led.

15

We've got Janet Parks, Jesse Lee Morgan, and Linda Morgan." Pictures of all three suspects as well as Dylan were posted on a whiteboard covering their west wall. With a Magic Marker, John drew a triangle from Janet to Jesse Lee to Linda; Dylan's picture was in the center.

"We know how they all come together," John said. "For Dylan's foster care. But what happened after that? Why did he disappear? Was he abducted by a stranger or possibly killed by the Morgans? If they had nothing to do with his disappearance, then why didn't they report it? And what motive would all of them have to keep this hidden?"

"Maybe one of the Morgans killed Dylan in a fit of rage or something," Tim offered as he sat on a desk facing their flowchart. "And Janet didn't discover he was missing until a long time afterward, because she wasn't doing her job. She then decides to cover it up, so she doesn't get in trouble."

"Possibly." Alan leaned back in his chair and clasped his hands over his stomach. "But that doesn't explain her being so adamant about not speaking to anyone. Once it was out, you'd think she would rather get fired than take a rap for murder, or kidnapping, or whatever. It doesn't make sense."

"A lot of this doesn't make sense." John balanced on the corner of a desk and placed the cap of the marker on his chin as he contemplated the possibilities. "For six years, Jesse and Linda have been cashing the checks for his care. They didn't seem too worried about being caught."

"Maybe they're just not very bright," Tim said. "After talking with them, that's a real possibility."

"They aren't that smart," John said. "That's for sure. But they just acted confident, too confident, like they really expected never to be caught. It's weird."

Gloria Davis crept into the room. "Excuse me, I'm sorry to bother you, John, but there's a young man in the lobby who asked for you. He says it's urgent. He has information about the Jacobs case."

"Let's see what the man has to say." Tim slipped on his jacket. "You never know, this could be the big one. The one lead that breaks this thing wide open."

"Yeah, I'll hold my breath." John and Tim walked from their cubicles, down a narrow hallway to Gloria's desk. On the side of her desk was a small, bulletproof window with a speaker attached, so Gloria could talk with people in the lobby and still have a degree of safety.

They watched the man for a moment. Looking to be in his late twenties, he gawked at a collection of police badges from around the country that were in a display case on the wall. His hands were shoved in his jeans pocket, and his black concert T-shirt hung untucked against his thin, milky-white body. His light brown hair was combed over neatly.

Tim and John ambled into the lobby. The man walked toward them and extended his hand.

"William Saldini." He shook John's hand first, then Tim's. "Which one of you is Agent Russell?"

"I am," John said. "I understand you have some information for us about the Jacobs case."

"Oh, I certainly do." William beamed and puffed his chest. "I have all the information you need."

"Really? What do you know about the case?"

"Everything. I know absolutely everything about this case, this Dylan Jacobs."

"How's that?" Tim asked.

"Because I killed him," William said, not blinking an eye.

"What?" John stepped back. He looked at Tim then back to William. "What did you just say?"

"I said I killed Dylan Jacobs." William sighed. "I killed him, and I've come to turn myself in." He stretched his hands out in front of him, palms up in the surrender position.

Tim snatched his left wrist, pulling William off balance. "Don't do anything dumb." Tim's powerful hand squeezed William's wrist so tight that he rose onto his tiptoes and let out a slight wince. "Do you have any weapons on you now?"

"No, I don't. I have nothing with me but my wallet."

Tim lifted William's shirt just enough to get his hand underneath. While still holding William's left wrist, Tim patted him around the waistband with his right hand, going around twice to make sure. As Tim ran his free hand up and down and around each leg, William held his right hand up higher.

"Nothing on him." Tim stood off to the side in a bladed fighting stance, still clutching William's wrist.

"I won't resist, officers. I won't give you any trouble. I've come to take responsibility for my crimes—my awful, hideous crimes."

"What's going on?" Alan sprinted into the lobby with his

pistol out of his holster and at his side. "What'd he do?"

"He just confessed to killing Dylan Jacobs."

William nodded his head in unison as John spoke.

"What?" Alan looked bewildered.

"He just con—"

"I heard you, I heard you." Alan waved his hand at John. "Well, what are we doing? Don't just stand there. Cuff him and get him inside. We don't need to be playing with him here in the lobby."

Tim pulled a pair of cuffs from his back pocket and clicked them around William's left wrist. William reflexively brought the right hand up as if well practiced, and Tim locked him in. With Tim on one side and John on the other, they ushered William Saldini into the office.

Gloria was backed into the corner of her desk and drew her hand to her chest as they whisked him by and led him into the interview room. Dull gray carpet covered the floor and walls of the cramped room. A small table with barely enough space to place a folder on it was against the wall opposite the two-way mirror with a video recorder behind it.

Tim pulled the chair out. "Sit!"

William sat in the stiff metal chair, specifically designed for discomfort. His soft, round shoulders rolled forward.

"I'm gonna uncuff you and put your hands in front." Tim removed his handcuff key from his pocket and knelt. "Don't give me a problem." His expression left no doubt about his intent— he was not going to be injured dealing with this prisoner.

William's eyes widened at the possibility of upsetting the bulky, angry-looking detective in front of him. Tim took his cuffs off.

"These things always hurt." William worked both wrists around.

"They're not built for comfort." Tim then cuffed him with his hands in front. "I'll be right back. Don't move." Tim met John and Alan just outside the door.

"Is the video on?" Alan asked.

"Everything's ready to go." The adrenaline rush wired John and sparked thousands of possibilities and more questions; he was thankful to be up-to-date on the case. He could do this interview from memory if needed.

"Tim, find out everything you can on this guy." Alan rolled up his sleeves. "I want to know every address where he's ever lived, every job he's ever had, his criminal history. Everything. I want to know who was at his fifth birthday party, for Pete's sake. Got it?"

"I'm on it." Tim jogged down the hallway toward his office.

"John, you got the interview," Alan said, his hand on his chin. "Work your magic on him. Let's see if we can wrap this thing up tonight. Be smart with him because we won't get this chance again."

"I understand." John stared into the monitor that was piped from the interview room into the office area. He spent several minutes just studying William, bobbing back and forth in his seat ever so slightly, like he was dancing to music no one else could hear.

William was weak. He walked, talked, and carried himself with a lack of confidence. That was a good thing for an interrogation. It also helped that he'd come to them to confess, but John didn't want to take that for granted.

He was torn. He wanted to wait for Tim to come up with some information about this guy, but he also knew that the window of opportunity for William to confess during a videotaped interrogation was wide open. If John didn't jump through it now, it could slam shut at any moment. Then it would be John and Tim's word against his in court.

He made sure his badge was clipped on his left side, so it would make a stronger impression and be right in William's face when he walked in. John grabbed Dylan's file and strolled into the room.

Towering over William, John extended his hand. "Let's see if we can start over. I'm Agent John Russell."

William took his hand, barely squeezing as they shook. William's hand was as soft as his demeanor.

"Who's the other guy?" Saldini looked at the door while biting his thumbnail. "I don't think I like him."

"That's my partner. He's a good guy. Just a little cautious, that's all. He's not one to mess with."

William still stared at the door. He had deep black circles around his eyes, which contrasted with his pasty white face like two eight balls jammed into freshly kneaded dough.

"William Saldini, is that right?" John scribbled his name on the rights form.

"Yes. You won't need that." He pointed to the Miranda form. "I know what my rights are."

"Well, I do need to do this. And you *need* to listen. You just told me in the lobby that you killed Dylan Jacobs. We need to talk about that." John wanted a starting point for the interview and wanted William to acknowledge on video what he'd said in the lobby.

"Yes, I did, because it's true."

"Okay, then. Let's get started." John read him his rights; William signed the form. John slid the form into his folder and shut it. It was going to be a good day.

"William," John said in a soothing whisper. "Why did you come in here today?"

"Because I'm a bad person." He looked down and shook his

head dramatically. "I...I've done horrible things, unspeakable things."

"I understand that. Tell me specifically why you're here today."

"I imagine you'll be calling the press on this." William peered out of the corner of his eye at John.

"Probably." John leaned back in his chair, his head cocked to the side. *That was an odd question. I've got to get him back on track.* He scooted his chair forward. "Now, tell me about Dylan Jacobs."

"Like I told you before, I killed him. I killed him, and I need to be punished."

"How did you kill him? Tell me about that."

William looked up and then shifted in his chair. John waited. The video was rolling, and he needed Saldini's answers to be clean, not appearing like John was leading him in any certain direction.

He paused for several seconds "I strangled him...yes, I strangled him."

John kept his game face on. He didn't want William to see his excitement about getting to the truth. He had to stay stone-faced, like nothing surprised him, like he knew everything he was talking about. "How did it happen? How did you find Dylan?"

"It was night." William rocked back and forth more vigorously. "I climbed in his window, and that's when it happened."

"Can you describe his house?"

William paused again, appearing to carefully consider the question. "I don't remember the house."

"Can you tell me anything about his room?"

Several more seconds ticked by. "It was dark. I couldn't see anything."

"In what city was Dylan's house located?"

"I...I don't remember." William dropped his head into his hands. He peeked up at John, then plunged his head into his hands again. "It was all so blurry, so crazy. I just keep seeing his face."

"Where is he now? Where can we find him?"

William's eyes widened. "I don't remember. Somewhere off the turnpike, I think, but I'm not sure."

"The turnpike is a long road," John said. "What were you near? Give me a landmark, someplace to start."

"I've blocked it out of my mind. I just don't want to remember it. It was so terrible."

"You don't remember where his house was." John sat upright. "You don't remember where Dylan is, and you can't give me any details about how it happened. How do you know we're talking about the same person, the same crime?"

"Because I saw him on TV." William perked up. "The boy. The blond boy. I killed him, I tell you. I did it, and I should be punished."

Tim knocked as he opened the door. "John, I need to talk with you."

"Not now." John scowled. "We're a little busy. Give me ten more minutes."

"No, John. *Now.*"

"Sit tight, William." John grabbed his file and headed for the door.

He nodded obediently, then turned toward Tim. A horrified look flashed over him, and he inched his chair closer to the wall, as far away from Tim as he could get.

John closed the door behind him. Tim carried a mound of freshly printed papers, and Alan's arms were crossed, his jaw muscles clenched.

"What's so important?" John moved away from the interview room so as not to be overheard. "The guy's spilling his guts."

"You're not going to like this." Tim flipped through several pages of his report.

"I get that feeling."

"I ran everything I could on William Saldini, date of birth March 29, 1976. He's only been in Florida for five months. Before that, all his addresses have been up in the Michigan area. As best as I can tell, he was nowhere near Florida when Dylan disappeared."

"Great," John said, "just great."

"Oh, it gets better." Alan snorted and ground his teeth. "Much better. I called a Detective Casey up in Lansing, where William's from, and he was real familiar with our boy." Tim shook his head. "Are you ready for this? They call him William the Confessor. He's confessed to nearly every major crime they've had up there in the last ten years."

"Tell me this isn't happening," John said, his mouth hanging open. "I should have seen it. His answers were just plain screwy. He couldn't tell me anything that made sense. The guy was making it up as he went along."

"According to Casey, William's even confessed to being on the grassy knoll in '63," Tim added, still looking at his notes. "And being in on the Brinks job, and having a role in the kidnapping of the Lindbergh baby."

John fell back against the wall and looked up, squeezing the last morsel of air out of him.

"And to top it off, he claims to be skyjacker extraordinaire D. B. Cooper as well."

"You can stop now." John said, still looking at the ceiling. "I get the picture."

"William will go for months without any problems, and then he'll get off his medication, and—*boom*—he shows up again."

"I guess he's off his meds," John said.

"I want this nutcase outta here," Alan snarled. "He's wasted enough of our time."

"I'd like to put something on him that Ajax won't take off." Tim glanced at the interrogation room.

"It won't do any good to charge him with filing a false police report," Alan said. "It won't even be worth the time. Just have him transported to mental health services. They'll commit him for a couple days and get him back on his meds—and outta our hair."

"I'll take care of it." John pushed himself away from the wall. John and Tim walked back into the room. William stopped rocking as they entered.

"I spoke with a friend of yours." Tim stood close enough to touch William, who leaned as far away from him as possible.

"Really, who's that? I don't know many people around here."

"Detective Casey in Lansing."

"Oh." William lowered his head.

Tim crossed his arms. "He told me you have the habit of confessing to crimes you didn't commit."

"That's not true. Detective Casey just doesn't like me. He never believes me, but I'm telling the truth. I should be punished."

"When was the last time you took your meds?" John asked, barely able to contain his anger.

"A few days." William shrugged. "Maybe a week."

"You're going to the mental health services tonight," John said, "and you'll be staying with them for a while."

"Will you take me there?"

"No." Tim stepped even closer, almost on top of him. "I'm gonna take you. We're gonna get real chummy. And if you ever call us again, I'm the one who's gonna show up at your house— every time."

"Could you please, please take me?" William pleaded to John.

John's anger abated some, and he pitied the sick young man sitting before him. But he knew if he took him to mental health services, William would probably call him all the time or be in their lobby at every major crime. If William thought he'd have to deal with Tim, he might be able to control his urge to visit them.

"Time to go." Tim reached under William's armpit and lifted him off the chair. "You've wasted enough of our time." Tim ushered him out of the room and down the hallway. William kept turning back toward John.

John shook his head. "This case keeps getting weirder."

16

C ome on, Frankie," Mama said, puffing and out of breath. "Get up the stairs. Hurry. Be quick, son."

The house quaked as thunder assaulted their home without mercy. Frankie bounded up the stairs two at a time, his mother close behind. Hand in hand, they sprinted down the hallway toward the master bedroom. She pulled the door shut tight, locking it. Sliding a cedar chest in front of the door, she wedged it in firm and secure.

A cut on her lip leaked a bloody trail, and a deep red abrasion covered the left side of her face. She wobbled toward the window on the opposite side of the room but had to steady herself against the bedpost.

After a couple of quick breaths, she pushed off and made it to the windowsill. She unlocked the window, struggled to pull it open, but only managed to get it partially up. Collapsing against the wall, she slumped to the floor.

She had nothing left.

"Lyn-e-ette." Frank drew out each syllable with torturous

intent. "Don't hide from me. I know you're up there." His footsteps pounded on each step like an artillery barrage slowly closing in on the enemy. Frank's hands slid along the wall of the hallway as he negotiated the darkened corridor. The doorknob jiggled and then turned.

Lynette scrambled to her feet and snatched the bottom of the window with both hands, jerked once, then again, finally yanking it open. She dropped to her knees and gasped.

"Frankie—" she waved him over—"get out now."

"I'm not leaving without you, Mama." He took her hand and tried to pull her conquered body from the floor.

"Open up, I say." The door bowed with each furious blow of his fist. The lightning cracked outside the window, drawing Lynette's attention away for a second. She looked back at her son and grabbed him by the shoulders.

"Frankie, he's crazy drunk." She squeezed him tight. "You have to get out now."

An ear-piercing snap reverberated throughout the room as the door split down the center. Frank's boot collided with the door again, and the cedar chest gave some ground. He forced both hands through the crack in the door and grunted as he tugged back and forth on the plank.

"Go," she said, tears falling on the dusty wooden floor. "Run. Please, Frankie, run."

"No, Mama, I—"

The door ripped completely apart, and Frank plunged through the splinters onto the chest, nearly flipping over it. Lynette pushed Frankie to the floor on the other side of the bed, out of Frank's view. She shoved Frankie's head underneath the bed. His body followed suit, as he slithered underneath.

Frank hoisted himself off of the chest and brushed broken pieces of the door from his flannel shirt. He sauntered toward

Lynette, who lay battered and defeated on the floor next to the open window, her back against the wall.

"Where's Frankie?" He swayed like a tree in a chaotic, angry wind. The stench of whisky and cigarettes trailed him into the room.

Lynette gazed at him, her eyes void of all hope, as the blood gushed freely from her lip. She remained silent, sealing her fate.

Lunging forward with surprising speed, Frank seized her throat with his left hand and squeezed, lifting her off the floor as she flailed helplessly against the assault. She gasped and clawed at his powerful arm. With his right hand, he pulled a .357 revolver from his waistband and placed the barrel of the pistol just underneath her eye.

"Where's Frankie?" he growled, teeth clenched, wringing ever tighter on her throat.

She tilted her head toward the window. "He's gone. Run away," she said as her face turned an ill blue. A mix of spittle and blood raced down her chin.

He slammed the back of her head against the wall, and she spilled onto the floor in a lifeless heap. Frank strolled to the window with his pistol at his side. The cool tempest breeze blew the drapes back and forth along the floor like dancers in a schizophrenic ballet. He wrapped his empty hand in the drapes and jerked the rods out of the wall and on top of Lynette, who quaked as they fell on her.

"I took all I'm gonna take from you, woman. You done pushed me for the last time."

Stepping in front of her, he raised the pistol. The hammer clicked as he cocked it.

Lynette rolled up onto her knees and folded her hands. "Our Father, who art in heaven, hallowed be Thy name. Thy kingdom come, Thy will be—"

The shot rang out.

"No!" John screamed as he kicked the covers from the bed. "He killed her; he killed her. Please, God, no. She's dead."

"What? What's happening?" Marie hopped from their bed and checked the room. "John, what is it?"

He sprang to his feet, his eyes darting from one end of the room to the other. His T-shirt clung to his chest from the sweat.

"It's okay, John." Marie lowered her hands. "It was a dream. Only a dream."

Standing in the middle of the room, John stared at Marie, as if he didn't recognize her.

"John, it's all right." She walked toward him, arms extended. He pushed her arms away.

"Don't!" He held both hands up, keeping her back. "Don't!"

With one more check around the room, he drew a deep breath and scurried into the bathroom, slamming the door behind him. Grasping the countertop with both hands, he stared into his pallid, trembling reflection in the mirror.

He splashed water onto his spent face, hoping to wash away the distant, vile memory. His heart throbbed, and the veins in his neck were swollen, fluttering frantically like the wings of a fleeing bird. The nightmare had not visited him since he was a child, but like so many things lately, it was back—and it hadn't lost its sting.

During those dark days of his childhood, when the tormenting memories were at their worst, his adopted mother spent a good chunk of her midnight hours comforting him from the torturous visions of his past. When he would scream out in agony and fear, she'd come to him and whisper hymns in his ear and dab his head with a washcloth until he could drift off again into something resembling sleep. She watched over him like that every night for over a year and a half.

It was during this time, too, that John discovered men's hands were created for more than inflicting pain and instilling terror. His adopted father, John Russell Senior, proved to be the most gentle, loving man he'd ever known—the antithesis of Frank Moore. He showered John with tender affection, pulling him on his lap at every opportunity, hugging him for no apparent reason, teaching him what being a man and a father really looked like.

The love and warmth of his new father carried him through the grim days of his childhood into a brighter time. John was mesmerized by everything John Senior represented, so he changed his name to honor the man he loved, the man who had rescued him from the pit. And when John Senior told him of his God, the Redeemer of all humanity, John sprinted toward Him with all the energy he could find—closing the final door on his past, leaving it dead and buried.

Slowly the nightmares of his childhood visited less frequently and then finally disappeared forever—until now.

But it was back, and so was Frank. *Why now, God? Why are You allowing this? What can I do to flush these things from my life forever?* For some unexplainable reason, this demon belched from the bowels of hell had returned and brought with him everything rotten and foul.

John's memories swung to his mother and her last act on earth that saved his life. Quite by purpose, he had not thought of it in years. The ache in his heart matched any physical pain he'd ever known. He forced his mind back to the present; the past held far too much anguish, and he couldn't bear to dwell there. Only a sheer act of will had kept him from that place for so many years.

He'd survived Frank once; he could do it again. If John was nothing else, he was most certainly a survivor.

Wiping his face with a towel, he walked from the bathroom a little more composed. Marie sat on the bed facing him. This time the tears were hers.

"We've got to talk about this. We need help, John."

"It was just a nightmare. No big deal. Nothing to get worked up about."

"What were you dreaming? What made you scream like that?"

He paused to consider his answer. He wanted to tell her, but some things hurt far too much to relive, at least for now. And he wasn't sure he could ever tell her. He doubted it would do any good anyway; it was his cross to bear, and in time it would pass, just as it had when he was young. He could wait this out. "I don't remember." Reaching around her, he took a blanket from the bed. "Sorry I woke you."

"You don't remember?"

John wrapped the blanket around himself and glared at her. "No. I don't."

"You yelled, 'He killed—'"

"It's not important, Marie," he said, cutting her off. "Especially at three in the morning."

"When *will* it be important? Give me a date and time when we can talk about it. Tell me when you think we can get this out in the open, and I'll be there."

"I don't want to argue. And we both need some sleep, so I'll be on the couch."

"But, John…"

He looked back, standing in the doorway.

"Can we pray about this?"

"You pray. I need some sleep."

For the first time in their marriage, John refused to pray with Marie.

"I love you," she whispered as he vanished into the darkened corridor.

17

The knock on the motel room door surprised Frank, who was almost asleep on his bed. When he stood up, pain fired up his legs and through his spine, freezing him in place for a moment. He moaned and grabbed his back and then started for the door again.

He fumbled with the lock, his hands weak and clumsy like they no longer belonged to him and had a will of their own. Finally getting a solid grip on the knob, he forced it open.

Marie stood in the doorway with her arms crossed and dark circles under her eyes. Her face appeared tense but certainly softer than the day before.

"So you come to holler at me some more, have ya, missy?" Frank reached for his cane propped beside the door. "Let me get outside so you can really give it to me again."

"That's not why I'm here." She stepped back. "I don't want to fight."

"Whoa," Frank said, exhaling and wiping his brow with a handkerchief. "That's a relief. I don't think I got the energy for a good screaming at, especially from you. You got fire in your guts, missy, and I pity the poor soul who tangles with you."

Frank smiled and lowered his head, attempting to get a glimpse into Marie's eyes, but she only gave attention to her shuffling feet and didn't respond.

"Since you're not here to holler at me, why are you here?"

"I want to..." She brushed her unkempt hair from her face. "To apologize. For yesterday. My behavior."

"I see."

"My behavior wasn't, well," she said, working her lips back and forth. "It wasn't fair. I shouldn't have said those things. I should have heard you out."

"Why the sudden change? Yesterday you were gonna have me arrested."

"I thought about what you said—a lot. As a matter of fact, it's all I've been thinking about. I couldn't sleep at all last night, and then John woke up and...well, I was just wrong. I want to hear what you have to say, if you can see your way to forgive me."

"I don't blame you, missy." He rested both hands atop the cane. "I might've done the same thing if I was in your shoes. I did kinda just show up. Everything considered, you wasn't that bad. You're looking out for your family; it's what you're supposed to do."

"That's no excuse, especially since—if—you're a Christian."

A jolt of life blazed through him, raising him to his tiptoes. "Are you a follower of Christ?" He took two steps out the door toward her. "Please tell me, is John a believer? I must know."

"Yes, we both are. Our whole family is."

"Praise God, Lord Almighty." He clenched his hands in front of his face, and tears rolled unchallenged down his cheeks. "Praise God, Maker of heaven and earth. I prayed every day for that. Every day for twenty-seven years, I prayed that my son would know Christ, and that the Lord would protect him and be with him. Thank you for telling me. Thank you so much."

Marie eased toward him and laid a gentle hand on his shoulder. "I think we need to start over. My name is Marie Russell, and I'm your daughter-in-law." She took his weak, knobby hand and shook it carefully with both of hers. "It's a pleasure to meet you."

"Would you like a cup of coffee?" He took a handkerchief from his pocket and wiped his nose. "There's a diner down the street. It's got lousy food but good coffee."

"I think we should. We have a lot to talk about."

Frank's hand trembled as he lifted the steaming cup of coffee to his lips. Marie tried not to stare at him, but the resemblance to John was uncanny, and slightly unsettling. He bore the same broad shoulders and long arms as John. But it was his eyes that intrigued her most, the same piercing blue eyes of the man she loved. Frank was definitely John's father. No question.

His hands caught her attention as well. They were large and probably once strong, like John's, but these hands had shed blood—much blood. As Frank raised the cup for another sip, Marie wrestled with the conflicting images of a now frail, withered old man who once murdered his wife and brutalized his son, his own flesh and blood. She felt like an actress in a surreal play.

The clatter of the bustling, crowded diner temporarily drew her attention away as the clanking of silverware on ceramic plates and the low murmur of the patrons echoed throughout the restaurant.

"What's he like?" Frank asked. "John. What's he like?"

"He's a good man. He's such a loving husband and father. I couldn't ask for any better."

"That's good." He bobbed his head up and down. Clearly uncomfortable in the diner, he sat up straight and proper in the booth and seemed hypersensitive with his manners, placing his napkin on his lap and keeping his elbows off of the table.

His last three decades were spent in prison, and he wasn't used to dining with a woman or anyone save guards and other prisoners. He'd passed from one dangerous and frightening world into another and was trying his best to adjust.

"John loves the Lord," she said. "He's strong and kind. He's a good detective, too."

Frank stayed quiet for a moment and sipped more of his brew. He seemed perplexed at what to say next.

Marie continued to stir her coffee long after the sugar and cream faded. She had a hundred questions. Most were deep and personal, and she feared the answers to the others. At least now she felt a connection to Frank. Something in her spirit assured her that he was truly a believer, but she still struggled with what to say. How could she ask him about the murder? Would he want to tell her? Would he tell her the truth? *Lord, give me the words.*

"What happened?" she finally said, breaking the silence.

Frank rested against the back of the booth and fiddled with a button on his red flannel shirt, as if he'd just discovered it. He swallowed hard and then took another sip of his coffee, while glancing over his cup at Marie.

"It was a long time ago." He placed the cup gently on the table.

"If you don't want to talk about it, that's okay. We can talk about something else. I can tell you about your grandchildren."

"No, no. We can get to all that." He held his hand up. "But

first I think we gotta get past this. I have to say what happened. Speak it, if this is gonna work at all."

"What's Frankie…I mean, John said about me?" Frank asked, his eyes focusing in on Marie.

"Nothing." She shifted in her seat. "Until the other day at the hospital. He's said nothing to me."

"The hospital?" Frank perked up. "Is he okay?"

"He's fine. He just had a…a problem. But he's okay."

Frank reclined, looking relieved.

"John told me only a little. All he would say was that you were his father and you…" She couldn't bring herself to say it. The words stuck in her throat as if they were too large, too awful to ever find their way out.

"Murdered his mama." Frank's voice quivered, and a glossy sheen filled his eyes.

Marie sighed and nodded her head, thankful that Frank spoke it for her. The dark subject was now out in the open, exposed to the light. The chasm between them evaporated like dew in the midmorning sun. "Yes, that's what he told me. But he wouldn't say any more."

"You didn't know before? He never said nothing about me at all?"

"Nothing," she said. "For the sixteen years we've known each other, he hasn't said a word. I mean, I knew he was adopted and all, but I always thought it was when he was a baby. I didn't know anything about this, or you."

Frank took notice of the ceiling. "That don't surprise me none. I imagine he'd wanna forget everything about me and his life, 'cept his mama, of course."

"That's why I came back to see you. John's not talking with me. He's still not telling me anything, and I'm worried about him. I've never seen him like this. And after yesterday, when I found out you're a Christian too, I just felt that God is opening this door. That it's time for healing."

"Every day since February 3, 1977, the day I accepted Jesus as my Lord and Savior, I've prayed for John. That God would give me a chance to make it right. I never dreamed He'd let me outta prison to do it myself. I figured I could write John a letter and ask him to see me or something. I never dreamed this. But that's God for ya. You never really know what to expect with Him."

His body convulsed, and he covered his mouth as he was besieged by a wheezing, coughing fit. Pulling several napkins from the holder, he masked his mouth again as another barrage of uncontrolled hacking overtook him. With his free hand, he fumbled in his shirt pocket, finally recovering a pill bottle. He slipped two pills quickly into his mouth, then downed a gulp of coffee.

Marie read the bottle on the table—Oxycotin. She glanced back at Frank, who was still holding the napkins over his mouth but seemed to have the coughing under control. His shirt dangled on his shoulders as if it were hung on a clothes hanger. His face was gaunt, and he just looked tired. After tending to her own dying father, she knew the signs too well.

She made eye contact with Frank. "You're sick."

He smiled and wiped his mouth with the napkins. "You're mighty keen, missy."

"Cancer?"

He affirmed her suspicions with a slight bow of his head.

"Where is it? The cancer."

Frank chuckled. "You'd be better to ask where it isn't. But that don't matter none. The only thing that matters is that I don't have much time. It's the only reason I made parole. They figured that I was gonna go off to the VA hospital, and that would be the end of me, and the state of Florida wouldn't have to pick up the medical tab. I suppose they thought it was a win-win for everyone."

"I'm sorry, Frank. Is there anything I can do?"

"Yes there is, missy. Help me meet with my son. Help me tell him how sorry I am. Help me make this thing right. Nothin' else matters to me now. It's the only thing I truly want. 'Delight yourself in the Lord—'"

"'And he will give you the desires of your heart,'" she finished for him. "It's one of my favorite Psalms." She smiled and took both of his hands and held them tight.

Her heart was open and yearning to help him, but she didn't see how it would be possible. "I don't know if I can do that. John won't even talk about it with me. If he knew I was here, he'd be really upset, to say the least."

"I don't want to cause you no heartache, but I don't have any choice but to ask. No one else can help me, and I don't think showing up again at your house would be smart."

"No. No." She shook her head. "That would be bad." She searched his eyes, which were transfixed on her. They were sincere, trusting, but also weary. She feared that they truly didn't have much time. The cacophony of feelings collided inside her heart like a derby smashup. She yearned to help this dying man, but she desperately wanted to honor her husband. The two emotions seemed incompatible, dividing loyalties. *Lord, what am I to do?*

In a place deep inside her, she felt that maybe helping Frank *was* honoring John. She would be giving him what he needed, not necessarily what he wanted—like medicine that doesn't taste good on the way down but ultimately leads to healing. Peace encircled her.

"I'll help you."

"Praise God!" He squeezed her hands. "Praise God!"

The waitress interrupted them, refilling both of their cups.

Marie sipped her refreshed brew. Frank told her of times past, John's birth, their life in Ocala, and a deadly night thirty-three years before. He didn't go into detail; he didn't need to.

Frank wore out quickly, and Marie took him by the arm and led him from the restaurant to his motel room.

Marie hoped that the more she discovered, the more she could help John. But her newfound knowledge only begged more and more questions, not the least of which was—what had she gotten herself into?

18

John and Tim pulled behind the crime scene van, which had just parked on the street in front of a wooden home. The house was blue like a robin's egg, not by design but by years of sun bleaching and neglect. An open carport with grease stains in the driveway was to their left as they faced the front. The windows were boarded up, and a For Sale sign dangled off its post in the front yard, which was a mixture of brown grass and dirt. The steps leading to the front door were in disrepair.

Barry Watkins stepped from the van and tied the yellow crime scene tape around the front fence and walked quickly along the sidewalk, unrolling the tape as he went, clearly showing that this residence belonged to FDLE's crime scene division, if only for the night.

Short and slightly overweight, Barry sported glasses and a goatee that consisted of more hair than was on top of his head. He walked, talked, ate, and slept crime scene work. He taped every show on TV about crime scenes and watched them faithfully. John and Barry worked together on a number of cases, including Gainesville, and Barry had earned John's trust. He knew that Barry would do whatever it took to find evidence. He once spent three days in a crawl space exhuming a body buried there and never once complained.

Even though Barry was stationed out of the Orlando office, John requested that he come with them to Fort Lauderdale to examine Jesse Lee and Linda Morgan's former home. Barry was the best and most dedicated crime scene analyst in the entire agency, and John wanted him to give it a once-over. Although the Morgans moved out several years before, it was worth a try to search for some evidence. Their best information so far placed Dylan at this address some six years before. They didn't have anything to lose.

A young brunette assistant, a little taller than Barry, got out of the van and helped him with the tape. They both wore the dark blue jumpsuits with FDLE Crime Scene plastered in neon yellow on the front and back. John would often tease Barry that he must wear it to bed because it was the only thing he ever saw him in.

The four huddled on the sidewalk. "All right, boss," Barry said. "What do you want done?"

"I'd like us to do a walk-through first—" he surveyed the front of the house—"to try and get a feel for the place. Then while you and Dawn are doing your magic, Tim and I will canvass the neighborhood to see if anyone remembers anything. That keeps us out of your hair for a time."

Barry nodded. "Fingerprints aren't a concern because we know Dylan was here, so we'll limit our search to serological evidence—blood, body fluids, and such."

"I know it's a lot to ask, six years after the fact and all, but do you think you can find any evidence?"

"If the scene is large enough, violent enough—" Barry rubbed his chin—"we might be able to locate some blood evidence with the ultralight source and luminol. Maybe even locate some cleanup spots. But it's a stretch."

"All we can do is try," John said. "We have DNA from his mother, so if you locate something, anything, at least it would give us a starting point. But six years may be too much for even *you* to find the one piece of evidence that breaks this case wide open." John grinned at Barry.

"Agent Russell." Barry held his hand vertically in front of his face, pulled the rubber glove on tight, then snapped it. "Do I sense a challenge here? What do I get if I find it?"

"The usual," John said, still smirking. "Dinner at the restaurant of your choice."

"Anything on the menu I want?"

"Anything."

"Dawn's invited also?" Barry pointed to his assistant with his thumb.

John paused, as if carefully considering the terms. "Dawn, too, of course."

"Then if any evidence is in this home," Barry said, his chin and chest out, "consider it found." He and Dawn pulled their protective goggles down in unison with the precision of a military drill team.

The four climbed the rickety, broken steps, and John used the key the realty company gave him to open the front door. With the windows boarded up and the sun going down, John strained to see into the front room. His hand searched along the wall for a light switch. He finally found it and flicked it several times, but to no avail; the electricity was still turned off. He pulled a small flashlight from his pocket and illuminated the barren room.

Dust from the floor rustled as a breeze slipped in through the door. Judging from the smell, a healthy breeze hadn't passed through the door in some time. The house had been on the market for eight months. The last owner was the third since the Morgans lived here. The odds of finding key evidence this long after the fact were about the same as him running into an Amish street gang. Who knows how many people had traipsed through the house since then? But if he didn't look, he'd never know. Stranger things had happened.

The floor creaked as they explored each room. They shone their flashlights from ceiling to floor, looking for anything obvious. Some papers, broken crayons, and clothes hangers littered the wooden floor.

John entered a small bedroom that could have been Dylan's. The white wall had suffered the abuse consistent with a four-year-old, foot smudgings and drawings scattered along the wall at varying heights and degrees.

Tim followed him into the room. "What do you think?"

"I don't know." John shone his light along the baseboard. "It doesn't look like it's been painted in a while. If anything splashed up during an attack, if there was an attack, we might be able to find it."

"If it happened here."

"Yeah," John said. "There's more *ifs* than *dids*. Let's get the neighborhood contacts done while we have a little light, and we can let Barry do his thing."

Tim and John hurried out of the bedroom and into the living room, where Barry and Dawn were setting up their equipment. Barry pulled out a laser wand with a cable running back to a small generator.

He handed Tim and John protective glasses with a yellow tint to them. "Put these on. You don't want to look at this light without them, if you ever want to see right again. I'm going to give it a test run."

John and Tim slipped the glasses on, and Dawn and Barry pulled theirs down as well.

Barry flipped the switch, and a blue laser beam shot across the room, splashing against the wall. The room transformed in an instant from the room they were looking at, with its distinctive hues and shadows, to a totally different room, like looking at a negative of a picture. The wall, which looked relatively clean before, now lit up with dozens of previously undetected spots and stains.

"Oh yeah." Barry shook his head as he scanned the room with the light. "It's gonna be a long night." He turned off the light, and John and Tim handed him their glasses and walked out the front door.

It took a moment for their eyes to adjust to the light of dusk. A black woman in her mid-thirties stood in the yard next to the house. She propped one hand on the chain-link fence and held a small child in the other as she watched the goings-on.

"Excuse me, ma'am," Tim said as he and John strolled toward her across the crispy brown grass of the front yard. "Can we speak with you for a moment?"

"Sure." Her expression was warm and inviting, a pleasant change from many of the people they contacted.

"Peggy Jones," she said, hand extended. "Looks like there's been some trouble here."

"We're just checking something out." Tim glanced over his shoulder toward the house. "How long have you lived here?"

"My husband and I have been here maybe..." She scrunched her forehead. "About ten years now, I think."

"Good." Tim pulled a paper from his file with pictures of Linda and Jesse Lee Morgan on it. "Do you remember these people living here?"

"Oh, yeah. I remember them real well."

"What kind of neighbors were they?"

"She seemed kinda nice." She pointed to the picture of Linda. "Quiet, but nice. But him." She stabbed the photo of Jesse Lee with her finger. "He's another story. Something was wrong with that man, I can tell you."

"What makes you say that?" Tim said.

"We could always hear him screaming at her and the kids or whoever. He just seemed mean. He would always give my husband and me dirty looks. I don't think he likes black folks too much. I said hello to him one morning, and he mumbled a word that I will not repeat. My husband didn't like him at all. He told me to have nothing to do with that man."

"Sounds like your husband has good instincts," Tim said.

John pulled a picture of Dylan from the file. "Do you remember ever seeing this boy here?"

"This is the boy from TV, right? The one that's missing?"

"Yeah," John said. "We're doing a little background on him and what might have happened to him."

"You know, he looks familiar, but they had all kinds of kids running through here. I'm not sure if I remember him from the news or what." She looked at the picture again. "I'm sorry. I wanna help, but I just can't be sure."

"That's okay," Tim said. "You've already been a big help."

"I've got one more question," John said. "When the Morgans lived here, did anyone from the Division of Family Services come out here and talk with you about them? Do a background check on them for foster family status or anything like that?"

"No." She shook her head vigorously. "No way. I would have remembered that and told them everything I told you. Those people shouldn't have had children of their own, much less taken care of someone else's."

"That's true." John took her hand again. "Thank you. We appreciate your help."

"I hope you find that boy, and he's okay and all. It's a crying shame people treat children like that. The Good Lord didn't put children on this earth to be treated like that."

"No, ma'am, He didn't."

"My husband and I will be praying for you."

"We can use all the help we can get," John said.

They walked back across the yard. The eerie blue glow of the laser light seeped through the edges of boarded-up windows like a specter from a time long past, passing back and forth across the living room.

John and Tim spoke with most of the neighbors on the street; the majority of them didn't live here when the Morgans did. No one remembered Dylan.

They made their way back to the house. Barry and Dawn were taking several paper bags of evidence from the home—pieces of drywall with stains on them, soiled clippings of carpet, and dozens of Q-tips used to collect the serological evidence from suspicious areas.

"Anything of interest?" John asked.

"Lots of little things," Barry said. "But nothing that stands out—like a large trauma scene or cleanup area. We'll have to send most of this stuff to the lab. It's hard to tell if there will be anything of value."

"Well," Tim said. "We don't know if we don't look."

Barry and Dawn took down the crime scene tape and packed the last of the evidence, then they were on their way.

A low peal of thunder growled on the horizon like the call of a lion in the distance. No one else seemed to notice. John did. He placed his hands in his pockets to hide his sweaty palms, and he fought to suppress the whirlwind of terror broiling just under the surface of his spirit. *Not now.*

With a deep, controlled breath, he checked the cloudbank off in the distance. "We probably should be going." The storm wasn't heading in their direction, giving him a slight reprieve, at least enough to keep him functioning. Tim didn't appear to notice John's angst—good. He didn't want to explain to him what he didn't fully understand himself.

As they walked toward their car, John said, "I don't get it."

"What?"

"Someone from DFS should have conducted neighborhood contacts for the foster-care checks. That's just basic procedure. From everyone we talked with, no DFS agent ever came out here to interview anyone. It's like the Morgans just slipped under the radar screen."

"Or someone slipped them under," Tim said.

19

Marie couldn't get comfortable. She tossed the bedspread off once again and lay silently in the night. She looked at the clock—1:30 A.M. She had to get some rest. John crawled into bed a little over an hour before, and she couldn't get back to sleep.

She turned to her side, facing John. He lay with his back to her, practically hanging off the other side of the bed. She placed her hand on his shoulder and ran it up his neck and back on the pillow. She hoped he'd stir, move, speak, anything. He was fast asleep or acting like he was asleep. She couldn't tell. Part of her hoped they could talk or hold each other, something that made them feel connected. The other part prayed he was finally getting the rest he so desperately needed.

In the week since Frank arrived, John hadn't had a night of uninterrupted sleep. Although he awoke screaming only the one time, most of the nights he would mumble in his sleep and toss and turn. His dreams tormented him. Several times, she'd found him sleeping on the couch in the morning. And, naturally, he didn't want to talk about it with her.

The day's events flashed through her mind like a kaleidoscope of shifting images and feelings. She felt criminal for meeting Frank behind John's back. In all the years they'd been together, she never did anything that made her feel like she betrayed her husband—until now. But what other choice did she have?

How would she get John to meet with Frank? It seemed impossible. She couldn't even get him to talk with her about what happened, his feelings, his desires. He just shut her out. They used to be able to talk about everything, share their deepest secrets and desires with each other. Now she felt as if she barely knew the man lying next to her.

She yearned to learn more about what happened. Frank had filled in many of the blanks, but she wanted to know more. She couldn't explain why. Maybe she could help John more if she knew every detail. Maybe she just wanted more facts of the life he closed off to her, worked so hard to conceal from her.

Her selfishness angered her, which wasn't helping her sleep. She pulled the covers back over her.

How could she be thinking about her needs right now? She had to focus on John, on helping him through this. If their roles were reversed, he would be more worried about her than himself, at least the John she thought she knew would.

She flipped back over to her side and tucked her hands under her head. Some of the puzzle was coming together, but much was still missing. Maybe if she went back to where it all started she could get some real answers.

She flopped onto her back and determined to find those answers—only a trip to Ocala would help her do that.

20

Marie drove past the sign that read "Welcome to Ocala, Tree City, USA." It was her first trip to the city where her husband grew up. Although she'd only driven a couple of hours to get here, she was surprised at the change in scenery. The palm trees and wetlands of Melbourne had been replaced by sprawling oak canopies with moss hanging off of them like lazy felines basking in the midmorning sun. She was even taken aback by a couple of hills, which were definitely foreign to the coastal areas.

Ocala felt slower than Melbourne, older and well established. Although many newer stores and restaurants lined the route, cattle and horses seemed to graze everywhere. Small ranches and dairy farms dotted the landscape like quaint postcards from Ocala's past.

Her cell phone chirped and displayed Cheri's home number. She picked the phone up off the seat. "Hey, I'm pulling into Ocala now."

"I just wanted to let you know that Kevin and I prayed for

the Lord's guidance and safety for you today. And don't worry about the boys. I'll pick them up from school, and they'll be here when you get back."

"What would I do without you?" Marie said.

"You'd be sad and lonely and at least ten pounds heavier."

"You're probably right." Marie chuckled. Cheri could always make her smile. "Thanks again for all your help. I'll let you know when I'm on my way home."

"I wish I could be there with you."

"You are." Marie smiled. They said their good-byes.

Marie glanced at her map and then spotted the sign for the Ocala Public Library. She pulled into a parking spot. What was she doing? She drove nearly three hours to get here. That would give her only a short time to complete her research before she'd have to turn around and drive back to pick up the boys. What did she hope to accomplish? She might not even find what she was looking for, if she even knew what that was. All she knew was that John grew up here, at least until he was seven. The events that had shaped and molded him were here somewhere, maybe well hidden, but here just the same.

She rubbed her eyes with both hands. The drive made her tired, but there was no time to rest. She picked up her notebook and hurried toward the brick library, which seemed fairly new and modern. She felt like she was back in college. Maybe the journalism classes she took would finally pay off.

She located the research room and found the microfiche for the newspapers. There was an overlap of two major newspapers that covered the area for the date she was looking for. Both the *Ocala Times* and the *Alachua County Herald* were up and running then. She chose the *Ocala Times* first.

She found the drawer for 1971 and ran her hand across the film boxes until she came to August. She pulled it out and opened the box carefully, sliding the spindle with the microfiche out into her hand.

Four microfiche reading machines lined the walls at the back of the room. She sat next to a woman maybe ten or fifteen years older than she was. The woman was preoccupied with a microfiche and had several rolls out on the table next to her.

"Is anyone using this machine?" Marie said.

"No." The woman pulled her notes closer to her, out of Marie's way. "Please use it."

Marie sat and placed her purse under her chair and her notepad on the table next to her. The screen on the reader was slightly larger than a normal TV. She used her fingernail to catch the lip of the microfiche to pull it out. It felt brittle in her hand. Would it break as she strung it through the reels and underneath the viewing platform? Turning the first knob, she gave it a test run.

Tiny images of photographs of each page of the paper blazed across the screen, and the high-pitched hum surprised her. She directed the reels slowly, and the pages passed by at a more discernable speed.

Adjusting the slide, she brought a blurry page into the frame. She tweaked several dials until the page eased into focus—August 1, 1971. Everything she was looking for would probably appear on August 9, since the murder happened on the 8th. She spun the reels forward as the pages turned into a blur of black and white and stopped on an advertisement.

The clothing ads brought back memories from her childhood—the bouffant hairdos, high-heeled shoes, and long skirts. She forgot about the clothes and the culture of her childhood in the late sixties, early seventies. Being a military brat, she missed out on much of the hippie movement, the tie-dye T-shirts, and the antiwar protests. Her family never stayed in one place long enough to make any attachments or follow any trends. One year they'd be in Europe, the next North Dakota.

She pulled the reels forward again, scrolling across the front page, then centered the frame.

OCALA MAN KILLS WIFE

In a fit of drunken rage, Frank Moore of Ocala shot and killed his wife late yesterday evening. The Moore's young son, Frank Jr., was found underneath the bed, traumatized from what he witnessed. Detectives have spoken with the boy—the only witness to the crime— but won't comment on what he might have seen or any statements he might have made.

Marie adjusted the frame closer to the bottom, so she could bring a picture into better focus. "Suspect Confesses to the Crime" was posted just above the picture. The grainy black-and-white emerged into clarity like a distant memory suddenly sharpened and brought to the surface by a familiar event.

Even though many years had passed, Marie knew the man in the picture in an instant. Frank stood defiant, angry, with his hands cuffed behind his back, being escorted from the Ocala police department by two detectives. His chiseled face was bruised and beaten, his left eye discolored and swollen. His expression radiated so much hate it gave Marie goose bumps.

She studied it again. She couldn't reconcile the man in the picture with the man she met the day before. Physically, it was certainly Frank—the same eyes and features. But the hateful scowl and defiance was foreign to the man she had coffee with, who spoke of the risen Savior.

God had done something powerful with this man for such a change to occur. She would have to delve deeper with Frank when she got the chance. She loved testimonies, and by the looks of it, Frank had some story to tell. She printed the front page and rolled the frames to the continuation of the story.

The picture on the second page was clear and centered. A tall, lanky man wearing a tie and long-sleeved shirt with a badge and pistol clipped to his side walked down porch steps with a boy in his arms. The detective seemed caught off guard by the picture. The caption below it read that he was Detective Randall Pollard. He was one of the men escorting Frank on the front page. She zoomed in on the small boy; his head rested on the man's shoulders.

Marie gasped, placing her hand over her mouth. Her eyes betrayed her. Lying like a rag doll, young John was the very image of Brandon at that age. Her head spun, and her stomach cramped. She took a minute to compose herself and then looked back at the photo.

John's eyes were dark, hollow, as if he weren't even conscious. His arms hung lifelessly at his sides, and his face was expressionless and empty like a mannequin.

Marie's hands trembled as she looked at the photo again. She was so tired. At first the tears fell slowly; she wiped them along her cheek and tried to calm herself. Soon, she burst forth, and the frustration, anger, hurt, and fear boiled over into uncontrolled sobbing.

The woman sitting next to her looked at Marie then around the room. She placed her hand on Marie's shoulder. "Dear, are you okay?"

"No." Marie dropped her head to the table. "No, I'm not."

21

John, Tim," Alan called from his office. "I need to see you
both, pronto."

They entered their boss's office, where an attractive
Hispanic woman was talking with Alan. In her early thirties,
she had a trim build and was wearing a brown suit that fit her
well. Her thick black hair was pulled back neatly.

John could see the outline of a pistol in her ankle holster,
but he didn't have to see that to know she was a cop. Just the
way she stood, with her shoulders back, chin out, marked her.

He'd often told Marie that he could spot another cop from
ten blocks away. They just carried themselves differently—
scanned a room when they entered for any signs of trouble,
only took seats at restaurants with their backs to the wall, and
always looked ready for a fight.

She was definitely a cop.

"Gentlemen, come in." Alan cleared his throat. "I'd like to
introduce Agent Roberta Sanchez. She's with our profiling unit
in Dade County."

Tim closed the door.

"Robbie." She spoke with a hint of a Cuban accent. She shook John's hand, firmly and confidently, then Tim's. "That's what everyone calls me, anyway."

John recently read an article about Robbie in the department newsletter. She was terrorizing the murderers and thugs in the Miami area, working a number of high-profile cases. She had almost a sixth sense when putting profiles together and was a rising star in the agency.

"Roberta," Alan said, "I mean, Robbie has come up with something interesting that might just tie into Dylan's case. Robbie, do you want to let them in on what you found?"

"My pleasure." She picked up a thick file from Alan's desk and thumbed through several pages. "I've been working a case in the Miami metro area of three abducted children—all boys. They went missing from south Dade County during the last eighteen months. We've found two of the bodies but not the third. Both were found murdered several miles from where they were abducted. The dump sites were similar—both wooded areas off the Tamiami Trail. The manner of death was consistent on both." She passed Tim and John a file folder. "The profile we put together indicates that the three crimes are related and most probably committed by the same perp."

John opened it. The first page had a booking photo of a suspect—Kenneth Willard Pate. With a crew cut and eyes that resembled those of a large carp, Kenneth's degenerate grin filled the page. His eyebrow was pierced with an ornate gold hoop, and his printout listed more tattoos than John had time to read.

"Kenneth Willard Pate," Tim said, looking at his photo. "Five foot ten, 170 pounds, brown and brown. Sweet-looking guy. What do you have tying him to our case?"

"He's a registered sex offender with a lengthy, nasty history. He's a real freak show," she said, and then a broad, mischievous smile overtook her. "And the show's about to come to an end. We have DNA. We got a positive match yesterday on these two homicides to our boy Kenneth here. I've got two signed arrest warrants with his name on them for first-degree murder."

"Sounds like you have a great case on him for your homicides," John said. "But, other than being a first-class deviant, what makes you think he might have any connection to our case?"

"Look at his address for 1998." She lifted up a page on his file.

"Cypress Street, Fort Lauderdale," John said.

"Two blocks from where Dylan lived at the same time." She handed him a map with both addresses highlighted. "The houses were just two streets away, and it was possible that Kenneth could have even seen Dylan's house from his."

John and Tim regarded each other and smiled. "This is good stuff. Real good stuff. This might be the break we've been waiting for. So when can we talk to this guy?"

"We got a tip that he's hiding out at a cousin's house thirty miles south of here in Vero Beach. We have it under surveillance right now. If he moves, we'll take him down. If not, he's got an early morning date with our SWAT team. Would you gentlemen be interested in joining us?"

"Now you're talking." Tim slapped the folder shut. "Waking up in the morning with the SWAT team and stun grenades—these are the days I love my job."

"Robbie," John said, catching her eye. "I think you've just become our new best friend."

22

Brandon passed John his dirty plate from dinner, and John plunged it into the soapy water in the sink, then wiped it clean.

"How's your arm?" Marie massaged Brandon's shoulder from behind.

"It feels okay. A little sore, but I think it should be all right by tomorrow."

"We'll soak it later," Marie said. "And then put a heating pad on it. If you get a good night's sleep, you should be able to pitch this weekend."

"I hope so." Brandon squeezed his right shoulder and rotated it around. "It's our chance to get back at the Braves."

"But if it still hurts in the morning," Marie glanced over her shoulder at John, "you can play out in the field, so you don't ruin your arm at age eleven, isn't that right, Coach?"

"He'll be fine, hon. He's strong and healthy. But if he looks like he's in pain, I'll take him out. Promise."

"I know, but it's my motherly duty to watch over him and my wifely duty to watch over you."

"And I do appreciate it," John said, bowing.

"Okay, boys," Marie said. "Time to get upstairs and do your homework."

They both bounded up the stairs, with Joshua pulling on the back of Brandon's shirt.

"How'd it go today?" Marie asked. "Any closer to solving this?"

"All right, I suppose." John dunked another plate into the sink. "We got a fresh line on a suspect. It sounds good, but we gotta check it out. I have to be up real early tomorrow. We have to be in Vero before sunup, so I might not see you in the morning."

"Oh." She struggled to figure out what to say to him. She was never good at being sneaky or sly. She usually blurted out whatever was on her mind. She planned all day about how to bring up in casual conversation that she thought it would be a good idea to meet with his murderous father. Of course, she wouldn't put it that way, but it always seemed to get back to that. She still felt treacherous for meeting with Frank. She wanted to walk carefully, but without being deceptive...or more deceptive.

"Have you thought much about the other day?" she asked as she wiped a dish dry. She opened the cabinet above the sink and stacked the plate on top of the others while she peeked over her shoulder at John.

"No. There's not much to think or talk about." He handed her another freshly cleaned plate.

"I just didn't know if you reconsidered—"

"I haven't." His blunt tone carried little hope for a change in spirit. "And I'm not going to, so let's just drop it, Marie." He handed her another plate, his eyes narrowed and his face reddened.

"I just don't think he came back to hurt you, that's all."

John gripped the edge of the sink and lowered his head, sighing long and loud. His knuckles went from red to white. "Hon, I don't ask a lot. I've never asked for anything before, but I'm asking now—Leave. It. Alone. Let this whole thing go away so we can get back to our lives."

"I want to…but I can't. I'm worried about you. All he wants is a chance to make things right, to seek your forgiveness." She tightened her lips and pulled her head back. Rats! She wished she could have taken her last words back. At that moment, she really regretted being married to a detective. He wouldn't miss such a misstep.

"How do you know what he wants?" John turned slowly toward her. His eyes sharpening like daggers, he cocked his head to the side for a moment, then righted it again. "You saw him. You met with him, didn't you?"

"I…I…" She took a couple of steps back. "I didn't mean to, honest. I was going to tell him to stay away. I never meant to talk with him. It just kinda happened."

"You lied to me." He pointed his finger at her. "You had no right." His face radiated his rage, and he took several deep, exaggerated breaths.

"We're married; we're a family, remember? Whatever affects you affects us all. That whole 'becoming one body' thing." Marie crossed her arms and stood firm as her anger rose. "Does any of that sound familiar?"

"Don't try that with me. Don't turn it back on me. I asked you to let it go, but you had to stick your nose in this. He kills, tortures, and destroys. That's all he can do. Don't you understand that? Stay away from him and stay outta this."

"He's not like that anymore. He's changed. He's become—"

"You have no idea!" John screamed so loud it made Marie

jump back. "You have no idea how evil that man is." John's eyes were savage and raging. "You couldn't begin to imagine what he did to me, to us. And I don't want to hear how he's changed. That's baloney. He can no more change than the devil can. He's that evil."

Marie stood motionless for a moment, still in shock over John's outburst. She'd never heard him even raise his voice, much less at her. Everything she thought she knew about John was now in doubt. She let several tense seconds pass to regain her composure.

"You're right, John. I don't know what it was like to live with him. I don't know how evil he was or what awful things he did to you and your mother. How could I? Someone would've had to tell me for me to know anything about that. Someone would have had to share that part of his life with me. And since that didn't happen, there's no way I could have known, is there?"

"I forbid you to see him again. I don't want you to talk with him or mention him to me ever again. You might believe his lies, but I know better."

"You forbid me?" She glared back at John. "What kinda talk is that? You don't trust my judgment or my motives? Since when have you felt like that?"

"Since you went behind my back to see *him*. You had no right, Marie."

Joshua peered around the corner, a frightened curiosity on his face. "Are you okay, Dad?" he said, timidly. "What are you yelling about?"

John stepped back against the sink and folded his arms. "Yeah, champ. Everything's fine. Mom and I are just talking."

Brandon stomped down the stairs. "What's all the commotion?" he asked, an ignorant smile covering his face.

"Nothing." Marie turned him around at the bottom of the steps, pushing him back up. "Now head up to your beds. We'll be there in a minute to pray."

"Come here, champ." John held out his arms to Joshua, who leaped into them. John squeezed him tight and held him for several moments. "It's okay. Everything is going to be okay."

Joshua wiggled in his arms. "Dad, you can let go now. I can't breathe."

John lowered him to the floor, and Joshua kissed him on the cheek, hugged Marie, then sprinted across the kitchen and up the stairs. John leaned against the counter.

"They're waiting for us to pray with them." She drew her lower lip in, and they just stared at each other for a moment, saying nothing. The tension lingered in the air like the stench of a burnt meal.

"I know you think you can fix everything, Marie. But some things you just can't." John looked older, with lines forming on his cheeks where his smile used to be. The gray flecks in his hair were more pronounced now. "Some people you can't fix either. It's just the way it is."

23

Two black vans turned onto the street with their headlights off and pulled to the curb in unison. "Do we have any movement?" Alan asked on the radio. He was balanced on a small bench that ran along the inside of the van with Robbie, rubbing shoulders in their cramped quarters. John and Tim hugged the bench that paralleled them. All of them were wearing their FDLE raid vests with trauma plates in them. They were going after a child killer, so no one was taking chances.

"All's quiet right now," the surveillance unit radioed back. "There hasn't been any movement since about eleven-thirty last night when the lights went out."

"Ten-four," Alan said. "All units, we're stepping off in two minutes, repeat, two minutes."

Alan turned to his team. "All right, people, one more time—SWAT is conducting the entry and search for our bad guy. We have the perimeter. Tim, John—you have the north side. Robbie and I have the south. Stay on the corners of the house so we can cover all the sides and the back and let SWAT do their thing," Alan barked out like an auctioneer while he scanned out the front windshield.

"We have the sheriff's department helicopter up and two marked units standing by if anything goes bad," Alan continued. "We'll be working off of channel three. Does everyone have that?"

"We got all this in briefing, boss," Tim said, smiling. "Don't worry. We've done this a hundred times."

"It's my job to worry." Alan checked his watch then looked back out the window, not even regarding Tim. "That's what they pay me to do."

John closed his eyes. He loved this stuff when he was younger, long before he understood how dangerous taking down a murderer really was. Kenneth Pate had a date with Florida's electric chair; he had nothing to lose by shooting it out with the cops.

God, please protect everyone today…even this Pate character. He didn't want to shoot him, although he would if he had to.

No matter how upset he was with Marie for going behind his back, he wished he'd apologized to her before he left. He was up and out before she even knew he was gone. If something went wrong, he'd hate to think that their last conversation was an argument. He'd hate to believe that the last night they spent together, he'd slept on the couch. Somehow he'd make it up to her tonight. But first things first: Kenneth Pate was waiting.

The condensation building on the windows was as thick as the anticipation inside the vans. Tim's smile appeared frozen on his face, and he adjusted his vest several times. Alan frowned, and Robbie bowed her head and appeared to be praying. Her long black hair was tied back in a tight bun. Everyone reacted differently under stress—some people got quiet and purposeful, others seemed almost giddy and carefree.

"All right, Robbie," Alan said. "This is your case, so you make the call when we're ready."

Robbie took a deep breath. "Ready."

"All units, we're stepping off," Alan called on the radio as he unholstered his pistol with his free hand.

Tim rolled the van door open smoothly, careful not to make any noise. Alan exited with his Glock at his side. Robbie crossed herself, then leaped out; John and Tim followed. Five houses separated them from their destination; as first light was cresting on the horizon, the team skulked along the shadows of the sidewalk toward their target.

The entry team hopped out of their van in front of Alan's team, taking the lead position. All seven members of the entry team wore Kevlar helmets and bunker vests that could withstand rifle rounds. Each thick vest was embroidered with FDLE SWAT in bold, unmistakable gold.

They scurried in a line toward the house. The lead man carried an MP-5 submachine gun up at the ready, covering the front windows for their approach. The man behind him held a large metal battering ram so heavy he carried it with both hands. The others followed behind, weapons drawn.

John and Tim peeled off from the group and jogged to the north side of the house, watching several windows that lined the wall. John stood on the front corner of the house, and Tim duckwalked underneath the windows to cover the back. Alan and Robbie split off to the other side of the home.

Sneaking up the walk with their weapons trained on the front door and windows, the entry team tiptoed into a line along the porch. The last officer in the line squeezed the arm of the man in front of him, and the signal that they were ready to move passed up the line.

The burley officer with the battering ram stepped in front of the door, nodded to the others, then drew the ram behind him. He launched it into the door, bursting it off its hinges and crashing onto the living room floor. Like a well-choreographed dance, he stepped to the opposite side of the door just as the second officer tossed in a stun grenade.

"Police! Search warrant! Everybody down!"

A brilliant light followed by an earsplitting explosion rocked the home. The entry team sprinted into the living room. "Search warrant. Everyone on the ground."

Another explosion shook the wall John leaned against, blowing out the window next to him, sending glass shards flying. He covered his face, then looked up to check if Tim was hit. He was still at the opposite corner and gave a John a thumbs-up.

"Get on the ground. On the ground," they heard from inside again as the team scampered from room to room. "He's running. Watch out, he's running!"

Suddenly, a body launched through the window, thumping the ground between John and Tim. The man rolled to his feet without slowing down and sprinted toward Tim, who put his arms out like a linebacker waiting for the perfect tackle.

Kenneth Willard Pate darted to the left of Tim, then bounded to the right. Tim dove and caught the bottom of his T-shirt as he fell to the ground. Kenneth dragged Tim nearly ten feet—his shirt tearing the whole way. With one quick spin, Kenneth was out of his shirt and racing for the back fence with Tim clutching the shirt in his outstretched hand like a prize.

John hurdled over Tim and sprinted after Kenneth, scaling the fence.

"He's running west through the backyard," John huffed into

his radio. "Foot pursuit." Kenneth disappeared over the privacy fence.

John leaped up and grabbed the top of the fence with his radio in one hand and his gun in the other. He struggled for a grip, finally able to pull himself over. He landed on the other side just as Kenneth slipped around the side of a house. The helicopter rolled a hundred feet over the home and then banked around.

John ran to where he last saw Kenneth, who was now at a full sprint down the sidewalk in only his shorts, no shirt or shoes. John pursued him, now nearly fifty yards behind.

"This guy's fast," John said as he stepped it out toward him. "Stop. Police!" Kenneth looked back, then sped up again. John wished he could drop his vest and gear, but that wasn't going to happen. His dress shoes weren't helping either as Kenneth pulled away. John struggled for breath, his lungs burning.

Kenneth galloped toward an intersection and then looked back at John, who was getting farther and farther behind. Kenneth smirked. As he crossed the intersection, a patrol car skidded directly in his path. His feet skipped on the roadway, and his arms flailed as he tried to stop. Crashing into the front quarter panel, Kenneth vaulted over the hood of the car. He twirled in the air and then smacked the pavement with his back, bounced, and rolled to the sidewalk.

The officer bolted around the front of his car, but Kenneth staggered to his feet, dashing off again but not nearly with the same steam he had before. Road rash complemented his tattoo-covered back, and he swayed to and fro as he scampered down the sidewalk.

John passed the officer, who was clearly not going to catch Kenneth. The officer jumped back in his car, squealing the tires and turning his car around in hot pursuit.

Gaining ground, John pushed even harder. Kenneth glanced back again, then cut behind a house with John on his heels. The helicopter buzzed over them again, the pilot giving their location over the radio.

Jumping two more chain-link fences, Kenneth came to another privacy fence. He grabbed the top and pulled himself up. John dropped his radio and dove, seizing his slick, sweaty ankle.

Kenneth shook it, then shook it again, breaking John's grip. Kenneth fell over the top of the fence, thumping onto the ground on the other side. John picked up his radio as he rolled to his feet. He bounded over the fence, landing in another backyard like a cat.

The yard was empty—no sign of Kenneth.

John could see the street in front and all along the sides of the house. He was right behind him; no way Kenneth made it out of the yard. A child's swing set, a shed, and several bushes covered the side fence.

He took several deep, controlled breaths and scanned the yard carefully. The sounds of sirens and his own heartbeat filled his ears. He steadied himself as the adrenaline caused his body to shake. *He's got to be here somewhere.*

The helicopter thundered again overhead. An officer tethered to the chopper held a rifle, leaned out, and pointed to the backyard where John was standing.

"Watch out," the voice came over the radio. "He's behind the—"

Kenneth screamed and charged from behind the shed, grabbing John's gun hand. John dropped his radio, and they struggled for control of the weapon. Kenneth's eyes were crazed, and his arms and body were glossy with blood and sweat.

Getting both hands on his pistol, John thrust his arms high in the air, trying to break Kenneth's grip, but he held on and yanked back. John felt the polymer grip slide in his hand. His heart sank.

"They're in the backyard directly below me," the pilot called over the radio. "Officer needs help. Get up here quick." He lowered the chopper almost to roof level, kicking up dust and dirt around them. The power lines stopped him from landing.

John shifted his body and rammed his hip into Kenneth, knocking them both off balance. They tumbled to the ground, and Kenneth rolled on top of him—the gun sandwiched between them. Kenneth panted his vile, scorching breath in John's face as their wet hands jockeyed for control of the weapon; John stared into a dragon face tattooed on Kenneth's chest.

The gun slithered farther from John's grip. He reached up with his free hand and pushed Kenneth's face away from him. John felt Kenneth's eyebrow ring in his hand. He twisted and yanked the piercing right out of his brow. Kenneth squealed and quaked but held firm onto the weapon.

Kenneth wrenched the handle to gain control; both of John's hands cinched down on the barrel, pushing it away from his head. The barrel passed across his face once, then back again. John locked his arms out, keeping the pistol pointed toward the ground to the side of him.

Kenneth leaned down, bit John's arm, and growled. John squirmed and jerked his arm from Pate's mouth. Kenneth pushed the pistol back toward his face.

John stared down the barrel of his own gun. *Lord help me!*

Tim and Robbie sprinted from the van toward where the helicopter hovered. Two more patrol cars screeched to a stop next to them. The radio was a garbled mess as every unit in the area called for a better location.

"Where is he?" Tim screamed, pistol at his side, frantically scanning the area. "Where are they at?" Two uniform officers jumped the fences with Tim and Robbie. They were still several houses away, running toward where the pilot was directing them.

The chopper hovered at rooftop level. An officer hung out the side with his rifle trained on the fight below, unable to get a clear shot. Tim, Robbie, and the officers stampeded to the last fence.

Crack! The shot echoed off the houses. Tim heard the words no cop ever wants to hear.

"Shots fired!" the pilot screamed into the radio. "Shots fired! Officer down! Officer down!"

24

Frank woke with a shudder, shaking his already flimsy motel room bed. The morning sun peeked through his partially drawn drapes. The pain in his spine throbbed in unison with every heartbeat. Placing his feet on the floor, he arched his back, hoping for some relief. There wasn't any.

The medication was on the dresser just a few feet away, but it might as well have been miles. His head swirling and his back on fire, he stood using the wall to balance himself. He grunted and doubled over, still trying to ease the pain, which bordered on unbearable.

"Lord help me," he whispered as he righted himself. Hands still on the wall, he tottered and wobbled his way to the dresser.

Hunched over, his gnarled hands fought with the pill bottle as he hurried to get the pills that might give him temporary comfort. The lid popped open, and the bottle fell from his hands, spilling the pills onto the dirty brown carpet.

Frank bent down to pick them up when a searing pain pierced his back. He stood, taking in small sips of air. Sweat gushed from his brow. *Not yet, Lord. Please, I haven't finished what I come to do.*

He shuffled toward the phone next to his bed. He stopped, trying to focus on the phone. Everything blurred to just a pinprick of light, then complete darkness.

He felt nothing as he crashed to the floor.

The electronic doors to the emergency room slid open as Marie trotted to the nurses' station. She was vaguely familiar with the layout of the hospital. Both Brandon and Joshua were born here, but it was a long time ago. She hated the smell of hospitals—the antiseptic smell of sickness and death, a palpable reminder of her own father's prolonged battle with cancer. She rubbed the goose bumps on her arms.

"Is there a Frank Moore here? They brought him in by ambulance."

"Let me check," the nurse said while she typed on the computer. "Are you friend or family?"

"Friend…" Marie stopped and thought for a moment. She hadn't really considered Frank as her father in-law. Her husband's father. This was all so new, so strange. She had a lot to get used to. "Family. Definitely family."

The nurse typed more on her computer. "Mr. Moore has been admitted. He's in room 332. Third floor."

"Thank you." Marie hurried to the elevators. She was glad she had given Frank her cell phone number. The call from the nurse, who told her how Frank had been found unconscious by the cleaning woman at the motel, surprised her.

Marie was also glad that John wasn't around when she got the call; that would have been tough to explain. But she was tired of the deception, the games. She couldn't do as John wanted. She still struggled with loyalty and obedience to her husband, but she felt she was being obedient, at least to his needs, not his wants. She couldn't leave the situation alone and hope for the best.

For thirty-three years John had buried his thoughts and emotions from the awful events deep in his soul, in a place he couldn't reach, that couldn't reach out and hurt him again. Maybe that defense mechanism served him well as a child, but he wasn't a child anymore. Denial and hatred had to end. There wasn't time to wait for John to come around on his own. Now, she wasn't sure if they even had thirty-three hours to work this out.

The bell sounded as the elevator reached the third floor. She scurried to Frank's room, near the end of the corridor.

"Hello, missy," he whispered as she entered the room. An oxygen tube ran from his nose, and several IVs were connected to his arms. A large abrasion covered his forehead where he must have struck the ground. Weak and medicated, he was still able to flash a large, grateful smile.

Marie grabbed both his hands with hers. "How are you feeling, Frank?" She stroked his hand with her thumb.

"Been better. But I'm doin' okay now. Got my meds."

"What did the doctor say?"

"He said I'm dying." Frank chuckled. "But I already knew that."

"That's not funny. Not funny at all."

"But it's true, missy," Frank said, this time solemn. "Have you talked to John yet?" He looked hopeful, like she was going to bring him the news he prayed for.

"Yes." She squeezed his hand tight. "But it didn't go well…he's not ready yet."

Frank turned his head away and focused on the ceiling. His

lip quivered and his eyes reddened. Several tears followed the lines in his face down his cheeks. "I suppose I understand. But I was hopin', praying, that somehow it could happen, you know, him coming to see me."

"Don't give up yet. There's still time."

"Not much. I'm fighting the best I can, but I don't know how much more I can take." He took several deep breaths. "Not that I mind going to be with my Lord. I look forward to that more than you know. But God opened so many doors. I mean, real doors for this to happen. I'm trying to figure out why He'd let me get this far only to fail."

"I don't know, Frank," she whispered. "I'm trying to understand it myself."

They shared a few quiet moments together. She searched deep into his eyes. All she saw was a man completely broken over his sin, over his wrecked life. She prayed silently for him, for John, for her, and the boys, for relief from the pain of an ancient wound that didn't seem like it would ever heal.

"You said before that you came to know the Lord in 1977," Marie said, hoping to change the subject. "How'd that happen, if you don't mind my asking?"

"Don't mind at all. It's a good story. You might not believe me, though."

"Try me."

He appeared to be contemplating his decision. "I was several years into my sentence. And I had a problem with another inmate, Bobby Johnson. I'll never forget his name." Frank wiped his mouth with a tissue. "I thought he stole some of my food from the commissary. So I was gonna fix him. We got in a fight, and I pulled my shank."

Frank stopped for a moment, probably not completely comfortable talking about the violence of prison life. And truth be known, she was a little uncomfortable hearing about it, but she tried not to let it show.

"It was a long time ago. I was a different man. Please understand that. The devil had a hold of me real bad. That part of my life gives me no pleasure to recall, 'cept that I get to give glory to our Lord for pulling me from there."

"I understand." Her hand returned to his. "It's okay. Please continue. I want to hear it."

Frank cleared his throat and drew another deep breath. "Like I was saying, I pulled my shank; it's like a knife, missy. I was getting ready to stick him. I'd already beat him down, and he didn't have any fight left in him. The rest of the prisoners were keeping the guards away and yelling and screaming for me to finish him off."

He paused again and worked his lips back and forth, seeming to struggle for the words. "I was just fixing to stick him when he started to recite the Lord's Prayer. That was the exact same thing that my...my Lynette said before..." He winced in pain but not from the cancer.

Marie took a tissue, leaned over, and handed it to him. He wiped his eyes, and she took his hand, holding it tight.

"I swear that I heard her voice. *It was Lynette's voice coming from his mouth.* I stopped cold right there and dropped my shank. I just stood looking at him. I didn't know what to do. He kept praying, and all I could hear was her voice."

Marie cocked her head; it wasn't quite what she expected to hear. "You thought you heard her voice?"

"No, ma'am. I didn't *think* I heard her voice. I *did* hear her voice. I was so scared I didn't know what to do. The next thing I know, the guards grabbed me and tossed me in solitary. I spent four months in solitary confinement, an awful place, to tell the truth. I thought for sure I'd lose my mind. I kept thinking about what happened, how I heard her voice, and how both Lynette and Bobby had said the Lord's Prayer to me. I remembered how Lynette had told me about Jesus plenty of times before that awful day, but I thought it foolishness...until then. The whole thing rattled me real good. For the first time in my life, I *knew* there was a God in heaven—and that meant I was in a lot of trouble. I was certainly headed to hell.

"And for the first time in my wretched life, I got on my knees and called out to the Almighty. I asked Him to save me from myself, my sins. I asked Jesus to be my Savior. Immediately, I felt God's love and forgiveness pour down on me like a waterfall. I wept for what had to be hours. I'll never forget that day as long as I live. I walked into solitary one man and left another."

Frank adjusted his body so he could face Marie better. "I may have been in prison for a long time, missy, but I was really set free on February 3, 1977."

25

Noooo." Tim barreled toward the wooden fence, Robbie and a swarm of officers trailing him. He sized up the fence as he prepared to bound to the top and pull himself over. But his rage and frustration gave him a better idea. Lowering his head, he rocketed toward the middle of the fence. A primal scream escaped him as Tim collided with the obstruction, smashing a section to the ground, breaching it for the rest of the troops.

Kenneth straddled John, the gun still smoking in his hand. Robbie leaped through the hole in the fence, and with two long steps, she punted Kenneth's head like a football, snapping it back and sending the pistol flying out of his hand. He fell backward off of John.

Kenneth staggered to his feet and looked up just in time to catch Tim's diving punch. His face exploded in a crimson mist. Tim swung for his head again but missed because Kenneth fell unconscious to the ground with a broken nose.

Officers pounced on Kenneth and mauled him like a pack of wild dogs, yanking and twisting his appendages in directions they weren't designed to go until he was handcuffed and hog-tied, with his legs bent back and secured to his hands.

"John!" Tim ran to his partner, still on his back, arms at his sides. "Please, God, let him be okay." Tim knelt beside him. "John, can you hear me?"

He made eye contact with Tim and wiped his face with his hand.

"Where are you hit?" Tim surveyed John's chest and head. A trickle of blood rolled from the side of his head to the ground right next to his ear. Tim couldn't tell if it was an entry wound or not. John's tactical vest was smeared with blood and sweat as well. He didn't want to move him, but Tim searched frantically for a wound to treat. "We need an ambulance up here now! We have an officer down!"

"I'm all right," John said, blinking hard and shaking his head, knocking the cobwebs out. "I think it missed." He tried to stand, but Tim kept him on the ground. John probed the wound next to his ear. "No hole, just a slight burn from the muzzle flash."

"Stay down until the ambulance gets here. They need to check you out." A chunk of dirt next to John's head was uprooted, courtesy of a 9mm round that came way too close.

Robbie knelt beside Tim, and Alan, who had just made it to the backyard, stood over them, out of breath.

"I'm okay." John stuck his finger in his ear and wiggled it around. He blinked several more times and shook his head again. "Really, I think I'm fine. It missed." He sat up, and Robbie and Tim took hold of him under each arm and raised him gingerly to his feet.

Alan stood in front of him with his hands on John's shoulders. "Are you sure you're all right? Are you positive?"

"Yeah," John said, standing on his own. "Although I can't

hear out of my right ear." He wiggled his finger in his ear again.

"We'll have you checked out to make sure," Alan said. "And then when I confirm you're *really* all right, I'm going to kill you myself for scaring me like that. I thought for sure we lost you."

Alan hugged John, squeezing him tight. "Don't ever make me have to explain to Marie how you got yourself killed. I've had to do that once before with another officer's wife, and I pray I never, ever have to do it again."

Four officers snatched Kenneth from the ground and carried him, each with a limb tucked securely under their arms. Kenneth groaned with each step, leaving a trail of blood pouring from his face.

Tim darted toward the neatly folded Kenneth. "You scumbag, I'm not done with you yet. You tried to kill my partner. Now you're mine."

Robbie stepped in front of Tim, putting her hands on his chest, holding him back. "He's not worth it, Porter. Let it go. He's got a date with death row anyway. He'll get his."

She was right. A little bit of "street justice" wouldn't do to Kenneth nearly what the state of Florida had planned for him. Tim didn't want to damage the case against him either, even though he struggled with getting at least another shot or two on him. But he knew all too well that down the road some attorney would say that poor Kenneth's rights were violated by the big, bad police. He growled as the officers passed by him toting Kenneth to the street, where a patrol car waited for him.

Alan picked up John's pistol and placed it in an evidence bag. All four detectives shared a collective sigh, then straggled out of the yard toward their vehicles.

John turned toward Robbie and Tim. "Thanks, you two. I'd be dead meat if you didn't show up when you did. I owe you both—big."

"I'm just sick that I'm this outta shape." Tim bent over catching his breath. "Ten years ago, I woulda caught that jackrabbit in the first block. I'm telling you both now, I'm hitting the gym this week. Never again will I be that far behind in a pursuit. No way." The excitement caught up with him. His lungs raged, and his side pounded in defiance; he felt woozy.

John put his hand on Tim's shoulder. "You got here just in time. By the way, nice kick, Robbie. It hurt me just to watch."

She smiled then limped forward. "Yeah, but I think I broke my foot on that knucklehead."

Alan waved at them to catch up. "Well, before we all get weepy, we need to book this clown."

The helicopter soared out of sight, and the early morning sun brought the neighborhood to life. Curious spectators watched from their yards as the commotion died down and all the officers left the area one by one.

John walked between Tim and Robbie. They put their arms around him. A new partnership was in the works.

26

Marie entered the city limits of Ocala again; this time she'd arrived a little earlier to do everything she needed before heading back to pick up the boys. She was a little less anxious this trip, though just as tired.

Pulling into the parking lot of the police department, she quietly prayed, again. One thing was for sure, this crisis was certainly helping her prayer life, though she could do without all the drama. The last blowout with John was bad. He had not spoken with her directly since. He got up on his own in the morning and was off to work before she woke the boys up. The only time she'd see him today would be at baseball practice, if he showed up.

Normally, he'd call her if he was going to work late or was off across the state. Lately, the only thing she could count on was not being able to count on him. Sometimes he would be there; sometimes he wouldn't. She could see that the burden he carried was crippling him. And that's what made her so angry. She was just trying to help. At least he could acknowledge that. She wasn't the enemy.

She clipped her black hair back tight, and checked her appearance in the mirror. The lines on her face seemed like gully trenches, and dark circles around her eyes made her look like a raccoon. She'd looked better, but she didn't really care. She had business to attend to.

It had been thirty-three years since Frank's arrest. She didn't know if asking questions at the police department would help, and she wasn't even sure if she could find Detective Pollard. Did he work for the police department anymore? Was he even still alive? But she couldn't shake the feeling that she needed to talk with him, that maybe he could help her understand.

The police department was large and modern looking, probably built in the last ten years or so. She walked into the lobby, which had a large waiting room with several sets of chairs and tables. Pictures of all of the officers covered one full wall, and the mission and vision statements for the department hung on another.

A bulletproof window with a speaker on it fed into the dispatch area, where Marie could see several people working at computer-operated consoles. She pushed the button next to the microphone, and a young black woman in her dispatcher uniform walked over to the window.

"May I help you?"

"I hope so," Marie said. "I'm looking for information on a homicide case from some time ago."

"When did it occur?"

"1971."

The woman crinkled her face. "I'd say that was a few years ago. I wasn't even born then."

"I know it was a long time ago," Marie said, "but is there

any way I can get information on it, like maybe a report or something?"

"I'll see what I can do. But I wouldn't get your hopes up. A fire several years ago at the old building destroyed most of the older case reports. Whatever survived was put into storage. Even if it wasn't lost in the fire, it will still take our records section time to locate it. Probably a couple of weeks."

"I understand." Great. She'd made her trip for nothing.

"Ma'am, if you'd like, I can put in a request. Maybe they can find what you're looking for."

"That would be nice." Marie held a copy of the newspaper article up to the window. The dispatcher copied down the date and information, and then she took Marie's name and address.

As they were finishing up, another dispatcher walked over and stood next to the younger woman. She was older and had gray streaks in her long black hair, which was tied behind her and dangled almost to her waist.

"I remember him." She pointed to Randall Pollard. "He was a detective here forever. He worked at the department when I first started."

"Is he still around?" Marie asked.

"Last I knew, he still lived in the area." The dispatcher leaned closer to the window and squinted to read the article.

"Could I get his address or his phone number? I'd like to talk with him about this. I think he could help."

"I'm sorry, ma'am," she said, sizing Marie up. "We're not allowed to give out information about any of our officers, past or present. You never know when someone might want to get a little, you know, revenge. We have to protect our people. You understand?"

Marie swallowed hard. "I'm certainly not going to hurt him. I just have some questions, that's all."

"You a reporter?"

"No, I just…" How could she tell this woman what she was going through? Would she understand? Would she care? "I just really need to talk with him."

"I'm very sorry, ma'am, but I can't do that."

Marie sighed and stood motionless. What next? Maybe she could look in the phone book, but it was unlikely a former cop would have his number listed—John and Marie didn't. She felt defeated and resolved to just drive home and find some other way to deal with it. Then she had an idea. What did she have to lose?

As the two dispatchers watched from behind the glass, Marie rummaged through her file until she found what she was looking for. She took the copy of the photo of Randall Pollard carrying John and held it against the window.

"The boy in this picture is my husband. I really need to talk with Mr. Pollard. It's important to me, to us. Is there some way you can help me?" Marie's voice quivered with emotion. The two dispatchers stared at her for a moment.

"Can you wait one minute?" the older woman said. "Please have a seat, and let me see what I can do."

Marie sat in one of the lounge chairs, leaned her head back, and closed her eyes. *Jesus, You are going to have to open the door on this one.*

The older dispatcher went to her seat and pulled a notebook from her stack of resources. She scrolled carefully through it and then picked up the phone and dialed a number. She looked at Marie several times as she talked on the phone. She hung up and walked back to the speaker and motioned to Marie, who jumped from her chair with renewed energy.

The dispatcher slipped a piece of paper through a small mail slot at the bottom of the window. "I was able to find a number for him." She smiled. "I just spoke with Detective Pollard, and he said he'd be glad to talk with you. I hope this helps."

"Thank you." Marie placed her hand against the glass. "It helps a lot."

27

John splashed cool water from the sink onto his face, the full weight of the morning's events hitting him. The adrenaline rush had faded, and his body ached as the soreness set in from his feet to the top of his head. His legs throbbed and seemed unlikely to hold him up much longer.

He checked the burn to his temple in the mirror and probed it with his finger. Gunpowder residue was embedded in his skin, giving the wound a shiny black hue. He still washed the burn thoroughly despite the sting. Another smaller burn had formed on his right hand between his thumb and forefinger where he pushed the pistol away at the last second. This, too, smarted under the cold water.

He lowered his head. "Thank You, Lord. You were looking out for me today—even though I don't deserve it…especially lately. Thank You. Help me do what I have to now. Give me the strength."

The Lord had spared him. Two more inches to the left and Marie would have been getting the news of his death about now. He looked at his watch—9:28 A.M. He couldn't get the old

Army commercial out of his head: We do more before 9:00 A.M. than most people do all day. He chuckled. With more than fifteen years in law enforcement, he'd never gotten so much as a hangnail. He'd been blessed and he knew it. Today was close.

John had no idea how he was going to tell Marie. He'd always tried to convince her that he left all the tough stuff to the other guys; he merely did the investigations, followed leads, talked with people. He conveniently left out certain aspects of his job, certain close calls. Now with everything else going on, he couldn't leave this one out. He'd left her out of enough and didn't want her to hear about this incident on the news or worse, at a department Christmas party two years from now. He would tell her...eventually. But there was still Kenneth Pate to deal with.

"You think you're up for this?" Alan said as John walked from the bathroom. "This guy did try to kill you. Can you interrogate him now and stay focused? Think of the case, not what you want. If you're not up to it, someone else can take over."

"I doubt Pate will say much anyway," Tim added. "He's got everything to lose and nothing to gain by talking with us. Besides, we have DNA on him. The case is solid."

"True." John straightened his tie. "But we don't have Dylan or Robbie's third victim. And he might be the only person who can help us."

John pointed to Kenneth on the closed-circuit TV monitor piped in from the interview room. He sat in the chair, his shoulders slumped forward, his head hanging down, like a fighter who couldn't stand for the final bell. Kenneth's crew cut held patches of dried blood, and a bandage covered his right eyebrow where John had ripped his piercing out. His face was swollen and discolored, and a Band-Aid decorated his disfigured nose, which had a piece of gauze protruding from each nostril. The EMTs had performed some minor triage on him. The scrapes and abrasions on his back and feet were covered by small bandages.

A large dragon tattoo covered his chest with its tail stretching around Kenneth's lean frame and curling onto his back. During their fight, John stared into the eyes of the dragon. He didn't like it much.

"See that?" Robbie pointed to the shoe imprint on Kenneth's face. "You can even see the tassel." She shared with the crowd around the monitor, one more time, her punting technique on the suspect.

"He's ready now." John pointed out on the monitor. "Look at his body language; it screams of surrender."

"Robbie, do you want the interview or should John do it?" Alan asked as they huddled around the monitor.

"John's the best interviewer in the state. I'd be a fool not to use him."

"Okay, it's your show, Russell." Alan crossed his arms. "Don't let it get personal, though. If I see you crossing the line, I'm gonna pull you out. Understand?"

"Got it, boss." Robbie handed him her files. He had read through them briefly before, but he wanted them in hand. It was more of a prop for Kenneth's sake. The more information he thought they had, the more likely he would feel inundated and confess. Like most things in police work, it was a gamble, not an exact science.

John straightened his clothing and appearance. He wanted to appear unfazed by the morning's events. He walked into the room, which was purposely small to make a suspect even more uncomfortable. Kenneth glanced up at John. A disturbed smile crossed his now puffy and unrecognizable face.

"Remember me?" John let the comment hang in the air like a fog bank on a dangerous road. He sat across from him, dropping his files onto the small desk.

"How's your head?" Kenneth said, smirking.

"Just a touch better than your face, it seems."

"Yeah." Kenneth snorted. "It's just like you cops to jump on a man and beat him for no reason." Kenneth glanced at the two-way mirror, playing for the camera. "I was just walking down the street, and you guys come out of nowhere and start knocking me around. Real public service."

"It sounds like a great story, Ken. Too bad the helicopter caught such outstanding video of the entire incident...even the part where you tried to kill me."

Kenneth leaned back in his chair and menaced John with his eyes. "What are you charging me with?"

"Attempted murder of a law enforcement officer and two counts of first-degree murder." John intentionally left off explaining who was murdered, hoping Kenneth would slip up and fill it in for him. "I'll explain the charges if you don't understand them."

"There's nothing *you* need to explain to me. I'm a whole lot smarter than you'll ever be. I'll beat these dreamed-up charges, you know that, don't you?"

"If you say so." John shrugged, dismissing him. He already discovered Kenneth's weakness and was ready to exploit it. John would wield Kenneth's own arrogance against him. "I still think it would be in your best interest to have an attorney or someone come in here and explain your charges to you. I'm not sure you completely understand what's going on."

"Lawyers are for idiots and chumps." Kenneth rose in his chair. "And I don't need anyone to explain anything to me. I've got a 160 IQ. I can think circles around you or anyone else, cop. You're just a lowly civil servant, try to keep that in mind while we're talking, if you can keep up."

"I am going to read you your rights anyway, so later you don't cry and whine that I tricked you." John was on the right path. He just needed to lure him a little more. "I still think you should have someone here to help you with this. It can be complicated stuff."

Kenneth scrunched his swollen face at John. "Give it your best, cop. You're out of your league."

John walked him through his rights, and Kenneth signed the bottom of the form with a dramatic swirl at the end of his name.

"Now get me a cigarette." Kenneth crossed his arms. "I'm dying for a smoke."

"I'll think about it. We've got things to talk about first."

"How hard is it? Just walk out and ask one of your little crony bosses if I can have a smoke."

"I *am* the boss…in here, anyway," John said, fully aware that Kenneth was trying to establish control of the interview. "I decide what happens in this room. And I said I'd think about it. You're not exactly on my good side right now, and you haven't earned enough points yet to get a smoke."

"Power hungry cops," he hissed.

"You're pretty fast for a guy who smokes. Did you play sports?"

"I was all state in cross-country," he said while he picked at one of the open wounds on his leg.

"Figures, you run like a rabbit."

John asked about Kenneth's employment history and sat back and listened. Kenneth bragged about his computer programming history and the numerous jobs he'd held. The angst disappeared from his voice as he was swept away in talking about his intellectual prowess and how no one truly understood his gifts. John let him build himself up to a mighty height. He nodded at the appropriate times, as if impressed.

"It seems like you're an incredibly bright guy," John said, nearly choking on the words. "That's why I can't seem to understand how you've been arrested so many times." John flipped through Kenneth's criminal history. "Not to be blunt, but most of your arrests are for sex offenses. You're even on the Sexual Predators list. How would a smart guy like you get caught up in stuff like that?"

"Most of those charges were exaggerated."

"What about the other stuff?" John pointed out one of his charges. "For instance, soliciting an undercover police officer for sex?"

Kenneth smiled and nodded. "Oh, that. That was no big deal. Everyone in America is a little too uptight about sex. Myths and fables still hold too much sway over the ignorant masses. But someday that will change. Someday we'll move out of the darkness of repressed thinking and into the light. Look at the Netherlands and Denmark. Those countries understand what true freedom is."

"Those countries also condone drug use, prostitution, and child pornography, among other things."

"So what? We have free will, and we should be allowed to express ourselves in any manner that *we* decide is right. No one should sit in judgment of someone else's personal preferences or tastes. This puritanical society is two hundred years behind Europe."

Thank God. John would need a brain bath after this interview. The arguments against all of Kenneth's diseased notions pounded inside John's head, demanding to get out and disprove everything this monster believed. But he wasn't here to debate, as much as he yearned to respond. Kenneth was waltzing right where he needed him to go. His perverse desires were becoming official video record. John imagined what some poor little grandmother on a jury would think when she heard Kenneth's deep personal thoughts. It wouldn't bode well for him.

"So someone should be able to have sex with whomever he wants?" John asked.

"Absolutely." A drop of blood from the gauze stuffed inside his nose dripped onto his knee. "It's about freedom." He paused, beaming at John, his twisted nature seeping out of his damaged face. "It's about *ecstasy.*" Kenneth blew a kiss into the camera. He smirked and turned back to John. "But I bet you don't agree. I bet you're one of those dinosaurs stuck in the mire of outdated notions of morality. Just a regular Johnny Law."

"I don't agree with you, if that's what you're asking. But I am trying to understand."

"I didn't think so. I told you that you couldn't keep up. You probably can't even understand what I'm talking about."

"Thankfully not." John pulled a photo of one of the victims from Robbie's file and slid it over the table toward him. "But I think our little talk might help explain what happened to him."

As Kenneth stared at the photo, the images of his own boys crept into John's mind. Thoughts of this monster anywhere in the vicinity of his sons sickened and enraged him, taking him off task for a moment. This couldn't get personal. He would have a purging prayer time later, but he couldn't let his disgust and anger get in the way. Things were going too well to lose it now.

Kenneth fixated on the picture for several moments without saying a word. He was clearly shaken. John let the silence taunt him. Kenneth chuckled nervously. "I don't know what you're talking about. I don't know this kid."

John flipped the photo of the second victim, then the third directly in front of Pate. "So you don't know these boys either?"

"Never seen any of them before in my life." He pushed the pictures back across the table toward John, out of his sight.

"Really, you've never seen them before? Is that something you'd swear to?"

"Absolutely."

"That's funny." John slid the FDLE lab comparison sheet over to Kenneth. "This says you knew at least two of these boys. We have a perfect match from your DNA from the Sexual Predators databank to DNA evidence taken from both scenes where these boys were found."

Kenneth stayed quiet, his fish eyes bulging.

"I find it interesting that when I told you that you were being charged with murder, you didn't bat an eye; you didn't ask who was murdered; and you never denied the charges—something innocent people always do."

"Well...because the charge is so ridiculous, I didn't see any need to deny it."

"Unfortunately for you, the DNA tests tell us everything we need to know about who murdered these boys and what was done to them." John's anger leaked out in his voice as he picked up the pace of his questions. How many lives had been destroyed by this madman? "And it puts you in the middle of this whole thing. For a guy with an allegedly high IQ, you left us with more than enough physical evidence to fry you with."

"If you got DNA, why are you even talking with me?" Kenneth said, wilting in the chair. "Why haven't you just shipped me off to jail? You must want something else."

"Maybe you really are a smart guy." John picked up the photo of Robbie's third victim and held it to Kenneth's face. "I want to know where he is. You're going down for the abductions and murders of two kids, and there's nothing you can do to stop it, and you know it. But there's one thing we *can* do today to make you not look like a thoroughly evil, depraved soul."

"What's that?"

"Tell us everything we want to know and lead us to this third boy's body."

Kenneth sat back against the chair. "I'm done anyway. If you don't jam me with the murders, you're gonna get me for trying to kill a police officer. Either way, I'm going to prison for the rest of my life. Why should I tell you anything?"

"Self-preservation," John said. "Purely self-preservation."

"How's my telling you *anything* self-preservation for me?"

"Because this is a death penalty case, and one way or another, this story will be told in front of a jury—a jury who could put you away for life or strap you into the chair, depending on what they think about you. We've got you solid on these charges, and it's not a matter of *if* you committed these despicable crimes, but only a matter now of *why*. And the why is that you are either one of two things—a sick soul who was unable to control himself and his urges, but when given the opportunity, you tried to make things right, tried to help return the boy to his family."

"What's my second option?"

"You're a vicious pedophile. An evil killer with absolutely no remorse, no concern for the victims or their families, and there's no reason why anyone on the planet should care one whit about what happens to you.

"You can help us find this boy and maybe, just maybe, someone down the road will feel sorry for you and take up your cause and fight for your life. But if you dig your heels in now,

I'm the one who gets to tell the jury who and what you really are. I will make you out to be the vilest murderer this state has seen since Ted Bundy. And they'll believe me, because when you had the chance to give the family at least a little peace, you didn't do it. You kept that little boy away from his parents and everyone who loved him. All they want is to have a proper burial for their son, and you were too cruel to help with that. Do you really want me to be the one to paint your picture in front of a jury? It will be ugly and accurate, trust me."

John scooted his chair almost on top of Kenneth, who cowered and could not look at him, his arrogance a distant memory. John turned his head slightly so Kenneth could see the fresh wound he'd inflicted. "What happened, Kenneth? How did we get here?"

Tugging on his lower lip, Kenneth appeared to be debating John's logic. "I hear voices, you know." He glanced at John to see if his feeder line was working and grinned. "They make me do things."

"I don't care if you hear the Beatles. Tell me what happened to those boys!"

"The voices make me do these crazy things." And then the dam burst, as Kenneth told in nauseating detail how he'd abducted the three boys, committed unspeakable crimes, then murdered them, hiding their bodies in various places along the Tamiami Trail. He blamed an insatiable drug habit and unnamed voices in his head for the wicked rampage he'd been on.

John didn't buy his story about "hearing voices," and he didn't think a judge or jury would either. But it didn't really matter at this point. Kenneth Pate was simply consumed by evil. Now they had him, and he was giving up everything they needed.

John stayed as monotone and nonjudgmental as he could

as the gruesome details spewed from Kenneth's mouth like a vile volcano. He wrestled with dueling emotions—part of him actually felt sorry for the pathetic person in front of him. What horrors befell him as a child to make him into the monster he was? The other part of him wanted to lash out in his flesh and beat him unconscious for the pain and misery he'd inflicted on so many people, so many lives wrecked because of him. But he had to keep his emotions in check. They were so close to everything they'd been working for—finding Dylan Jacobs.

Kenneth finished confessing about the third murder. He then agreed to lead investigators to the body. John thought he could hear Robbie cheering in the other room. All her hard work was about to pay off. At least she could give the family some peace by returning their son to them. It seemed an awful consolation prize, but still it was something.

John gave him a piece of paper, and he drew a map to the location, a wooded lot next to a convenience store leading out of the Miami area. All three of Robbie's cases were sewn up nicely. He felt good to be able to help her clear the cases out; he knew the pressure all too well.

John loosened his tie and let out a sigh, wondering if he had anything left. His brain was soiled and numb, but he still had to move forward. The interview had lasted for more than three hours, but this was the time he'd been waiting for.

He opened his file and slid a picture of Dylan across the table, stopping just in front of Kenneth. "Tell me about *him*."

Kenneth leaned down and stared at the picture long and hard. He looked back up. "Never seen him before."

"That's what you said about them…at first," John said curtly, pointing at the pictures of the three other boys. "Do we really need to go down that road again?"

"What are you trying to do, blame me for every missing kid

in the state? I'm telling you, I don't know anything about him."

"Fort Lauderdale. Does that jog your memory?"

"Agent Russell," Kenneth said, as if they were friends discussing politics over tea. "I would tell you. What do I have to lose? I'm a dead man anyway. But I'm not holding back. I've never seen this kid before."

"You lived just two blocks from him when he disappeared. You could practically see his house from yours."

"I might be crazy, but I'm not stupid. I remember what I've done and what I haven't. I've never seen this kid before."

His denials were strong and clear, not like the ones from the earlier cases. But Kenneth was a depraved child killer, so his word didn't hold a lot of weight with John.

"Would you take a polygraph test on this?"

"Sure," Kenneth said. "A polygraph. DNA. The SATs. Whatever you want. I'm not about to take the rap for something I didn't do. I've got enough stacked against me."

"Great. We'll get it started right now." John sighed. He would have another detective administer the lie detector test because he knew what the answer would be.

Kenneth Willard Pate had nothing to do with Dylan's disappearance.

28

Driving slowly down the street, Marie skimmed the addresses for the home of retired detective Randall Pollard. She had no idea what insights he could offer, but he was a part of the puzzle, this strange, entangled series of events that long ago determined a boy's fate, and a man's destiny. As John told her many times, you never know what someone's going to say until you talk with them. She slowed even more as the numbers closed in on her destination.

The neighborhood was older, with small, well-kept homes, and most of the yards were tightly groomed. She pulled up to 465 Huntington Lane. A battered blue Ford pickup with a faded camper shell on the back was parked underneath the carport. A series of fishing rods lined the back wall next to the truck, which didn't surprise her because his mailbox was shaped like a bass with a lure hanging from its mouth.

Marie strolled up the narrow walkway to the porch area, where she could see into the living room through the screen door. The TV blared a news report to an empty room.

"Hello." She knocked twice on the door. "Is anyone home?"

"Coming," a gruff voice called from a back room.

Waiting for those few seconds, Marie's pulse accelerated. She still didn't know what to expect. How would she explain everything to this man? What would she hope to gain? Maybe nothing. But if she didn't take this opportunity, she'd always wonder what she might have missed. Under different circumstances, she thought John would be proud of her investigative skills. Unfortunately, the circumstances weren't different.

An elderly man rounded the corner into the living room from a darkened hallway. He wore shorts, a T-shirt, and flip-flops, and he carried a small oxygen tank on his side with a strap slung over his opposite shoulder like a purse; two tubes ran from the tank up to his nose. The lush, wavy hair that adorned his head in the picture had long since vanished. The gangly former detective hobbled toward the door.

"I'm coming," he wheezed, a cigarette poking from his lips and keeping time like a conductor's wand as he spoke.

His grin was broad and seemingly permanent, not unlike the largemouth bass that served as his mailbox. "You must be that lady."

"Yes, I just came from the police department. Is this a good time for you? I can come back later if you wish."

"No, no." He unlatched the screen door and held it open for her. "Please come in. I don't get too many visitors these days. It's nice to have such a pretty young lady here to see me."

The living room was clean and well kept, but the pungent stench of cigarette smoke watered Marie's eyes the second she entered. A row of pictures lined the shelf next to the door. One showed Randall with his arms around a younger man and woman, both in police uniforms. She assumed them to be his children; they bore his distinctive smile. Another picture was of an elegant, elderly woman with a black ribbon across the bottom of the frame.

She browsed his bookshelf, which lined an entire wall. Several rows were dedicated to the classics—*The Adventures of Tom Sawyer*, *Of Mice and Men*, *Lord of the Flies*—with some books of poetry mixed in. All the other rows were dedicated to philosophy and religious studies of all types, from Ayn Rand to Billy Graham. Several bass fishing magazines covered the coffee table.

John once told her that one of the first things he did when he went into someone's home was to scan the bookshelves. He always said, "You are what you read." That being true, Randall Pollard could prove to be a very interesting person.

"Please, sit." He pointed to the sofa with his extended hand, and he sat on a chair next to her. "Make yourself comfortable."

She plopped down on the couch, kicking up another round of latent smoke. Not wanting to embarrass him, she struggled not to cough.

"So you want to talk about one of my cases." He took a long, affectionate drag on his cigarette. "I thought most of my work had been long forgotten." Though his speech was slow and deliberate, hampered by wrecked lungs, his dark eyes knew no such restrictions. They seemed to breach her spirit with powerful clarity. His penetrating, probing stare was all too familiar—he had cop eyes.

She stared at his cigarette, then glanced at the oxygen tank. Randall caught her gaze.

"I know, I know. It doesn't make any sense to keep smoking while I'm sucking on this tube. But I've been smoking for over fifty years. If I quit now, it might just kill me." He laughed, which quickly turned into a sharp, choppy cough. "Besides, who wants to die healthy?" He took another long draw.

Marie smiled and nodded as if she understood. She didn't. But she wasn't here to argue health issues with him. She opened the file on her lap and pulled the news clippings out.

"I know it was a long time ago, Mr. Pollard, but do you remember this case?"

"It's Randy." Sitting forward, he squinted to read the article. His face shifted from uncertainty to recognition, and he smirked as he leaned back in his chair. "Oh yeah, I wish I didn't, but I do. Frank Moore—that scumbag. Shot and killed his wife. Woulda killed his son, too, if he'd found him. I remember the case…well, very well."

Marie's heart skipped. How different would her life be if one second was changed in that awful night? Everyone in her life who mattered wouldn't exist. No John. No Brandon. No Joshua. She closed her eyes and shuddered. This might be harder than she thought.

She reached to hand him the article, but he put his hand up. "Don't need to see it. I remember everything about it, I mean *everything*. Why would you be interested in this case? It was so long ago."

"The dispatcher didn't tell you when she called?" Marie said, tilting her head.

"Nope. She just told me that you weren't a reporter, but you did want to speak to me about a case. She also said you were a very nice lady and I should talk with you. She was certainly right about that."

Marie blushed and then giggled. Randy was charming, much like John. Maybe being a detective ingrained that in a person after so many years of talking to people in the worst times of their lives. Or maybe it was the other way around. Maybe those kind of people were attracted to being a detective. She wasn't sure.

"F-Frank's son. He's…well, he's my husband."

Randy jolted, as if he'd just been jabbed with a needle. "Really? Imagine that." He sat back in his chair. "I always wondered what happened to him. How he turned out and all." His smile transformed into a curious grin as he regarded Marie. "Why didn't he come with you?"

Marie shifted on the sofa and laid the file next to her. "Some things have come up. Things that made me want to know more about this, to be able to understand."

"In other words," Randy rubbed his chin with his forefinger and thumb, "your husband doesn't know you're here."

She nodded. Retirement had not dulled his perceptive skills; he nailed her.

Randy pulled another cigarette from his pack and lit it. He blew smoke toward the ceiling and watched it, as if it were something mystical.

"Excuse me." He lifted himself from the chair. "I have something that might be of interest to you."

He ambled down the hall, and Marie fanned the fresh wall of smoke from her face. She heard several thumps in a back bedroom that sounded like boxes being moved. After a couple of minutes, Randy returned carrying a photo album.

"Can I sit here?" He pointed to the space next to her on the couch. She slid over, and Randy used the corner of the coffee table to help him sit. He opened the album to the first page, where a faded yellow newspaper clipping that matched her copy covered the front.

"I knew I had this back there. I always made a copy of the homicides I worked, so I could have it available, you know. I never trusted our records section to keep this stuff. And to tell you the truth, I once thought about writing a book about all these cases. But that's another subject."

He turned the next page, and on it was the photo of Frank being escorted by Randy and another detective. He pointed to Frank's beaten and swollen eye.

"He resisted—" Randy smiled like a Cheshire cat—"a lot." His giggle changed into a cough.

Frank's black eye certainly matched the size of Randy's fist. He turned the page again, and there was the picture of Randy carrying John. He'd kept good records.

"What's he like, your husband? How is he?"

"He's a good man, a detective with FDLE."

"Really?" Randy said, beaming. "You're not messing with me, are you?" He took his cigarette from his mouth. "That makes sense, I suppose. If you think about it, with his life and all. He could go two ways—be a criminal like his daddy or be a cop. Boy that's good news. I needed to hear that."

"He's such a good husband, a good father. I couldn't ask for any better."

"Well." He scooted his body around to face her. "Then I have to ask again, why are you here…without him? Something is definitely going on. This is causing you a lot of pain."

She wouldn't even try to argue; he could see through her facade.

"Frank is out of prison, and he's come to see us," she said matter-of-factly. "Frankie changed his name to John when he was adopted, and John wants nothing to do with him. Anyway, this whole thing is tearing us apart. I was hoping you could give me some insight. I don't know, something to help me understand what John went through. It's all I know to do to help him…us."

"Frank Moore is out of prison?" He scowled, took a deep drag, and exhaled dramatically. "That animal doesn't deserve to be out. We had a great case against him, and just when they were gonna light him up like a Christmas tree, the Supreme Court up and rules that the death penalty is unconstitutional. The governor commutes all death sentences to life in prison without the chance of parole, and that snake skates out of his date with death. Now it looks like he's skated again. It's just not right. Don't people keep their word these days? Life should mean *life*, as in, you die in prison." Randy smashed his cigarette in the ashtray and ground it down to a crinkled butt.

Marie didn't dare mention Frank's conversion or try to defend him, at least right now. Randy drew several exaggerated breaths, his tirade apparently wearing him out. She turned back to the photo album and ran her finger across John's limp body in Randy's arms.

"Can you tell me about that night? Whatever you can remember."

"I told you before, I remember everything about that case. Most I couldn't tell you a thing about. They've long since been forgotten. But for years I couldn't stop thinking about this one. I even dreamed about it. But the bigger question is, are you ready to hear it?" His caution floated between them like the rings of his cigarette smoke.

Marie considered the wisdom of moving forward. Would this help? Would this answer the questions she had? She didn't know. But she did know that Randy could shed light where only darkness dwelled for her. Little pieces of her husband's puzzled childhood could be put into place to make what was blurry, clearer. That was worth seeking—even if it was distressing.

"I'd like to know. I think I need to know."

"Well, okay then." He crushed another cigarette into the ashtray. "We got the call about ten-thirty that night. Dispatch called me at home and said there had been a murder, and I needed to come in. As soon as they told me the address, I knew what happened. We all knew about Frank Moore. As a matter of fact, I had arrested him about six months before for beating up a man at a bar. He savaged the man so bad he nearly killed him.

"That night, though, the neighbors had heard the fighting and then a gunshot. They called the police. Frank was gone by the time our patrol officers arrived. I got there, and we worked the scene for about two hours. It was a particularly gruesome scene. Lynette Moore was still lying on the floor." Randy stopped and wheezed several times to catch his breath.

Marie put her hand on his knee. "Take your time. There's no hurry."

He waved at her and took several more breaths. "That's when we, I, found the boy still in the room." He stopped again, appearing to choke up. "I have to tell you, I never seen anything like that. I looked under the bed for any spent shell casings or such, and there he was, catatonic, still looking at his mama's body on the floor. God only knows how long he'd been lying like that."

Randy shook his head and leaned back against the sofa. Several moments passed as he composed himself. "Well, as you can imagine, I screamed like a little girl and jumped up. Scared my partner half to death. I thought for sure we had a double on our hands. I reached back down and checked for a pulse; I was shocked when I found one. I pulled the boy from under that bed and ran downstairs with him. That's when they took that picture."

He pointed to the tattered newspaper and then turned away for a moment. A depressed silence filled the room. He pulled another cigarette from the pack.

"Marie, I've never seen anything like that. He was just

staring ahead, all vacant, like a doll. It freaked me out bad. I had nightmares for years about his eyes."

Marie took his hand in hers as tears pooled in the aged detective's eyes. This wasn't easy for anyone. She never imagined the effect it had on Randy also. Breakfast wasn't sitting well in her stomach.

"We turned the boy over to Family Services," he continued. "Then we caught up with Frank later that morning. He was hiding out in a shed about a mile away from his house. The homeowner found him in there sound asleep and called us. He'd been so drunk the night before that he didn't wake up until he was cuffed and on his way into the patrol car."

"I thought he resisted arrest?" Marie pointed again to Frank's battered face.

"Oh, he certainly did." Randy smirked and bobbed his head up and down. "But that didn't happen until we got him back to the station. He resisted then…several times."

Marie studied the photo of Frank and then looked at Randy, who was still smirking. What was his definition of "resisting"? Given the anger he'd expressed at Frank some thirty-odd years later, she felt pretty sure she knew what he was talking about. She let the comment die an appropriate death by simply staying quiet.

"Where are my manners?" Randy smacked his hand against his forehead. "Can I get you anything to drink? I make a pretty mean cup of coffee."

Marie checked her watch. "I'm sorry. I don't think I have time. I've got to leave soon. I don't want to hurry you, but what happened to John after all this?"

"Oh, yeah. We built a powerful case against Frank. He confessed, and he had the gun on him when we apprehended him. We were real fortunate that everything fell into place. So the state attorney and I decided not to use the boy to testify against his daddy in trial. We didn't think that would help anyone or that he would be a good witness, even if he was capable of testifying, which I doubt he was."

"So he didn't have to go to court or anything?"

"No. We got a rock solid conviction without his testimony. It's the only case I can think of where we didn't use an eyewitness to a murder to testify."

"Interesting." Instead of bringing comfort, the new round of information clawed and tore at her spirit. *John...I can't imagine what you went through.*

"This might help you." Randy handed her his thick notebook.

She flipped through the pages. It had the original police reports, copies of the newspaper accounts, and witness statements.

"Wow, this is great. You have everything here."

"I don't have a need for this stuff anymore. Looking at everything now, maybe I held onto it all these years for a reason. Now that reason seems clear to me. So I'm passing this on to you."

"Thank you," she said, captivated by the pages before her, like peering into a viewfinder to the past. "I'll take good care of it. I promise. If you ever need it back, just call me." She scribbled her name and address on her pad, tore off the page, and handed it to him. "Maybe you'll want to write that book you were talking about."

Randy shrugged. Marie picked up her folder, the notebook, and her purse as she stood to say her good-byes. Randy lifted himself from the couch and took her by the hand.

"There is one more thing." His eyes locked onto hers. His face was serious and hesitant, not looking like he wanted to proceed further.

"What is it?"

"We did a lot of follow-up investigation in this case. We talked with the neighbors and people who knew the Moores. You've got to understand something before I go on—it was a different time back then. We didn't have the laws in place that we do now to protect children. And most people didn't want to get involved in other folks' business."

Marie wasn't sure where he was going, but she let him continue.

"Some of the neighbors told us that they heard Frank beat his son and his wife nearly every day. They heard screams of anger and pain constantly coming from that house. I wish I could tell you that the murder was the only traumatic event your husband experienced, but I can't. For what Frank Moore did to his family, he should have been strapped into the electric chair and sparked until he died. No child should grow up carrying those memories—no child."

29

Let's go, boys," John's voice called from behind Marie, who was standing on the baseball field watching the team chase each other around, waiting for the coach to arrive. "Start the warm-ups. I'll be right there." John slammed his car door and pulled the tie from around his neck as he jogged onto the field.

"Sorry I'm late, hon." He pecked her cheek as he passed.

"Wait." She grabbed his hand and pulled him toward her. "What's with the bandage? What happened to the side of your head?"

"Brandon—" John looked out to the field where the team was waiting—"warm them up, and then start batting drills. I'll be with you in a minute."

"Okay, Dad." Brandon called the team together, and they began doing jumping jacks in cadence.

"Daddy!" Joshua charged him with a stick-sword and stopped several feet away and began jousting with him. John grabbed the stick and pulled him close, hugging him for several seconds. "How'd you hurt your head?"

"It's a long story, champ. Why don't you run along for a minute and let your mother and me talk." As quickly as he had come, Joshua sprinted back toward the bleachers to play underneath.

"What did happen?" She inched closer and raised her hand toward his head. He jerked away as she attempted to touch it.

"It's no big deal. I'm okay. I'm fine."

"But what happened?" He was avoiding her, and she knew that was never good.

"I'm late enough as it is, hon. I need to get the boys ready for Saturday. It's going to be a big game."

"You're not coaching anything until you tell me what happened to your head." She squeezed his hand tight.

"You really don't want to know. It'll only upset you, so there's no reason to go into it now. I'm fine. We can talk about it tonight."

"It sounds pretty bad. Is it going to be on the news?"

"Probably. Now I really have to get to the team."

"Fine." She let his hand fall. "Go coach. After all, there's always later." She waved him off. "I seem to hear more of what's going on with you these days on the TV news than from you. I hate that."

"We'll talk about it later." John walked backward, the bandage sticking off the side of his head like a third ear. He pulled his tie the rest of the way off, stuffed it in his pocket, and trotted toward the players.

Marie watched John interact with the team, running them through various drills and jogging alongside them as they ran the bases. She could tell he was limping slightly and was not his usual self. He winced several times when he reached to catch a ball. He had a story to tell, but his silence frustrated her.

She ambled to the bleachers with her hands in her pockets, then sat on the cold, hard metal. It didn't matter what time of year it was, the bleachers were always bitter, unforgiving, much like their relationship right now.

A small flower slithered up through the metal seats near her feet. The flower shook and then Joshua's head followed behind.

"Thank you, sweetheart." Marie took the flower from him. "It's very pretty. We'll put it in some water when we get home."

"Is Dad's head okay?"

"He's fine. It's nothing to worry about."

"Did a bad guy hit him?" He looked at her with eyes much too innocent for the answer she assumed.

John never spoke much with the boys about his work—or with her, for that matter. Every morning they would kiss him and tell him to be careful, but he didn't share what he would do during the day. Brandon respected that, but Joshua always wanted to know how many bad guys he would catch that day. John told her he feared that Joshua would be the one to follow in his footsteps. He promised Marie he'd do everything he could to dissuade that. But it was going to be tough.

"I don't think so," she said. "So don't worry about Daddy. He'll be fine."

"If a bad guy was going to hurt Dad—" Joshua peered over the metal seat—"I would jump in front of him and fight him with my sword."

"I know you would, sweetheart." She lifted him onto her lap. "So would I. We won't let any of those bad guys hurt Daddy, will we?"

"No way," Joshua decreed, his stick held high in the air.

"Frank Moore," the heavyset black nurse said with a note of anger in her voice, "you're one of the most stubborn men I've ever tended to."

He folded his shirt and placed it in his suitcase, the bandage from the IV port still on his hand. "Don't take no offense to it, Martha." He closed the suitcase and zipped it shut. "The treatment and the company's been just fine, but I don't have much time, and I don't plan on spending it here. Got too much to do."

"You're not well enough to be out there tending to yourself. And you shouldn't be doin' anything right now but taking care of yourself."

Frank shook his head and waved his hand at her. "Not much of me left to take care of. I think I just let myself get too dehydrated. I won't do that again. Got my meds. I should be fine."

"Who's that nice young lady that came to visit?" she said as she pulled the sheet from his bed.

"That's my daughter-in-law," he said as pride filled his being.

"Maybe your son and daughter-in-law can take you in. It's better than going to some old nasty motel."

"Well, that's not an option." He hoisted his suitcase off of the bed, teetered a bit, and dropped it on the floor.

"Maybe they could help you to find a home or hospice center."

"Thank you for your concern." He walked over to her and took her hand in both of his. "You've been very nice and helpful. I couldn't have asked for better care, Martha. I'll keep you in my prayers."

She smiled and shook her head. "Frank Moore, you are something else. With all you got going on, you're going to pray for me? There aren't too many men like you left in this world."

He smiled, then shuffled toward the door. Martha pulled a business card from her shirt pocket and scribbled a number on it.

"Here's my card. If you need help, my pager number is on the back. I have to tell you, Frank, I fear you'll end up in the street or something. That's no kinda place for you. I'd like to help if I can."

"You already have."

"Well, put yourself in this wheelchair and let me cart your stubborn self out." Frank climbed into the chair and pulled his suitcase onto his lap.

The gentle hum of a hymn as enchanting as soft pipe organs from heaven emanated from Martha while she wheeled him toward the elevators.

30

Marie jiggled John's foot as he lay on the couch with a quilt covering him. For the third night in a row, he'd left their bed to sleep on the sofa. Before he left, he tossed and turned most of the night anyway, so she knew he didn't get anything resembling sleep.

"John, it's time for church. We need to get going. The boys are ready. If you don't hurry, we'll be late."

"I'm not gonna make it today," he mumbled without opening his eyes. "You all go on without me."

"You missed last week, too."

He didn't answer; his eyes remained shut. Marie didn't want to push the issue, but she huffed in frustration as she sat next to him. She watched him sleep for several moments. She was really trying. After everything that happened this week, she hoped and prayed that would shake John out of his funk. That he would see how God had protected him and saved his life.

When John finally told her what had happened, she could hear the emotion in his voice—how he'd nearly been killed with his own gun, how Tim and Robbie got there just in time to save him. They even prayed together for the first time in weeks. She felt that it could be the beginning of something powerful in his life, and maybe, just maybe, the beginning of healing with Frank.

But the nightmares continued. Almost every night since, John would wake and go to the couch. He hadn't screamed like the first time, but twice he leaped from the bed—shaking, disoriented, and scared.

She could see the spiritual nature of the battle they were in, but John didn't seem to see or understand, or even want to. He hadn't been doing his Bible studies or going to church with them. She couldn't remember the last time he'd read the Bible to the boys. Well, actually, she could remember—the day Frank showed up nearly two weeks before.

Brandon and Joshua thumped down the stairs and into the living room. Marie tucked Joshua's shirt in and tried in vain to push a cowlick down on his hair. With one more quick lick of her fingers, she slicked it to the side of his head.

"Dad's not ready yet," Brandon said. "Isn't he going with us?"

"Not today. He didn't sleep well last night."

Brandon raised an eyebrow. He walked over and kissed his father gently on the forehead; Joshua followed his lead. They loaded up in the van and sped toward church.

Marie and the boys rushed down the aisle as Pastor Phillips entered the pulpit. They sat in the pew just behind Cheri and her children. Cheri took hold of Marie's hand as she sidestepped to her seat.

"You okay?" Cheri whispered as her husband prepared to speak.

Marie couldn't answer. She shrugged, squeezed Cheri's hand, then sat down. Kevin was in good form. He'd been teaching a series on the nature of man: fallen, sinful, and in desperate need of a Savior. Marie often said that Kevin could make a sermon on baking a broccoli pie sound fascinating and compelling.

She struggled to stay focused on the sermon, but her mind drifted in and out as nearly every point seemed to bring her back to John. For the first time since they'd been together, she truly feared for their marriage. She had no idea how to break through to John or how to communicate with him. After talking with Randy Pollard, she knew that his wounds were deep, deeper than she'd first imagined.

She prayed more frequently than she had in years. But at every turn, John seemed to grow more and more distant, trying purposefully to push her away. And if that wasn't bad enough, he was pulling away from God as well—which frightened her the most. If she tried too hard to pull him back to her, he might only push away more. If she did nothing, she might lose him for good. It seemed that everything she tried was wrong.

John was slipping away, Frank was dying, and she was floundering in a sea of frustration and despair.

Tears rained down her cheeks as the choir closed the service with "Holy, Holy, Holy." As the beautiful melody echoed through the church, Marie suffered quietly. She cried out in her soul for some relief, for direct intervention from the Savior.

After the service, the crowd filed out of the sanctuary, and Marie and the boys fell in line. Kevin and Cheri greeted everyone. The line would often slow down or stop altogether as he would inquire how people were. Even though the congregation numbered nearly five hundred, he knew everyone's name. He could meet a person once years before and still remember his or her name.

"Hey, Marie." He cupped her hand in his. "John didn't make it today?"

"No." She didn't offer any more.

"How are you holding up? Cheri and I have been praying for you both every day."

"I...we're doing fine, I suppose," Marie said, feigning peace and putting on her church face.

He scratched his neatly groomed beard. "Is everything really okay?"

She bit her lip to keep the surge of emotion and frustration inside. It wasn't the time or place to break down. But Kevin's incisive, truth-seeking eyes caught hers, and she could no more hold back her emotions than she could hold back the wind.

"I'm not fine. Everything's not fine at all." Her face turned hot, and she trembled.

"Come here." Cheri wrapped her arm around Marie like a warm blanket, and they walked over to a bench.

"Boys, why don't you come with me to the playground for a while?" Kevin walked with them to the back parking lot of the church as they glanced back in concern for their mom.

Marie crumpled in Cheri's arms, weeping uncontrollably. Dumping her latest woes in her friend's lap, the two shared some much-needed fellowship and prayer.

31

John strolled into his office to see a new cubicle being set up alongside his. A pair of legs jetted from underneath the new desk—a woman's legs. She had a walking cast on one foot and a suede shoe on the other.

"Robbie, what are you doing under there?"

"Fixing my desk." Her legs flopped with each word.

"Your desk?" He bent down to see what she was working on. "The Pate case is finished. I thought you'd be back in Miami by now, soaking up that south Florida sun and finally getting some rest."

"She's not going back to the Miami office." Alan walked into the room, coffee mug in hand. "With the Pate case wrapped up so nicely, which by the way I'm putting you all in for a Unit Citation, since everyone did a great job with that slimeball. Even though Russell tried to give me heart failure." He punched John in the shoulder.

"Anyway, since Robbie's freed up now, I called the director's office and asked that she be assigned to help us out on the

Jacobs case. They agreed. She agreed. So it's official—you all are a task force."

"Excellent," John said. "We could use all the help we can get."

"I've put together some ideas I'd like to run by you, if you're interested." Robbie plugged in the keyboard to the back of her computer. "That's it." She scooted from underneath the desk. John extended his hand. She took it, and he lifted her to her feet. "I think this will work."

"How's the foot?" John said.

"Doc said two bones were broken." She sat on her freshly built desk to take the pressure off her foot. "It'll be a month or so before I'm running around again. I only hope Pate's face hurts as much as my foot does."

"I'm sure he's still feeling that kick." John laughed. "It was one for the books."

Tim entered the room scrunched over slightly at the waist. Upon seeing everyone, he straightened his gait.

"Hey, Tim," John said. "Robbie's been transferred to our office to help with the Jacobs case."

"Great." He walked over and shook her hand, welcoming her with a forced smile. "It'll be nice to have a girl on the team."

"Girl?" Robbie said, hands on her hips. She scanned the room. "I don't see any girl here."

Tim held up his palms in surrender. "Don't get all feminist on me. It's just an expression."

"Well, in that case, it's nice to be working with the *boys* here in Melbourne."

"So it's gonna be like that, huh?" Tim turned and shuffled toward his desk. "You're gonna fit in fine around here."

As Tim passed, John caught the slight whiff of alcohol and mouthwash. Tim's eyes were red, swollen, and his steps were careful and purposed. After the pleasantries were exchanged,

Tim moseyed to his chair and plopped down. He leaned back and placed his hands on his face.

John gripped his shoulder. "You okay?"

"Yeah, just a late night."

"I'll get you a cup of coffee. Alan made it, so it should be drinkable."

"Thanks." He looked at John. "I appreciate it."

John grabbed the Marine Corps mug from Tim's desk and headed for the break room. As the aroma of freshly brewed coffee tickled his nose, John worried about his partner. It wasn't the first morning he'd come in looking like a train wreck from the night before. John was sure all the upheaval in Tim's life didn't help. In the last two years, Tim had been shot and gone through an agonizing divorce that estranged him not only from his ex-wife, but from his daughter as well—his only child.

Although his tough mornings weren't alcohol induced, John sympathized with Tim and wanted to be there for him during this difficult transition in his life. John made his way down the hallway and back into their office. Robbie adjusted several items on her desk, and Tim was still in a reclined position.

John placed the brew in front of him, his hand on Tim's shoulder. "Take your time with this. We'll have a meeting later in the morning, whenever you're ready."

"Sounds good." Tim passed the cup underneath his nose several times, which seemed to breathe some much-needed life into him. He savored his first sip. For the first time that morning, a genuine smile surfaced on his face. "We can start now. I'm good."

"Fair enough." John walked to the dry board, took a marker from the tray, and crossed a line through Kenneth Pate's face. As John predicted, Kenneth passed his polygraph. Although lie detectors weren't 100 percent accurate, John was comfortable marking him off the list of possible suspects, at least for now.

They needed to focus their energies back onto their first set of suspects—namely Jesse Lee Morgan. He was the only one they hadn't properly interviewed yet. John really didn't want to talk with Jesse Lee cold. He'd seen how mean and defiant the man could be. If John didn't have any evidence, even weak evidence, Jesse wouldn't tell him anything. If he'd never been arrested before, they might be able to bluff him. But with Jesse Lee's record, that wasn't an option.

Alan, Tim, John, and now Robbie pulled their chairs close; each brought their legal pad out. Gloria came in and gave him the latest stack of messages of alleged Dylan sightings. John rummaged through them quickly before they started, searching for anything that looked promising. The messages were pretty much the same as they'd been receiving since the beginning of the case: Dylan was spotted in a grocery store or a truck stop in Nowhereville, USA; someone saw him at a fruit stand or visiting a next-door neighbor.

While most of the people who called the tip line sincerely believed they had seen Dylan, experience told him that most were overactive imaginations in people who truly wished to help. Some, of course, were mentally unstable, like William Saldini. But somewhere in the volumes of information they had was the one lead that would make wading through the other garbage worth it. So they would follow up on every lead and try not to judge it before they fully investigated it.

"Well," John flipped to a fresh page on his notebook, "Mr. Pate didn't shake out like we hoped, but it's sure nice to have him off the streets anyway. The world is a better place without him in it."

"Amen," Robbie said. "I can't tell you how long this case has been dogging me. I really appreciate the time and effort you all put in on that case. Now maybe I can return the favor."

"I'm sure you will," John said. "I had really wanted to hold off talking with Jesse Lee until we could come up with something a little more solid connecting him to Dylan's disappearance, but I think we'll have to move his interview up on the list. Let's do an extensive background on him for the next two days, and maybe we can get to him by the end of the week. Since he's a parole violator, he was shipped right back to prison after he took a poke at Tim, which I'm sure he regrets now."

Tim chuckled as he lifted his brew to his lips.

"He's currently residing at Okeechobee Correctional Institution down near the Everglades, so it's going to be a couple hours' drive to get there."

"I was thinking." Tim clutched his cup in both hands, as if he were using it to warm them. "We talked with Linda and got nowhere, and we talked with Janet and got nowhere."

"True." John nodded. "What's your point?"

"Well, we know what they said, or better yet, what they didn't say. But *Jesse Lee* doesn't know that."

John cocked his head and frowned. He scanned the room and the broadening smiles on his team. "What do you have in mind?"

"Play the part of the tape for Jesse where Linda said it wasn't her idea. Then stop the tape. Let it stress him out, and then we make like she told us everything."

"You have a very dark and devious side to you, Porter," John said. "I've never been much of a poker player, but I think it might be time for a good bluff."

"I like it." Alan rubbed his chin. "I like it a lot, especially since we have nothing to lose. This creep's not likely to spill his guts out of the goodness of his heart. He needs a little...encouragement."

32

Marie heard John's car roll down the driveway toward their house; with each passing second her pulse quickened. She wondered, again, if she had done the right thing. The last few weeks caused her to question everything—her judgment, her motives, her commitments to John and the boys, and her relationship with the Lord. She fought against a flurry of self-doubt with each new step. She had made so many mistakes.

John walked through the door, and his face confirmed her fears. He was not pleased.

"I thought that was your car," John said to Kevin, who was sitting at the dinning room table with Marie. They thought it best that Kevin come without Cheri, so it wouldn't look like they were ganging up on John.

"Hi, honey." She held her smile a little longer than normal. "Kevin's dropped by to see us."

"Hey, John." Kevin rose from the table, and they shook hands. "Good to see you. It's been a while."

"Yeah. It has been a while. What's going on?"

"Always the cop." Kevin slipped his hands into his jeans pockets. "I can't put anything past you."

Marie folded her arms and stared at the floor. She scraped the carpet with her foot, as if erasing a pesky, imaginary stain. There was no way to say that the pastor was here just for a visit. John would know that she told Kevin. But what were her options? And at this point, she really didn't care.

"I thought we might need to talk a bit," Kevin said. "You haven't been in church for a while, and when I asked Marie how everything was going...well, she told me."

"I'm not surprised." John eyed Marie, who continued to focus on the floor. "But this is something we're working out. It's between us and our family, Kevin. It doesn't concern the church."

"We're all family. Church family, at least. But beyond that, we've been friends awhile now, and frankly, Cheri and I are worried. Marie told us what happened with your father—"

"He's not my father." John tossed his briefcase on the couch. "He may have fathered me, but he is *not*, nor has he ever been, my true father."

After a few moments of uncomfortable silence, Kevin said, "I understand. But can we sit down and talk about it?"

"There's not much to talk about." John loosened his tie and pulled it over his head. "As far as I'm concerned, this is finished. He goes his way; I go mine. No problem."

"I know you're angry with...him, but you might want to consider that God has opened this opportunity to heal, to put this behind you, to reconcile."

"I have put it behind me. I spent my whole life putting it behind me. I also decided a long time ago to put *him* behind me. And that's what I'm doing."

"That's not quite what I meant."

"I know what you meant, Kevin. I've got it under control. We don't need any help."

Marie stood off to the side, her arms still folded. "If you have it so 'under control,' tell him about the nightmares."

"We can talk about this later." John glanced toward her. "I don't like having every aspect of our lives brought out to our friends."

"I didn't come to make things worse," Kevin said. "I just wanted you to know that we care about you and we're praying for you. I'm always available if you need to talk. We could just go out and get a cup of coffee or something."

"Maybe sometime," John said. "But right now we're fine. We'll get through this. It'll just take some time."

"Will I see you in church this weekend? You all need some good fellowship, and we miss you."

"We'll see." John walked to the front door and opened it, an unmistakable cue that it was time for him to leave.

Kevin strolled to the door and looked back at Marie. Then he took John's hand. "I'm here if you need me. Call anytime. I can be here in a snap."

"I know. We're fine."

The door shut and silence blanketed the room. She could tell John was fuming, but she didn't care. He'd blown off his best friend and strongest confidant. She was running out of options.

"He's become a believer, John."

"Who?"

"Frank. He's been a Christian for over a quarter of a century."

"That's not possible." He cocked his head and scowled at her. "Light has nothing to do with darkness."

"You might not want to believe it, but it's true."

"Is that what he told you when you met? I suppose you believe him now?"

"He did and I do. You should find out for yourself."

"He's a liar, Marie. You can't trust anything he says or does. There's no truth in him. I know everything I need to know about that man."

"What would John Senior do? Would he hold onto this hate like you have? Would he let this consume him?"

"You don't know what you're talking about. You've never *really* known either man. If you did, we wouldn't even be having this conversation." John stepped around her and bounded up the stairs to their room. The door slammed behind him.

"That went well," Marie said.

33

John shuddered awake as he struggled to recognize the form standing over him as he lay on the couch. He blinked hard twice and then looked again. Marie's outline came into focus. In her nightgown. He flung the blankets off and sat up, resting his feet on the floor.

"What is it?" John wiped his face with his hand. His hair jetted in different directions like porcupine quills.

"Tim's on the phone." She handed him the cordless. "He said it's urgent."

John yawned. "What time is it?"

"Four-twenty in the morning."

John took the phone. "Hey, Tim, what's going on?"

"We'll have to postpone our little visit with Jesse Lee."

"Why? What's happened?"

"They found a body just outside of Jacksonville off of I-95." Tim paused for a couple of seconds. "John, it appears to be a little boy, and he's been there for some time. It could be Dylan."

"Okay." The possibilities whirled in John's head. "Let's get everyone together, and we'll head up there."

"I'm way ahead of you. I've already called Robbie. She's good to go. We'll pick you up in thirty minutes."

"I'll be ready."

John turned the phone off and passed by Marie without saying a word. He jogged up the stairs to their bedroom. The anticipation chased the fog from his head. If this was Dylan, at least it would be some break in the case, though the likelihood of physical evidence at the scene was small but a possibility nonetheless.

Marie meandered upstairs and leaned against the doorjamb of their bathroom, watching John get ready. He nicked himself twice as he hustled to shave. He slapped a fresh Band-Aid on the burn on the side of his head, which was healing better than expected.

"You have to go out?" She broke the silence.

"Yeah, they found a body in Jacksonville. Could be Dylan, so I have no idea when I'll be back. I'll call when I get a chance."

"I figured it was something like that." She sighed. "I hate these early morning calls. They're never good news."

"Why don't you get some sleep?" John cupped the water from the faucet in his hands and tossed it on his face. "I've gotta get going."

"You really expect me to sleep now?"

"I guess not. But you could try."

"Just be careful...please."

"I will." He wiped his face with the towel and felt the Band-Aid to make sure it was secure. "I've never had a dead body hurt me before."

Marie didn't laugh; she just looked tired. John wanted to say something, anything, but the gulf between them was deep. There were so many things he wanted to tell her that it felt as if he would burst. Shame made him pull back. Marie was always there for him, and she deserved better.

But she couldn't understand. She would never know what it was like to live in terror every day, all day, and to see the things he saw. He knew evil intimately, and he was thankful that she had no idea. He didn't know how to explain it, nor did he have the desire to. He just knew that he'd do everything possible to keep that evil from descending onto his home, to keep it far away from Marie and the boys.

After a few excruciatingly still moments, she turned and shuffled over to their bed, where she slipped under the covers.

John finished dressing and packed a small overnight bag, just in case. He'd learned the hard way to be prepared for extended stays at crime scenes.

As he walked out the front door, Tim pulled down his driveway. Robbie leaned against the back door, asleep.

"Let's get going." Tim held up a Styrofoam cup of java. "I got some pick-me-ups for us and sleeping beauty back there. And, John, I've got some bad news."

"What's that?"

"She snores," Tim said with a chuckle. "And I mean loud. Listen."

John opened the passenger door and a horrific noise emanated from the backseat. That couldn't be Robbie.

"It's like a herd of moose or something. It's just so unnatural."

"Let's get going, Tim." John crawled into the passenger seat. Before long, they were rocketing up Interstate 95 toward Jacksonville with Robbie serenading them with her guttural bellowing.

"Went to the gym yesterday." Tim turned toward John. "Ran on the treadmill. Well, I wouldn't exactly call it running, but I was on the treadmill. You wait and see. Two months and I'll be lean and back to my old self. No jackrabbit's gonna get away from me again like that slime Pate did. No siree."

"I don't doubt that." John hoped to relieve some of the guilt Tim was feeling. He was surprised that Tim was still upset about Kenneth Pate. John didn't feel any animosity toward Tim. In fact, he was thankful that he and Robbie were there. A second later, and he would have been history. But being partners was a difficult thing. You always felt responsible for the other person's safety. Hoping to change the subject, John pulled the case file out. The three-hour drive gave them time to catch up on the case and to put together a game plan.

As the sun inched over the horizon, Robbie finally woke up. She sipped her lukewarm coffee and spoke very little. John figured she wasn't a morning person. It would take a while for them to get used to working with each other.

As they traveled toward the scene, they passed a giant billboard of Dylan's picture and the 1-800 tip-line phone number for information about the case. *Lord, we could really use a break.* Dylan's eyes seemed to follow them as they roared past the sign.

John attempted to study his file, but other things kept his mind at bay. Marie couldn't really believe that *he'd* become a follower of Christ. Not that man. She always wanted to think the best about people, but he knew the truth. He shook off the thought and rubbed his eyes.

How he wished his father were still alive. While growing up, John always sought his counsel on everything important. He missed that now. His father knew the environment John was raised in better than anyone. In the same situation, John Senior probably wouldn't meet with Frank either...well, maybe he would. But he was a special man.

John's dilemma wasn't all about forgiveness; it was just as much about protecting his family. Frank was a destroyer. He could be playing a game just to get close to John and his family for one last, final blow. His true father would see it that way too, wouldn't he?

When they approached exit 13, John could see the FDLE crime scene van, the crime scene tape, and several Jacksonville patrol cars. They pulled off at the junction, which was in the most rural part of Duval County.

The command post was set up at an abandoned gas station. The gas station sign, though visible from I-95, was rusted, and the plastic portions were smashed out. Several satellite trucks from local news agencies crammed into the parking lot, jockeying for position with the police vehicles.

"This looks like it's gonna be a production." Tim pulled into the parking lot.

A red-haired detective in his mid-thirties approached their car with a half-eaten bagel in hand. "Can I help you?"

"Agent Porter." Tim held up his badge. "We're with FDLE."

"We've been expecting you. Detective Will Brant, Jacksonville PD. Glad you could come and take a look. This could very well be your missing boy, but we're not sure."

Tim, John, and Robbie exited the car, stretched, and made their acquaintances with Detective Brant.

"Where's the body?" John said.

"Right there about thirty, thirty-five feet from where the crime scene van is parked." He pointed to the wooded area just off the pavement of the gas station. "He's not far into the wood line."

"Who found him and how?" Tim asked.

"A couple traveling from New York got a flat on the interstate last night," Detective Brant said. "They pulled off here. As the husband was changing the tire, nature called. He took his flashlight into the woods and walked right up on the body. If freaked him out pretty bad. He was hysterical when he called 911. He wasn't a lot better when we arrived."

"I can imagine." John turned to Robbie and Tim. "Are we ready to have a look?"

They nodded and walked over to the FDLE crime scene truck, where Barry Watkins was retrieving another roll of yellow scene security tape. His assistant, Dawn, crouched about twenty feet off the pavement and planted a red flag to mark an item of interest.

"This is a big scene," Barry said. "Real big. Maybe a hundred, hundred and fifty yards, scattered about. We're going to have Search and Rescue walk the length of these woods." Barry's hand panned the whole area, and he beamed as the complexity of the scene became apparent.

"Nice to see you, too," John said. "Where do we walk in?"

Still chattering about how he was going to work the scene, Barry guided them to a small path at the edge of the parking lot. They walked in a line, careful not to tread off the path. One way in, one way out—it was the only way to keep the scene from being trampled. Barry and Dawn planted flags in the ground wherever they could see items to collect. The whole area was staked out like a football field: marked, painted, and measured.

John followed Barry just past the first set of pine trees and saw palmettos. As they rounded a small set of scrub, they saw a tiny cowboy boot sticking out from behind a tree. John lifted a silent prayer to protect his mind and his spirit and keep him focused. He had to detach from a scene like this and couldn't afford to get caught up in the emotions of viewing a dead child; he had to be viewing evidence.

After years of viewing death scenes, he knew what to do to stay focused, but it wasn't always easy. In fact, it was never easy. He eased around the tree to get a better look, placing each step with great care.

The full picture came into view—the small, lifeless skeleton of a boy half covered by pine needles and leaves. One cowboy boot lay next to him; the other was under a bush some ten feet away. A tattered shirt lay in pieces around the scene. It might have been red and white at one time but was more of a faded pink now. A small pair of blue jeans lay intact with the bones; a blanket and a small teddy bear lay next to him, also suffering from the elements. The boy's skull was half buried in pine needles and other debris.

John, Robbie, and Tim all squatted simultaneously. Several seconds passed before anyone spoke while they soaked in the scene.

"The victim's in pretty good shape for being out here in the woods," Tim said. "I once had a body that was spread out a quarter mile or so. This isn't too bad at all. Looks like we'll recover most of the bones."

"He's been down at least a year." Robbie leaned forward to examine the skull. She placed her legal pad on her knees and began a sketch of the scene. "Probably longer, but I'm going to say at least a year."

"I would agree on that," John said. "I'm also surprised that the animals didn't do more damage, but that's good for us."

John stood and wiped his hands on his pants. The noise from the interstate hummed through the forest in a hypnotic rhythm. Several cars passed along the local road right beside them. How many countless people drove this route every day, oblivious to what lay just a few feet into the woods? A mere line of bushes had concealed this dreadful, heinous secret for who knows how long. But now the secret was revealed, and it was their job to figure out the rest.

"What do you think?" John asked.

"Whoever did this has an attachment to him." Robbie

nodded her head as she thought about it. "He's not buried; he's laid out here real nice, as if someone were laying their child down to sleep. Look how his legs are positioned." She pointed to the blue jeans. "Yep, it's like he's been laid out here real nice...careful. Not the mark of a stranger."

"He's got a blanket and teddy bear here, too." Tim rose and jammed his hands in his pockets. "That's just odd. No stranger is going to do that." He surveyed the scene from one end to the other. His thick jaw muscles flexed back and forth. "Whoever would do this to a child . . ." He drew a deep breath and exhaled dramatically. "I'd love to get my hands on him. Five minutes. No, maybe ten. That would be a good day."

John understood Tim's anger; he felt it himself. Only he wanted the suspects caught and convicted—justice was the best revenge.

Examining the scene boosted John's confidence in his team's abilities. Their observations were acute, sharpened by years of experience. He didn't know Robbie well, but she had just put away a serial child killer and now was making some pretty keen, off-the-cuff interpretations of this scene. Whoever dumped this child definitely had some sort of attachment to him. Now it was just a matter of confirming if they were looking at Dylan or not.

Taking in the area, John wrestled with conflicting feelings. He wanted this to be Dylan. He wanted the case to be over so he could move on, have some closure. It was wearing him down mentally, physically, and emotionally. But another part of him didn't want it to be Dylan. He held the faint hope that he would still find Dylan alive, as remote as that chance seemed. If this wasn't Dylan, who was he? How did he get here, and who murdered him?

Rarely was there a win-win situation in police work. Their

job was to clean up the messes created by other people. Good news didn't bubble out of their office often. The best they could hope for in most cases was a lose-bad/lose-a-little-less scenario.

The injustice of the scene started to wear on him. Why did it seem that the innocent and helpless always suffered while the wicked prospered? This boy before them met with a horrible fate, while Frank Moore survived for so long on this earth. That wasn't right or fair. But there were lots of things John didn't understand.

"We've got the medical examiner on the way." Will Brant popped the last bite of his bagel in his mouth. "What else do you need us to do?"

"We'll let crime scene do their thing," John said. "Depending on what the ME says, we'll have to wait for the test results. Based on the amount of decomposition, it's going to be tough to establish cause of death. Looks like DNA will have to speak for the dead on this one."

34

You really should be in a hospital." Marie leaned against the dresser in Frank's motel room. "This is no place to be, not when you're sick and all. You need to be getting some treatment."

"I'll go to the VA once I'm finished here, but not a minute sooner. I'd rather die in this room than abandon my destiny. I still got strength enough to pray, and that's all I need."

Marie caught herself before she said something she'd regret. Seeing full well where John had gotten his stubbornness, she wasn't happy about it. It made her sick to think that Frank was spending his last days in a dump of a motel. Time was the true enemy here. Frank kept losing more and more weight. She was surprised that he could get around or even stand the pain. He was strong, determined, this much she was sure of.

"Maybe we should pray together."

"I'd like that, missy."

Marie knelt next to him and took his hand, and they petitioned the holy Lord together.

⁓

"Why can't the state put these places closer to civilization?" John said, taking a break from his folder. The narrow two-lane road seemed little more than a glorified gator trail through the swampland of south Florida. Reeds, cattails, and telephone poles blurred into a mesmerizing backdrop as their car barreled toward Okeechobee Correctional Institution, less than three miles away.

"Because civilization doesn't want them close," Robbie called from the backseat. She leaned her back against the door with both legs lying across the seat, keeping her walking cast elevated. She had scrawled "This shoe's for you, Ken" across the side of the cast. "Nobody complains when you build a prison in the swamp. Try to build one in the city and see what happens."

"This suits me just fine," Tim said. "I can't think of a finer place for these fellas than out here, among the gators and snakes and bugs. Seems right to me." He slackened his tie and wiped a small amount of sweat from his forehead. Even with the air conditioner at full tilt, the brutal Florida sun bore down on the car without mercy. It was going to be a long, hot summer.

"Okeechobee Correctional Institution two miles away" a lone sign read.

"I've looked at Jesse Lee's criminal history and reports," Robbie said. "He's going to be a tough one. All his crimes are about anger and control. Half your battle with him will be keeping him from taking control of the interview."

"We've had a brief experience with his anger," John said, "and I think you're right." She'd crawled into Jesse Lee's head pretty well.

"Another thing, I'm staying out of the interview room on this one."

"Why's that?" Tim tried to look at her over his shoulder. "We could use your expertise in there. It seems like you've got him figured out."

"He doesn't like or respect women." She shrugged. "He has several domestic violence charges in his past. I would be a distraction."

"Well, I'm not a woman, but I'm pretty sure he doesn't like me either." A disgusted look seeped across Tim's face. "Maybe I should stay out as well."

"No. It would be good if both of you are present. It'll keep him off balance. The best chance we have of getting him to confess is to make him think he's caught, and it's in his best interest. He's got to move into the bargaining stage where he's trying to wheel and deal. Only then will he tell you anything."

John organized mental notes of how to approach him. Robbie was proving to be a godsend. Her skills on reading people were phenomenal.

They hadn't identified the boy found in Jacksonville yet. Even if it turned out to be Dylan, they still didn't know how he got there and what happened. But talking about that with Jesse Lee was way down the list. First they had to build the historical perspective of Dylan's care. Only then could they zoom in for the kill. If they got to that stage, John would be ready.

They had a rush order on the DNA comparison, but it would still take time; time they might not have. Every day that passed gave Jesse more time to refine his story, if he had one. They didn't need DNA results to speak with him now. Should they get to that point, the crime scene pictures would be enough. The test results would only confirm what he said or help convict him.

John loved the new technology. Law enforcement could do

more things now than they ever dreamed possible just a few years before. But ultimately, real police work revolved around extracting information from people. Evidence rarely spoke for itself; it needed a story attached to it, a framework to slide the individual pieces of the puzzle together into a coherent, ordered picture that unequivocally pointed to a suspect. Right now, they had no story to tell about Dylan, no facts. They did have a set of random circumstances and hunches, but nothing that would ever fly in court.

Jesse Lee Morgan's interview was paramount in a case that had more holes than a colander. John was tired, and they hadn't even started the interview. Lack of sleep was catching up with him. *Jesus, please prepare the way for us.* Jesse Lee's heart would need to be softened if anything meaningful was to come out of this day.

He opened his eyes as they pulled into the parking lot of Okeechobee Correctional Institution, a sprawling complex of buildings and barbed wire rising forth from swamp.

They collected their notepads, files, and tape recorders and walked into the administration building. They had called ahead for an appointment, and it appeared that Jesse Lee's schedule was free.

After showing their IDs and signing in, they were escorted from the administration area by a guard. Three solid metal doors later, they were in a small room that appeared to be used as a spare office or processing area. Another door was on the opposite side of the room, where they brought the prisoners in. Some chairs and small tables filled the room. John and Tim arranged the room to their liking.

"I'll wait out in the hallway and take some notes," Robbie said. "Keep his back to this door, so I can wave at you through the window if I need to talk with you."

The guard opened the door for Robbie. "He's coming up now."

A few seconds later, Jesse Lee appeared in the door window. A guard with a flattop haircut loomed behind him. The guard was so large and muscular that he dwarfed Jesse Lee, whose eyes darted from John to Tim back to John. He didn't look pleased to see them. The metallic buzz announced that the door was open, and the guard walked Jesse into the room.

"I'm gonna take your leg shackles and cuffs off," the gargantuan guard said, "but don't give these gentlemen any problems. Got it?"

"I got it," Jesse said, still eyeing the two of them.

The guard walked to the door. "I'll be just outside should you need something."

"That will be fine." John turned to Jesse. "Thanks for seeing us."

Jesse just looked at John's outstretched hand, not offering his own. "Magilla gorilla shows up at my cell telling me I got visitors. What choice do I have but to come."

"Well," John said, pulling up a chair, "you're here now, so have a seat."

Jesse glanced at Tim, who stood behind John. Tim held his gaze, showing that he wasn't going to be intimidated by some two-bit felon with a soft midsection.

"What took you so long to come and see me?" Jesse said. "I expected y'all here last week."

"We've been busy," Tim said. "By the way, Linda told us to tell you hello."

Jesse glared at Tim. Message received. He didn't look happy that they'd talked with his wife before him. "Really, what else did she say?"

The foundation was laid. Now it was time to move in carefully. "We talked about lots of things."

"Like?" Jesse dropped the chair back on all fours and threw his arms on the table, listening intently.

"I'd love to tell you. If fact, I plan on telling you, but we can't talk until I read you your rights."

"I know what my rights are."

"Great. Then you won't mind hearing them explained again. That is, if you want to hear what I have to say." John felt better about the interview now. He'd whetted Jesse's appetite with the talk of Linda's interview. Jesse pretended not to be anxious to hear what they had to say, but John could tell he was ripe.

"I'll hear you out," Jesse said.

John put the tape recorder on the table and carefully walked Jesse through the Miranda warning. He signed the form.

"So what did she tell you?" he said with the ink still wet on the form. "You going to tell me or what?"

John signaled Tim, who had another tape recorder in his hand. Without a word, he pressed the play button. Linda's scratchy, timid voice echoed throughout the room.

"*What happened to Dylan, Linda?*" John's voice came through. "*Help us help you.*"

"*It was Jesse's idea,*" Linda clearly said. "*I didn't want anything to do with it, I swear.*"

Tim shut the recorder off.

Sighing, Jesse sank back into the chair. "Women."

"We had quite the talk with Linda," John said. "She had a very interesting story to tell us. She's also a nice young lady, I must tell you."

"We got along very well." Tim and John shared the moment.

Jesse lowered his head, looking defeated. John tried to stay calm.

Then Jesse perked up and stared at the two. "Play some more."

"That's all you get," John said. "Just a tidbit."

"I don't know what else is on that tape."

"That's right—you don't. That's in my pocket. I'll let it out when I'm ready." John couldn't let Jesse start dictating what was going to happen. And they didn't have anything else on the tape to play, except for Richard Cromwell interrupting them.

Jesse rocked back and forth with his arms crossed. "If you had something on me, you'd charge me, not ask me what happened."

"Maybe we want to give you an opportunity to tell your side," John said. "Maybe we want to compare what you say with what Linda told us to see who's lying...and who's not. You're already arrested. We're in no hurry to charge you."

"And maybe you don't have anything, and you're here on a fishing trip." Jesse squinted.

"It's your life. If you want to roll the dice and look like the bad guy, that's fine with me."

Jesse stopped speaking but continued rocking. After a few tense moments, he said, "Enmity."

"What?" John said, his eyebrows crinkling.

"I want enmity." Jesse flashed a snaggle-toothed grin, as if he were holding a royal flush. "If I don't have enmity, I don't talk." He folded his arms and puffed his chest out.

"Well, Shakespeare, I think you mean immunity," Tim said.

"Okay, immunity. Without it, this conversation is over. They're going after me with the Career Criminal Statute because of the trumped-up resisting charge." He scowled at Tim. "If they convict me of fraud and resisting under that statute, I'm going up for thirty years. I can't do thirty years. I want enmity."

"Immunity," Tim said.

"Whatever. I want it."

John scooted closer to Jesse. "You're living in a fantasy world if you think they're just going to let you walk outta here."

"And you're living in a fantasy world if you think I'm ever going to tell you anything about that boy without it! You can't use anything Linda told you—if she truly told you anything—because she's my wife. It can't be used, and you know that. Don't play me like some rookie punk. Either you come in here with a deal from the state that gets me outta here, or you get outta my face about this whole thing."

"Outta your face?" John rose from his chair and towered over Jesse. He fisted both hands on the table, which creaked and bowed under the pressure. State would never agree to immunity. If they gave Jesse Lee immunity and later discovered that he killed Dylan, they would never be able to prosecute him. They wouldn't budge—even if it meant never finding Dylan.

Too many helpless children had been hurt in John's life, and too many times he'd been unable to do anything. It had to stop. Now.

"What kinda sick soul are you?" John said, his pulse racing. "Have you no sense of decency? No shame? We're talking about a little boy here!"

"I've got nothing to say." Jesse teetered on his chair, his hands folded on his distended stomach. He flashed an obnoxious, pompous smirk.

"Oh, you've got plenty to say," John said. "And you're gonna say it. Today."

"In your dreams."

John lunged around the table and seized Jesse's throat with

both hands, jerking him from his chair and slamming him against the wall. "You're gonna tell me where Dylan is right now, or I'm gonna reach down your throat and drag it out of you."

Jesse grabbed John's arms, and his eyes bulged, froth bubbling from his mouth.

"Whoa, whoa." Tim grabbed John's shoulders and yanked him back. "Chill out, John. Let him go. We'll find Dylan; I promise. This slime isn't worth it."

The buzzer sounded, and the door flung open as Robbie, the giant guard, and two other guards sprinted into the room.

"I told you to behave yourself," the huge guard said. He snatched Jesse from John's grip. The guard twirled him around, mashing his face into the wall. Jesse screamed and winced as the guard ground his forearm into the back of Jesse's neck, smearing his face along the unforgiving brick wall. The other guards wrenched Jesse's arms behind his back. "You don't attack a cop in here, Jesse Lee. You should know that by now."

John stepped back, and Tim and Robbie shuffled in front of him. John sighed.

He was in big trouble.

"It's not his fault," John said, catching his breath. "I started it. He didn't do anything."

The guards paused their assault on Jesse and looked back carefully at John. They released some of the tension but continued cuffing him. They escorted a dazed and beleaguered Jesse Lee from the room.

Stunned into silence, Robbie and Tim gawked at John, who drew his hands to his face. "I can't believe I just did that. I messed up big. I lost it. I just lost it."

"It looked to me like he was getting ready to swing on you." Tim held his fist up in a fighting stance. "Isn't that right, Robbie?

Yeah, it looked like he was going to jump up at any second. He's already swung at me once, so you *had* to defend yourself."

"Don't go there." John held up a hand. "I know what you're trying to do, but I'll take responsibility for this. I'll take my lumps, but I'm definitely not going to drag you two into this."

"We're partners," Robbie said. "We *are* involved in this. We'll be here for you if this goes bad...if there's an internal investigation or anything."

"We probably need to go." Tim placed a hand on John's shoulder. "Before they turn us into guests rather than visitors." His expression was a cross between sympathy and shock.

"This place gives me the creeps anyway." Robbie put her hand on the small of John's back and led him to the door to the outside world.

The ride home was quiet. Robbie and Tim were in the front, John in the back. The sky had darkened; trouble invaded from the north.

Great, just what I need now. John closed his eyes and took several controlled breaths. *Not now, please.* The peals of thunder in the distance rattled him. He twitched slightly, hoping Robbie and Tim wouldn't notice.

Their small car was on the outskirts of Okeechobee when the storm unleashed its full wrath. Soon the fury engulfed their car, the wind rocking it to and fro, and rain tapping on the roof to an ever-increasing beat. Sweat leaked from John's face like a rusty pipe. His chest tightened. The first round of heavy thunder erupted. John clenched the seat, digging his fingers deep into the upholstery.

"Man, this is bad." Tim leaned forward and squinted to see. "I haven't seen a storm like this in years."

Robbie looked back at John, now splayed out in the backseat. "Are you all right? You look like you're going to be sick."

John bobbed his head but didn't speak. He panted as the thunder collided with the car again. *I've gotta get outta here.* His heart pounded. His mind reeled.

"Stop…" he wheezed, "…the car."

"I can't stop, man. We're in the middle of nowhere, in a storm no less."

"Stop the car now!" John fumbled with the door handle and pounded on the door with his fist.

"Hold on! I'll find a place to stop. Get a grip." Tim leaned even closer to the windshield. "John, there's a gas station right here. I'm pulling in now."

The car skidded underneath the covered awning. John leaped from the car before it stopped. He lost his footing but caught himself with his hands, keeping himself from falling face first onto the pavement. He pushed to his feet and sprinted into the gas station, past the attendant, and into the bathroom, locking the door behind him.

The booming echo vibrated the tiny building. John covered his ears with his hands and fell back against the wall, trying to silence the rage of the storm. The deafening barrage pounded against his spirit. His chest constricted, as if a gigantic python were squeezing the life out of him.

The room closed in. Dylan's face came clearly into focus, then morphed into Frank's sadistic smirk from so many years before. John threw up in the toilet and backed against the wall, sliding down. He crumbled into the corner, quaking with each round of thunder.

Slowly, more and more time passed from each angry storm blast. John's chest loosened, and he was able to breathe again.

He cupped his hands over his face. He was losing it. Big-time.

"John, you all right?" Tim tapped on the door. "You've been in there a half hour."

"I'm fine," John said, finally able to speak in more than a whisper. He scrambled to his feet. "Just give me a couple more minutes."

He turned on the faucet and drenched his face with cool water. The rumbling in the distance caught his attention momentarily. He doused his face several more times. For the first time, he noticed the stench of the small bathroom. This attack had exhausted him. He didn't know how much more he could take.

Fear of facing his partners kept him in the bathroom for several more minutes. He made a vain attempt to straighten his clothes and then opened the door. Tim, Robbie, and the station attendant stared at John, whose chalky complexion and disheveled appearance caught them by surprise.

"You okay, John?" Robbie said, her head tilted. "This thing with Jesse Lee is going to pass. It's going to be all right. We'll be here for you."

"It's not that. We...we just need to get going."

The attendant continued to stare at John.

"Don't you have something to do?" Tim leaned into the attendant's personal space. The man pulled a rag from his uniform pocket and began wiping down the counter.

John staggered toward the car as Tim and Robbie glanced at each other with raised eyebrows.

I'm truly losing my mind.

35

Tim, Robbie, and John shuffled through the back door of their office. Robbie led the way, carrying her briefcase as she picked up the pace toward her desk. John and Tim lagged behind. John's shirt was partially pulled out, his tie was loosened and crooked, and his hair clumped in different directions. He had looked better after his fight with Kenneth Pate.

Alan emerged from his office, stopping them cold in the hallway. His face told John everything he needed to know—he was in big trouble.

"We need to talk, Russell." Alan pointed to his office. "Now."

"Boss, that Jesse Lee was crazy. You should have seen his eyes." Tim pointed to his own, making dramatic gestures. "John was provoked."

Tim trailed John into Alan's office as well. "I need to talk with John…alone."

"But, boss—"

"No buts, Porter. Outta my office."

Robbie poked her head in the doorway and tried to slip past Tim. "It's been a difficult case, Alan. Lots of stress. We've all felt it."

"This isn't group therapy, people. Both of you, out...now!"

Tim paused, then turned to John and placed his hand on his shoulder. "I'll be at my desk."

He and Robbie took an inordinate amount of time crossing the three feet of carpet to the door, giving Alan plenty of time to ask them to stay and defend John; both looked disappointed when he didn't. John sank into the chair like a torpedoed battleship slowly submerging into the abyss.

"As you can imagine, I got a call from the warden of Okeechobee Correctional Institution." Alan placed both hands on his desk and used them to ease down onto his chair. "It wasn't a pleasant call, John. It's never pleasant when I'm told one of my agents is *persona non grata* at a state prison."

"What's going to happen now? Am I suspended?"

"Not yet. The gracious Mr. Morgan hasn't filed a complaint yet, and neither has the warden, who I don't think is going to. But Jesse Lee is another matter. I'm sure when he talks with his attorney, there's a good chance he will."

John stared out Alan's window. He'd never been the subject of an Internal Affairs investigation, and he didn't like the thought of it. He figured that when the time came, he'd just tell what happened and take his lumps. Maybe suspension. Maybe worse. But what if he lost his job? Was criminally prosecuted? How could he tell Marie...the boys? How could he have been so stupid?

Alan clasped his hands in front of him. Although he rarely displayed his emotions, Alan was clearly perplexed and uneasy. John had worked for Alan for many years and had never put him in this situation. It was new territory for them both.

"What happened, John? Talk to me."

"I can't work this case," John said, still unable to make eye contact with Alan. "I can't find this kid. You've got to give it to someone else. I just can't handle it anymore."

"I can't give it to someone else. You're too deep into this now. No one else could be brought up to speed in time. Besides, I was asked to put my best people on it, and, John, you're my best people."

"Let Tim and Robbie take it over. They're good cops; they can finish it out."

"Not an option. Tim's still too new to the agency, and Robbie hasn't been with the case from the start. This case is all over the news, and I've got people from the governor's office calling me every day for updates. We're all under the microscope here. None of us can walk away from this case until it's finished—no matter how it turns out."

John sighed and shifted his eyes to the ceiling. No relief. He couldn't even get suspended to get off the case. John tugged at his already loose tie; it was strangling him.

"I don't mean to get too personal, but is everything all right at home?"

John wasn't sure how to answer. He and Alan had been friends for a long time, but John had shared nothing about what was happening with him. Not with anyone. He wouldn't start today either. "It's been better." Truly the understatement of the year.

"Let me give you some hard-learned advice. Don't let this job ruin your marriage. I've wrecked two now, and believe me, it's not worth it. Marie is a doll, and you'd be a fool to let this interrupt your life. Cases come and cases go, but in the end, your family is all you have."

"It's not just this case. There's…well, there's a lot going on. That's all. It's just too much for me right now. I need a break."

"You're a good cop, John. A professional. And I'm expecting you to act like one. I'm asking you as your boss and your friend to pull yourself together and finish this case. If you need time after that, you can take as much as you need. But we're all under the gun. We've got to get this thing done—and done right."

John let his head fall back and thump against the wall. "Is that all?"

"Yeah. Now go home and get some rest. You look terrible. I'll let you know if IA contacts me."

"I wish I could get some rest," John whispered as he lifted himself from the chair.

Frank squeezed the dashboard with both hands as Marie hit the brakes a little harder than normal in the congestion on I-75. He still couldn't get used to traveling so fast. He sat back and avoided looking out the side window. The blur of the passing trees and cars made him nauseous. Since walking was the fastest he'd moved in three decades, seventy miles an hour seemed like light speed.

"Sorry about that." Marie turned to check on Frank. "This traffic is terrible."

"It's okay, missy." His heart throbbed, and he wiped his face with his handkerchief. After composing himself, he opened his manila folder and dumped the papers onto his lap. He sifted through them until he found what he was looking for. "It should be our first right after we get into Ocala, if this here map is right. I'm sure plenty has changed since I was there last."

"A lot has changed, but I'm sure once we're in town, it'll come back to you."

"I can't thank you enough for giving me a ride way out here. You've been so good to me. Don't know what I'd do without your help. I thank God for you."

"We're family." She smiled. "That's what families do. So sit back and don't worry about it. I'll drive you where you need to go. I'm getting to know my way around Ocala pretty well now."

Marie was such a beautiful young woman, full of grace, and more than a little spunk. After their rocky first meeting, he didn't think she'd ever talk with him again, much less help him. He knew why his son loved this woman so, and her character spoke volumes to the kind of man his son had become.

Frank just wished he could know John, even a little. If he could talk with his son for one hour, he'd be ready to leave this earth. He wanted to hear John's voice, hear him laugh, or see him smile. Frank tried to imagine what that would be like.

During their time together, he asked Marie what seemed to be a million questions about John and their life. He worried she might tire of talking about it, but she never did. She answered every question as best she could. But even with all the knowledge he now had about his son, it still couldn't replace a relationship.

Maybe he'd hoped for too much. Maybe all the days and nights he knelt on the hard cement floor of his cell until his knees bled, crying out to God to give him a chance to reconcile with his son, was too much as well. The most he'd hoped for was his son to visit him in prison and give him a chance to seek the healing balm of forgiveness.

But when he was diagnosed with terminal cancer and the chance of parole seemed likely, he had dreams—deep, vivid dreams. One recurring dream haunted him every night: Frank would come home to their old house in Ocala, and little Frankie would be waiting on the porch for him, as if the awful event never happened. As soon as Frankie saw him walking down the driveway, he would sprint from the porch, down the dirt driveway, and then launch himself into Frank's arms. Frank would squeeze him tight and never let go.

He often woke up in his cell weeping uncontrollably.

Frank prayed for God to stop the dream from coming, because it seemed cruel and impossible. Then the parole hearing came. And he won. Freedom would be his, and the faint chance to see the dream come true.

After experiencing John's rage, he realized his dream was silly and unrealistic. His crimes were too cruel and sadistic to overcome; the scars and wounds he caused were too deep. He hadn't had the dream since that day.

"We're getting close now." Marie made the second right just inside the Ocala city limits.

He strained to check the numbers on the mailboxes and to scan the terrain. "You're gonna have to slow down, missy. It's been so long."

"Just let me know if you recognize something."

His past collided with his present as he tried to sort everything he was seeing. Much of the landscape looked familiar, but with so much new construction since he'd left, he couldn't be sure. Several newer housing developments occupied space where cattle used to graze, and convenience stores dotted the roadway like telephone poles. Ocala was not the same city it had been three decades before.

As Marie plodded along the roadway, Frank searched for something to spark his recollection.

He gazed across a small field between a housing

development and a grocery store. "Stop! Hold it here." A faint recognition flashed across his mind as he studied the field in detail. "Pull over. I wanna see something."

Marie parked the van on the side of the road. "Is this the right place?"

"I wanna get a closer look." Frank opened the door and was clambering down before Marie could get out and around the van.

Frank used his cane carefully as he hobbled toward the dilapidated fence, along a footpath, and through the fence toward a clump of trees. Marie shielded her eyes from the late-morning sun and searched the horizon.

"This is it," Frank said with a note of excitement. "We're here." He walked faster than his cane would take him, taking two or three steps before the cane even hit the ground. "Our house was right there." He pointed to just beyond two great oak trees and in among a cluster of saw palmettos.

As he got closer, he could just make out the foundation. Marie intertwined her arm with his as she helped him along the trail. He was grateful; she kept him steady on the rugged path.

"Are you sure, Frank? It's been a while."

"I'm positive." He knew the spot well. He had helped build their house. Although it hadn't been much of a home, it was a sturdy house. He was a good carpenter, even if it was in between jail stints and drinking binges. It was the only thing in those days that made sense in his life, and he helped build many of the homes in Ocala.

"I see it now," Marie said as they walked up onto the foundation where his home used to sit. Now only the cement pad remained with a small oak growing where their living room used to be. Vines and vegetation covered the pad as well, leaving small portions of exposed and barren cement.

Frank used his cane to flip over a board that lay just off the path. It was charred on one side. "Must have been a fire." He poked the board several times. Walking the perimeter of the foundation, he visualized how their home looked so many years ago.

He leaned on his cane and fought back the emotions. Everything was destroyed—his house, his wife, his son, and his life. All were gone, wrecked, demolished, crushed. Nothing was as it used to be. He struggled to control himself as he turned in a circle, taking it all in, however agonizing. He couldn't go back. But if he could, what he wouldn't give to change what he had done. Not only that horrific night, but his life all the way around.

He wondered many times how different his life would have been if he'd only met his Savior years before. Prison taught him not to get caught up in the could-have-beens, but standing on the cracked, broken foundation of his home, his life, it was hard not to speculate and dream.

Marie strolled around the edges of the base. She picked up a stick and jabbed at the cement.

"Frankie's…I mean, John's bedroom was up there." He pointed up and to the right.

Marie looked in that direction, as if contemplating the design of the home. "Thank you."

"I thought you'd want to know, missy." He looked at his watch. Almost lunchtime. "We probably ought to get going."

Marie helped him off the foundation and back onto the pathway. Halfway back to the van, he stopped and turned around. Tired and winded, his legs wobbled with each step. He didn't have any more energy. Each day was more difficult than the last.

It wouldn't be long now.

As he gazed down the road that used to be his driveway, he seared the image in his mind. He could see where the porch was, see where Frankie sat in his dream. *Jesus, my home's destroyed, but my dream is still alive. Please heal my son. Let me hold him one last time.* He turned toward the van.

He would never be back here again.

36

John left Alan's office dejected and exhausted. He trudged down the hallway, toting his briefcase and Dylan's file with him.

Tim propped himself against the wall, pretending to be reading a case file, and Robbie stood in a doorway looking at the ceiling, as if she were inspecting it for leaks.

Checking up and down the hall, Tim whispered, "How'd it go? Are you suspended?"

"No, not yet anyway. I couldn't even get myself off this lousy case."

"You're gonna be all right," Robbie said. "Chances are that slime Morgan won't even file a complaint. I doubt it was the first time someone choked him."

John shrugged. "It doesn't matter." He walked to his chair, plopping down hard. "I've really blown it. I'm just sick over this."

"I've got an apartment here now." Robbie reached into her pocket and handed him a piece of paper. "This has my home phone and pager on it. Call me anytime if you need something.

We've all been doing this a long time, and sometimes we just need to sit down and talk about it."

"Thanks. I'll be fine, but I appreciate it."

Robbie gathered her things. "Well, I'll see you guys in the morning. I've gotta finish getting caught up on this case." She headed out the door, leaving Tim and John.

"Maybe we can start fresh in the morning?" John asked.

"Want some coffee or something before I go?"

"No thanks, Tim." The day's events flickered before him. They were stalled, in more ways than one. Since Jesse Lee wasn't talking, there were no fresh leads to follow up.

He failed Dylan. He failed Robbie and Tim. He failed himself. All the people who knew anything about Dylan were keeping mum. And John had nothing that could make them talk.

Linda faced fraud charges. Neither she nor Janet Parks had a criminal history, so even if they were convicted, they'd serve a small amount of time, if any. Jesse Lee was going up under the Career Criminal Statute, which would probably keep him in prison for the rest of his life. There just didn't seem to be any way that they'd find Dylan now.

At least the guy responsible would be in prison. But what if Jesse Lee wasn't responsible? What if something completely different had happened? Dylan was out there somewhere, and one or all of these people knew where he was and wouldn't tell anyone to save their own hides. How could these people sleep at night? How did they justify their existence?

John arose from his stupor. "You know, Tim, I'm beginning to think you were right."

"Right about what?"

"When you said that we can't help these people, because most don't want to be helped. I didn't believe it before, but I'm starting to now. The world is going to hell in a handbasket, and there's not one thing we can do to make it better. These people are just nuts, and nothing's going to change that."

"Don't tell me that, John." Tim's normally jovial face contorted as if he'd swallowed something putrid. "Don't put that on me. I know we've been partners only a short time, but there's something I've gotta get off my chest."

"Might as well." John shrugged.

"When I first started here a few months ago, my life was in ruin." He shook his head. "I was still recovering from my gunshot wound, recently retired from Orlando PD, and my wife had just left me—all within the same year." Tim rubbed his stomach where the old wound was. "I was in a rough place."

"I remember."

"Well, up until now one of the things that has been getting me through is you."

John cocked his head back. "How's that?"

"Every day I'd come in here, and you would have that stupid, happy, full-of-life expression on your face. Nothing ever seemed to bother you. And then I met Marie and your family, and I saw nothing but joy in your life. At first it upset me." Tim leaned over and picked up the picture off of his desk. "Since the divorce, my own daughter, Ruby, won't talk with me. The little girl I held in my arms and promised that I would be there forever won't have anything to do with her father."

John had seen her picture many times, although Tim hadn't said anything about her. She was a beautiful young woman, eyes full of energy and joy, and she bore Tim's high cheekbones and deep, trenchant smile.

"She's very pretty."

Tim handed him the picture to examine closer. "She's brilliant, too, like her mother. She's a freshman this year at

Florida State. She won't take my phone calls, John. All I get is her answering machine or a hang-up. We were happy once. Close and strong. But not anymore."

John passed the photo back to Tim, who wiped the dust off the frame and placed it carefully on his desk.

"John." Tim rolled his chair closer to him. "I let my hurt, anger, frustration, and *pride* destroy our family. When the demons of this job came calling, I went to the bottle and everywhere else except to my wife and daughter. Ruby has every right to be angry at me. My wife, too. I'm angry with myself for letting it happen."

"I'm sorry, Tim." John didn't know what else to say. He knew the man had been through hell. John's mind leaped from his own troubles for a moment.

"Now here we are, and I don't ever see that same silly Christian smile anymore. Not since we started working this case. I don't mean to rag on you, but you're pulling me down to a place I don't want to go back to. I just started feeling like my old self, and then this happens. I used to be able to look at you and see something bright and possible in the world. I want to see it again, John. I *need* to see it again."

Tim spoke more truth than John had heard in a long time. It wasn't just this case that haunted him, but he didn't know how to tell Tim. Where would he start? His situation was different, too. But he yearned to return to the sweet place of peace. He would get back there…somehow.

"Thanks," John said.

"Don't thank me. This isn't about you. It's about me feeling better." Tim winked and then gave a wry smile. "I'm available if you need me, 24/7." He rose and put his hand on John's shoulder. "See you tomorrow."

"I'll be here."

Tim gathered his things and headed out the door.

Worn out and alone, John stared at his computer. *If I could only find peace, but it doesn't look like that will happen anytime soon.* He pulled a sticky note from his monitor with a message to call Barry Watkins.

John didn't realize how much his life was open to inspection of those around him, what a witness simply trying to live a God-honoring life was. He and Marie prayed together for Tim on several occasions. John had spoken with him about the Lord as well. Now, after his meltdown on Jesse Lee, John feared his entire testimony was destroyed, and he lost, maybe forever, the respect of those around him.

John picked up the phone and dialed Barry's extension at CSI.

"Watkins," Barry answered.

"Hey, it's John. You left a message."

"Yeah, and it's not good news, or it is, depending on how you look at it, I suppose."

"My day can't get any worse. What do you have, Barry?"

"I got the DNA comparison back from the body in Jacksonville."

"It's been a long day. Just give me what you have."

"The body isn't Dylan."

"Why not," John huffed. "Nothing else is working out in the case, so why should we be able to recover his body? Why should we get one iota, one shred of physical evidence to help us out?"

"You okay, John? You sound like something's up."

"Just fine. Great. Never been better. So if it's not Dylan, who is he?"

"We linked him to a boy missing out of South Carolina, Bradley Frazier. The authorities up there have always suspected the mother's boyfriend. At least now they have some decent evidence to go on. We'll be working with them pretty closely on this one. I just wanted to let you know."

John didn't speak; he couldn't. He didn't want to thank him for the information, even though it wasn't Barry's fault. He forced the burning knot back down his throat. "Okay, Barry. I'll be in touch." He slammed the phone down before Barry could answer. He didn't want to talk with anyone right now.

Why? The single word pinged through his head like a bullet ricocheting in a metal room. Why had he failed in everything that mattered? Why was everything he touched falling to pieces? Why had God's hand been lifted from his life?

Closing his eyes, John dared what he hadn't done in weeks—he petitioned the Lord for help. There, alone among the cubicles, track lighting, and the things of work, God's Spirit fell upon him in a way John hadn't felt since he first received Jesus as his Savior. He basked in the long-missing serenity and comfort of union with his Lord.

A gentle curiosity tugged at his spirit. He pulled up the Department of Corrections website and clicked onto the Recently Released file. After typing in the name, the digital image of Frank's face filled the screen. John turned away, unable and unwilling to look for any length of time. Was it possible? Could this man be changed, transformed from beast to servant?

John didn't doubt the God who spoke the universe into creation and could do all things. But he certainly doubted this man. John knew him too well. It wasn't possible…or was it? He chased the thought from his head and closed the screen.

In that brief moment, John felt in the depths of his being the Lord's leading—and something he'd known the whole time. *I can't do it, Lord. Not now, not this man. Please…there must be some other way.*

As quickly as the peace had descended on him, it

disappeared, like a puff of smoke in a gentle wind. His gaze locked onto the picture of Dylan that served as the background on his computer. An empty, cavernous void took the place of the brief tranquility that had visited his soul. He directed the cursor to Dylan's file, opened it, and started typing.

It would be another long night.

Oak Hammock Memorial Gardens was beautiful and serene, as far as cemeteries went. Frank took a piece of paper from his folder and read it carefully. He pointed toward the northern corner of the graveyard.

"The investigator's report says it's over in that direction." Frank opened the door and slid from the van, his eyes focused on his destination, his steps tentative and measured.

Careful not to push him too fast, Marie strolled alongside him, linking his free arm with hers. She worried he might fall on the uneven and sometimes slippery ground. His slender arm trembled in her grasp.

Frank stopped, wiped the perspiration from his face, and rested for several seconds. He glanced at his directions and then resumed his trek toward the corner of the cemetery.

"It should be in this section." He paced off the count given to him. The rows of plots seemed like an endless forest of crosses and tombstones, nothing outstanding to use as a landmark.

Marie read some of the gravestones. Many were from the early 1900s, and some went as far back as the late 1800s. The inscriptions on the older stones were weathered and faded, difficult to make out. She was intrigued by what was written about these people who'd passed so long before. It must have been difficult to live in wild Florida in those days.

One read, "Galen Worthington Foster, Good Husband, Good Father, Good Christian."

Another read, "Charlene Mack, Too Good for This Earth." Most of the stones just had the date of birth and death on them. Nothing ornate or poetic, just the prosaic writings of official history. The kind of information that told when they lived but not how.

Frank ambled through the maze of headstones until he came to a small site, stopped, and checked his papers. He leaned forward to read the name on the small plate at the head of the plot that was nearly covered with grass and dirt—"Lynette Jewel Moore. Born: July 24, 1936. Died: August 8, 1971."

He teetered; his papers tumbled from his hands as a guttural gasp leaped from his mouth. Sliding down his cane, he collapsed to his knees and buried his face into the ground around her grave.

Placing her hand on his back, Marie knelt beside Frank, who was hunched over and near prostrate. "Lynette, I'm sorry! So sorry. Please forgive me! God forgive me for what I done." He squeezed the earth until it squirted from between his fingers. His body quaked, and he wept uncontrollably and begged the forgiveness of the long dead.

Rubbing his back, she sat with him as he mourned in a way he hadn't had the chance to do in thirty-three years. His broken cries filled the graveyard, attracting the attention of several visitors. Marie made eye contact with them and nodded, assuring them that Frank was indeed okay. Broken and in pain, but okay.

She got comfortable in the grass around the grave as Frank's lamenting told her that they would be here for a long, long time.

37

O h, boy," John said. "This is not good."

Ryan stepped to the plate again and knocked the clay off his cleats with the bat. He'd been killing them all day. A home run and two doubles already.

"Time out." John made a T with his hands. "Time out, Ref." John headed toward the mound.

"Dad, don't pull me," Brandon said. "I can get him this time. I've got Ryan figured out. He doesn't hit curves well. I know I can slide one by."

"You've pitched a good game, son, but it's time to give someone else a try. Your arm's tired, and this kid's the best hitter in the league. We're gonna need something fresh for him."

"Dad, *please*. Let me try. I can do this. I feel good."

"I'm taking you out, and that's all there is to it. You haven't had good luck against him, so give me that ball."

"One more set," Brandon said. "If I can't strike him out, I'll take myself out."

"Don't question my judgment again. We're not playing around here. Now give me the ball and get to the dugout."

Brandon reluctantly handed the ball to John and then jogged to the dugout.

"Thomas," John called. "Come on in and finish this up."

The boy ran from third base and began his warm-ups on the mound. After several pitches and a shake of his arm, he indicated he was ready to play.

John walked back to the dugout and looked at Marie, who sat with Joshua in the stands. The ball cap hid her eyes, but he could still sense her mood—it wasn't good. She'd been quiet most of the day, from the time they got up and even through the game. Something was brewing.

Ryan stood in the batter's box, steady and determined. As Thomas pulled the ball to his chest preparing to pitch, the blond batter hunkered down in his stance. The ball whizzed through the air, colliding with the bat. The crunch was so loud John thought for sure the ball would be deformed. He watched their season end as the ball landed a solid ten feet outside the back fence.

Ryan jogged the bases as his team greeted him at home plate. John's clipboard fell to the ground. Brandon stared at John, who couldn't look him in the eyes.

The other players stomped into the dugout, some hurling their gloves to the ground.

"Settle down," John said, amid the cheers of the winning team. "Settle down." He cleared his throat and then panned the faces of his disappointed players. The parents huddled around the dugout, waiting for him to speak. "I…I'm sorry. It's been a good season…but maybe next year. I think we should just go home now." The words lumped in John's throat. He didn't know what else to say. Maybe if he hadn't missed so many practices. Maybe if he'd done something different...

John and Brandon gathered the bats into the bag. Marie walked away with her arm around Joshua, well ahead of him.

The blond bomber and his mother approached Brandon. "You pitched a good game, Russell." He extended his hand. "Really, you're the best pitcher in the league."

Brandon reluctantly shook hands. "Thanks. Good game yourself."

"All the boys played well this season," Ryan's mother said to John. "I wanted to thank you too, Coach Russell, for being such a good role model for these young men. You and your team have really exhibited class and sportsmanship this year. Some of the other coaches have been, well, a little excitable, but you've always maintained your composure. It's good for the boys to see that, especially with your being a policeman. There's a little too much craziness in sports sometimes...and the rest of the world, for that matter."

John feigned a smile. "Thank you." Right now he didn't feel much like a role model of any kind, to anyone, especially his own son.

Pausing for a moment, she seemed to have more to say. Standing behind Ryan, she combed her fingers through his blond hair. But John tossed a glove in the bag and bent down for another, not in a chatty mood.

"We really should be going, Ryan." She took him by the shoulders and turned him toward the parking lot. "Dad's waiting in the car. Take care, Coach Russell. Thanks again."

Ryan and his mother waved their good-byes, and John nodded and forced another smile. He and Brandon shuffled quietly to the van, carrying their bats, gloves, and burdens.

John fired up his home computer and logged onto his work intranet. Within minutes he was reading reports from across the state and the nation about discovered bodies or missing persons. He jotted down locations and descriptions of cases that might be related. There were few. Most of the unidentified bodies were adults, usually female, but he scribbled the notes anyway. Anything that could be close. He had nothing else to go on. The case was in desperate need of CPR, and if left in its current state, Dylan would never be found.

Everything around him seemed to be collapsing. He was probably going to face an Internal Affairs investigation, maybe even a criminal prosecution for grabbing Jesse; Marie wasn't speaking to him; and the vision of his father hovered around him like a demonic specter from the past. It wasn't a coincidence that his life began falling apart after Frank's arrival.

If there was one good thing in all of this, at least the old man hadn't shown up at his house again. After his warning, John wasn't sure if Marie saw Frank again or not. They hadn't talked past the pleasantries of living in the same home in days. She would drop little hints about his father, little tidbits to try to draw him into a conversation, but John wouldn't bite.

Part of him felt sick about that, the other part felt confident that he was doing the right thing. His father was a destroyer. It didn't matter what he now claimed to be; John knew the truth, and he must protect his family.

He clicked into an interesting case of a body uncovered in Montana. Not a likely pick, but he read it anyway.

"Dad, are you almost done?" Brandon was reading over his shoulder. "I wanna play Cyber Sports."

"Not right now, son. I've got work to finish."

"When will you be done?"

"When I'm done. Probably not till late."

"But, Dad, you've already been on-line a long time."

"Go do something else, Brandon. I'm working, and I need a little peace and quiet."

Joshua buzzed by John, firing multiple rounds from his toy machine gun.

"Boys, please go in the other room."

Joshua grabbed Brandon's leg and wrestled him to the ground. They rolled around just feet from John's chair.

"I *said* go in the other room."

Brandon threw Joshua over, and he crashed into John's chair.

"That's it!" John pushed away from his desk and grabbed Brandon by the shirt, yanking him off the floor. "I've had enough. Don't you listen?" John swung his hand back.

Marie screamed as she sprinted toward the tussle. "Don't you dare!"

John froze, hand still raised. Horror covered Brandon's face as he recoiled from his father's grasp. John staggered back and brought his hand to his face. "What have I done?"

He walked toward his son with both hands extended. "Brandon...I—"

Marie leaped in front of him. "Don't even think about it." She had one arm around Brandon, the other pointing at John. Glaring at him with her chin down, she stood planted in front of John, ready for war. "That's enough! We've all had enough! John Russell, you need to leave and get your head straight. And don't come back until you're ready to deal with this, and I mean *really* deal with it."

"But Marie...Brandon...I..." He stepped toward them again.

Marie pulled both boys into her bosom as they backed away from John. "Go, now! You need to leave."

John turned and headed to the front door, where he stopped to see his shocked family. His mouth agape, John fell into the night.

38

L ord, help me," John said, driving toward the beach. He'd always loved the sound of the waves, the roar of the powerful, ominous ocean. As he crossed from the mainland onto Melbourne Beach, the salt mist enveloped his car like smoke from an unseen fire. On this night, the ocean's sound gave him no comfort. It just added to the noise in his tortured mind.

He traveled along Route A1A until he found a remote beach access. He parked his car and then trudged along the boardwalk. The ocean was angry tonight; a storm loomed just offshore. Colossal waves crashed vengefully above the normal water line, digging jagged gullies out of the dunes. A young couple passed him on the boardwalk. They held hands and exchanged loving looks, oblivious to him.

John wandered onto the beach, hoping to find an area away from the lights.

He had business with God.

John was surprised by the amount of people walking the beach this time of night and searched the dark horizon for any vestiges of light, but none were found. Even if a ship were on the horizon, he couldn't see it through the dark, menacing storm just off the coast.

He bowed then shook his head. "Lord, help me. I'm falling apart. Everything in me is pulling in opposite directions. I can't take it anymore. I have nothing left. I think I'm losing my mind."

His pained soul replayed the look on Brandon's face over and over again. He wanted to throw up. Never in his wildest dreams did he think himself capable of that. He raised his hand to his own son in anger—something he swore he'd never do.

John had spent his life fighting against the legacy of his father, so the sins that haunted his childhood would never, *ever* creep into their home. He convinced himself that he could be a better husband, father, and Christian than Frank. But for the first time in his life, John realized that the dreadful memory of Frank Moore had helped shape him into the man he'd become, whether he liked it or not.

The heat lightning skipped from cloud to cloud over the ocean like searchlights scanning for enemy planes. A massive wave broke on shore and raced toward him, reaching for his feet. He stepped back twice to keep from being drawn into the murky surf. The salty vapors stung his eyes.

"I know what you want, Lord." He jammed his hands in his pockets as the wind whipped his hair about. "I've known it since Frank arrived. But I don't understand. Why? Is there no justice in the world? Couldn't he have died in prison? He should have paid for his crime. Why after all these years have You allowed this man back into my life?"

John shivered as the first tears tumbled down his cheek. "I can't do it, Lord. I'm not strong enough."

His thoughts collided with each other as John struggled

with what he'd done and what God wanted him to do. God was making it painfully clear that he would have to deal with this man again.

John rocked back, then collapsed to his knees into the sand. His weeping was drowned out by the call of the ocean. With his head lowered and his arms raised, he called on the only One who could ease his pain. "I'll do as You wish, Lord. I'll meet with him…but only if I know You're in this. Please let me feel You again."

"Did you sleep in those clothes, Russell, or what?" Tim said as he walked into the office. "Come to think of it, you did wear those clothes yesterday. Did you stay here last night?"

"Yeah, but I didn't get much sleep."

"Go home and get cleaned up," Tim said. "You're not going to miss anything around here."

"I'll be fine." John sauntered into the bathroom, doused his face in the sink several times, then looked in the mirror.

He'd seen heroin addicts who looked better.

John would definitely have to go home, shave, and clean up. He checked his watch. Better wait a bit longer to give Marie time to get the boys off to school. Hopefully, he could pop in and out. He wasn't ready to see them yet.

He made it back to his desk just as his phone rang.

John stared at it. It had to be Marie. He'd turned his pager and cell phone off last night. What would he say? It rang again.

Tim grimaced. "You gonna get that or just keep watching it?"

With another ring, John tentatively pulled the receiver to his ear. "Agent Russell," he said in a low whisper.

No voice answered him, although he could hear breathing on the other end.

"Hello." He glanced at Tim and shrugged. "Is someone there?"

"You're the detective who's looking for Dylan, the little boy missing from state care?" It was clearly a woman's voice.

"Yes." He reached over and turned on the tape recorder connected to his phone. "That's me. Who are you?"

Another pause with only breathing on the other end. "That doesn't matter right now," she finally said. "I have information I think you're gonna want to hear."

"Really." He rolled his eyes. "I'm listening."

"Not over the phone. I want to meet...in person."

"I don't like meeting with strangers. I want to know who I'm dealing with. Who are you and what do you have to tell me?"

"This is hard enough," she said, her voice cracking. "Don't make it any harder on me. Just meet me at Veterans Park in forty-five minutes. And come alone. I'll only talk with you."

"How will I know who you are?"

"You won't, but I'll find you. Be there in forty-five minutes—alone." The caller hung up.

John stared at the receiver before hanging up. "That was weird." He rewound the tape and played it for Tim. Robbie walked in and listened, too.

"What do you think?" John said.

Robbie shook her head. "You need a shave."

"No, about the caller."

"Sounds strange. But the only way you'll find out if she's got good info or a loony is to show up. And now you only have thirty-five minutes," Robbie imitated the caller's dry whisper.

"I don't like it," Tim said. "It doesn't feel right. Why would she want to meet you alone? She won't tell you how to identify her. It sounds like a setup."

John flopped back in his chair, considering his options. He wasn't in the mood for another lunatic to surface in this case. But something in her voice intrigued him—a sense of urgency and desperation, a small ring of validity. If she was crazy, she was playing it well. This could give him a little time before he went home to clean up.

"Can you guys cover me if I meet her?" John twirled a pen between his fingers.

"There's some good parking at Veterans Park," Tim said. "I'll keep my rifle up front with me in case she gets freaky. But keep your eyes open. I still don't like it."

"We'll leave now to set up before you arrive." Robbie picked up her purse and strung it over her shoulder. "She won't even know we're there."

"We better get going." Tim reached for his coat. "Our secret squirrel informant awaits."

39

Not wanting to drive directly into the parking lot, John found a space along the side of the road near Veterans Park. He'd given Tim and Robbie a five-minute head start. He didn't like someone else dictating where they'd meet. If the caller had stayed on the phone longer, John would have convinced her to move the location, taking her out of her comfort zone. Since she knew where he would be and when, he was sure he'd be watched as soon as he arrived. Cops liked to watch people first, not the other way around, especially when the person seemed odd, if not unstable.

Tim's car was backed into a shady spot across the street, which gave him a full view of everyone and everything in the park. Over a dozen children ran around the large playground that covered the middle of the park next to a granite memorial to the veterans of foreign wars from Brevard County. Flags from all branches of the Armed Services circled the monument, and several sidewalks wrapped around and through the park like stitches on a baseball.

Carrying a legal pad, Robbie strolled along the walkway,

appearing to admire all the tranquility the park had to offer. Her hair pulled back in a ponytail, she looked like a young professional on a break from work. She chose a bench shaded by a colossal oak. She sat, crossed her legs, and started writing on the pad, blending perfectly into the surroundings.

John walked into the park, careful not to move too quickly. As he moseyed along, he scanned the faces of the many mothers watching their children play. He maneuvered around several women pushing their strollers on the sidewalk. Standing next to the monument, he rotated in a circle, searching for his potential informant. All the faces blurred together, and everyone in the park seemed to belong.

"I hope this isn't a wild goose chase," John mumbled. He glanced toward Tim, watching him through binoculars. John looked around again, then shrugged. Maybe she was running late. Maybe someone was just playing a game with the police. It wouldn't be the first time.

He sat on a bench in front of the playground. The soft breeze carried the joyful chorus of children playing, a small treat for an otherwise miserable twenty-four hours. A thirtyish mother broke from the collection of chaotic children, sat next to him, and crossed her legs.

"Nice day." She adjusted her ball cap that covered her eyes and stared away from John toward the children.

"Yeah." John said, giving in to the feeling that he was being messed with by some maladjusted, going-to-be-in-really-big-trouble-if-he-ever-caught-her practical joker.

The serene morning did little to soothe his growing angst. He checked his watch. Ten minutes late. Chances are she'd never show. He searched the parking lot one last time for anyone who might be watching her stunt come to fruition. He only saw Tim leaning back in the front seat of his car. The park was close to home; John could be there in five minutes and clean up. He'd wasted enough time for one day.

Sighing, he stood, stretched, and eyed Robbie, who was still pretending to be writing. He started to his car.

"Wait," the woman on the bench next to him said.

He shifted toward her but couldn't see her face, which was covered by the brim of her hat.

"Don't leave, Coach Russell." Her trembling voice sounded familiar.

John cocked his head. "You're the one who called me?"

"Yes." She removed her hat, revealing the woman he'd spoken with just the day before at the ball field.

From her cloak-and-dagger routine on the phone, he half expected a seedy, drug-addicted informant—like most he'd worked with—traipsing through the park, completely out of her element. This woman was a normal part of the community, far removed from the world that would have any information about Dylan Jacobs. Although it wasn't even cool, she wore a white sweater and pink pants. Her light brown hair was clipped back, and she had soft, motherly features.

John raised his hand, trying not to be too obvious, signaling Tim and Robbie that this was the woman they were looking for. He sat back down on the bench.

"I talked with you yesterday after the game, didn't I? You're the team mother for the Braves, Terri—"

"Terri Bennett."

"Why didn't you tell me who you were in the first place?"

"I was debating." Her arms drew tighter around herself.

"Debating what?"

"If I was going to tell you what I came here to tell you."

"Well, why don't you just let it out, then we'll both know what in the world you're talking about."

"It's not that easy." She appeared to choose her words carefully. "I almost said something yesterday, but it didn't feel right. It wasn't the right time. I needed confirmation."

"Okay, Terri." John checked his watch again. "I don't have the time or the patience for a game of twenty guesses. If you have something to tell me, just say it. If not, stop wasting both of our time."

"You have no idea how hard this is." She squirmed on the bench and turned away for a moment, lowering her head. Then she regarded John again. "What would happen if you found the boy—Dylan? What would happen to him?"

"Alive or dead?"

"Alive."

John perked up and gave her his full attention. "Is he alive?"

Terri closed her eyes. "He's alive."

"How do you know?" John bent forward, planting his elbows on his knees. His brain shifted into overdrive as he moved into interview mode. This did more to wake him up than a half-dozen lattes. "Where can I find him? Is he safe? Do you know this for sure?"

"I know everything about him."

John's enthusiasm plummeted like a skydiver in freefall. The painfully fresh memory of William the Confessor declaring nearly the same thing leaped from his mind. He settled back and surveyed Terri's face again. Although obviously in pain, she didn't seem deranged or unstable. But he didn't want to get too excited yet. He didn't want to be dragged down that road again.

"How do you know everything about him?"

Terri paused again. "Because a mother knows everything about her son, Coach Russell. That's a mother's job."

"What?"

"Dylan Jacobs is my son. And he is alive and well...incredibly well. Better than he's ever been before, I can assure you."

His mouth agape, John stared at Terri. "But...but how's that possible? We're gonna need to verify that."

"That shouldn't be too hard. You know him. You talked with him yesterday, and he's right over there." She pointed to a large blond boy atop the monkey bars. She waved at him to come over. He jumped from the equipment and sprinted toward them.

"He doesn't know anything about this," she said quickly as he approached. "And I'd like to keep it that way, at least for as long as possible. Please don't say anything. I need to be the one to tell him...at the proper time."

John nodded.

"What, Mom?"

"Look who's in the park today." She turned to John. "Coach Russell, you remember *my* son...*Ryan.*"

"Hey, Coach Russell. That was a close game yesterday."

"I...I..." John was staring at the same boy who slammed homers against his team all year long. The resemblance slapped John in the face. How did he not see it? Everything fit, except the scar on his lip, which had disappeared. The veil had been lifted; he could finally see.

John cleared his throat and extended his hand. "You have a mighty strong bat." He shook Ryan's hand. "You were a thorn in our side all year."

Ryan blushed. "Thanks." He turned to his mother. "Can I go play now?"

"Go ahead, honey. Coach Russell and I have some things to hash out. I'll let you know when it's time to go."

"Okay, Mom," he said, already sprinting toward the playground again. "See ya later, Coach."

Stunned, John didn't know what to say. He'd expected to

find Dylan in a shallow grave somewhere in the thousands of miles of swamp in Florida, not healthy and doing well in John's own town. But he still wasn't completely convinced.

"Well, it sure looks like him. Except for the scar on his lip."

"It's amazing what plastic surgery can do these days," Terri said, smirking. "It's him. On the news, you said you had DNA from his mother. Compare it and you'll find I'm telling the truth."

"I do have to verify your story. And if what you're saying is true, we'll have a lot to talk about."

"As much as I never wanted to share this with anyone, especially someone from the state, I know now I *must* tell what happened, even though you'll try to take him away from us." Terri grimaced and squeezed herself even harder.

"But no matter what happened before, Detective Russell, he's our son now. And even if the paperwork isn't exactly right, my husband and I will fight you with everything we have."

Terri resisted the tears that welled in her eyes as she locked in a stare with John. "God has blessed us in the last few years, and we have plenty of money. My husband is meeting with an attorney as we speak."

"Whoa, whoa." John held up his hands. "I'm not the enemy. I'm not looking to ruin anyone's life or take anybody away. My job is to find out what happened and to find Dylan…period."

"You say that now, but why weren't you investigating that sham of a foster home he was in? You should have seen the filth and nastiness those children endured. The only regret I have is that we couldn't have taken more of them with us."

"Why did you wait so long to tell us?" John put his arm along the top of the backrest. "Why didn't you come forward when this first came out?"

"Yeah right, and have the state say our adoption wasn't legal and put Ryan back where he was…back into that cesspool? I don't think so. If it were up to me, I wouldn't be telling you anything right now." The muscles in her jaw worked back and forth as she continued to scowl at him. "I would have kept this secret until I died, you can trust me on that."

"Well then, why *are* you telling me?" John couldn't figure this woman out. She definitely didn't want to be here spilling her guts to him, opening herself up to all sorts of legal and personal troubles. But she was doing it anyway.

She turned away, adjusted her hair, and shook her head. "You wouldn't understand."

"We'll have to get to know each other, so you might as well try me. You've got nothing to lose at this point, and you'd be surprised what I understand."

She squirmed and pressed back against the bench. "Since this has been in the news, I've been praying like never before. And then *she* came back. She hasn't bothered us in over three years. But every so often she'd return and want more money, with more threats, and then more money. I'd pay a million dollars to keep my son out of this mess. But the last few days I've been struggling with what to do. Then last night…I had a dream."

40

Marie prayed as she searched the park. She wasn't surprised when John called, but she did find it odd that he wanted to meet in a park. That wasn't his style. But a lot of things about John surprised her lately. She'd never seen him lose it like he did the night before.

She struggled to understand what he was dealing with. She had attempted to keep the peace and gently support her husband, but that wasn't working. She wasn't pulling punches anymore. He was going to get help...or else. Marie wasn't sure what "or else" meant, but she was tired of waiting for him to come around, to see that he needed to forgive his father and how his hatred was destroying their life.

"Please, Lord, give me the wisdom and the strength to know what to say and how to say it." Her mind was a whirlwind of thoughts and desires. She wanted to run up and hold him, never letting go. She wanted to shake him until sense returned. But she decided just to listen. She would be quiet, God willing, and hear what he had to say. "And please, Lord, help me keep my big mouth shut."

Slumping on the bench like a deflated balloon, John still wore the same clothes from the day before—although now they were bunched and wrinkled. His thick brown hair curled and protruded in different directions, obviously untouched by a brush this morning. She so wanted her husband back, the man she'd fallen in love with, the same man who swore he'd love her forever. She eased toward John, just to the right of his peripheral vision. His head was bowed, and his elbows rested on his knees.

Standing about twenty feet away, she watched him for a couple of moments. He didn't move. She stepped closer, catching his attention.

"Hey, hon," he said in low tone, not able to look her in the eye. "Thanks for coming."

"You thought I wouldn't?" She crossed her arms and kept her distance. *Keep it together. Let him speak. Just let him speak.* Inhaling through her nose, she exhaled a cleansing, calming lungful of air.

"Marie, I—"

"John, we can't go on like this," she blurted out as the dam burst. "I know you've been hurt. I know you went through hell…"

"Marie."

"But this has got to stop. It's killing us. All of us. Think of Brandon and Josh, what they've seen happen to…"

"Marie."

"…their father. How it's impacting them. It's not just your life. You're not a little seven-year-old boy anymore. This is pride, pure and simple."

"Marie, please stop," John said, his hand up. "Can I say something…anything?"

She corralled her dangerous tongue, barely holding back

the litany of feelings and pent-up emotions. She brushed the hair out of her face and pursed her lips, knowing that only a force of will could keep her from interrupting. Closing her eyes, she peacefully consented to listen.

"I've had a very interesting morning. I just had a nice talk with Dylan and his mother."

"Dylan who?"

John cocked his head, then smiled. *The* Dylan."

"As in missing boy Dylan?" A smile crossed her worn-out face, too.

"Take a look." John pointed to Terri and her son throwing a ball in the field next to them.

"That's Terri and Ryan from Little League? Are you sure? What happened?"

"It's a long but interesting story. The gist of it is that they illegally adopted Dylan from Linda and Jesse Lee Morgan through Janet Parks. An attorney set up a meeting for what she and her husband thought was a legal adoption. When they got to the Morgans' house, they knew something was screwy. But Terri saw Dylan and felt God screaming in her soul to rescue him, that he was to be theirs. They adopted him even though it wasn't on the up-and-up. They changed his name, plastic surgery removed his scar, and voilà—Ryan Bennett was born."

"Praise God." Marie stepped forward and took his hand. It was warm and strong. She hadn't seen a smile on John's face in so long that she almost forgot what it looked like.

"Everyone figured Dylan didn't have any family, so what was the harm. Janet could erase all memory of him from the Department of Family Services, the Morgans and Janet got their money, and the Bennetts got their child. If everyone stayed mum, no one would ever be the wiser."

"How did you find out?"

"That's the really interesting part," John said. "Mrs. Bennett was never going to tell anyone. She and her husband would have died before they'd put their son back into that situation again. Then last week Janet Parks threatened to expose them if they didn't pay her more money. Terri and her husband struggled with what to do. Until last night—when she had a dream, a dream in which God told her it was time to come forward, time to make everything right. Imagine that. They decided to be faithful to God's call, regardless of the risks to their family. That's when she called me."

"That's great news, hon. Fantastic news. So what's going to happen to the Bennetts?"

"I think we can help," John said, checking the horizon, as if he were already formulating a plan. "The adoption might not have been on the up-and-up, but Dylan has been in a good environment. They have been loving parents, good citizens. I think we can find a way to make this work. As a matter of fact, I know we can. I gave her my word that I'd do everything I could to help. And I plan on keeping it."

"What about Janet Parks?"

"I've got a special plan for her, too, but one thing at a time."

John shifted in the bench and squeezed her hand. He looked Marie in the eye for the first time since they started talking. "Dylan was right here the whole time. In our town. Right under my nose. What are the odds of that? I should have seen him, but I couldn't get past myself."

He cleared his throat and pulled her closer to the bench. "I never meant to hurt you, Marie. Years ago, I made a promise to myself and God that I would never hurt you or our family. I broke that promise, and I'm sick about it. I thought I was protecting our family, but all I was doing was being a stubborn, angry fool. I've done everything wrong. I've completely blown it."

Marie laced her fingers with his. "I've never given up on you, John Russell. Not for one moment. I love you, the boys love you, and we're all in this for the long haul—together."

"I know what you want me to do, what God wants me to do. But I have to be honest, Marie…from the depths of my soul, I hate him. And I've hated him for so long that I don't know if I could ever stop."

His face clouded over, and he turned away from her. "I've spent my life forcing the memory of that man from every part of my being. I thought if I pushed him so far down and ignored what happened, it would go away, and someday I'd be healed from my wretched past with him. I never imagined he'd be back. Never."

Marie listened as John poured out his heart. God blessed her with the gift of silence.

John wiped his eyes and gritted his teeth, looking very uncomfortable. "Frank worked construction back then, and in the summers when the storms came and I heard the thunder, I knew he would be coming home from work early. The storms always brought that man home. That fear has haunted me my entire life. I'm tired of being afraid of thunder and the memories of that man, and I'm really tired of wrestling with God. It's like trying to swim upstream at Niagara Falls—impossible and exhausting."

"So that's why." Marie nodded. "The anxiety attacks."

"I've always known the cause. I've just been helpless to stop them. It's embedded in my psyche or something. A glitch I can't seem to erase or get rid of."

Marie leaned over and kissed the top of his head. Her lip quivered as a surge of gratitude and peace overwhelmed her. She felt God's presence with them like she hadn't in a long, long time. John shared a part of his past with her. Healing was within reach.

"I don't know why God allowed this man back into my life. After everything Frank has done, I'd be lying if I said I understood it." John exhaled dramatically and glanced at the ground. "I can't guarantee anything, hon…" John paused. "But I'll meet with him."

"That's all I ask. I'll be there with you." A wry grin formed on Marie's face. "You will be unarmed, I hope?"

"I think that would be a good idea." John chuckled nervously.

"I might have to frisk you before we go." Marie smiled and slid onto the bench beside him.

John wrapped his arm around her and pulled her close. They watched the children play in the park, which seemed much brighter and more alive now. Terri Bennett walked with Ryan across the field toward their car. She looked back at John once more, and he waved at them. She seemed at peace. Her secret was out, and yet she was leaving with her son.

"You've got another thing to take care of," Marie said.

"I know." John kissed her. "I'm going to take care of it later tonight."

41

Brandon smacked the ball into the net set up in their backyard. He grabbed another ball from the pile, tossed it in the air, and smashed it into the large batting cage.

With his coat draped over his shoulder, John slowly approached his son from behind. The pines were blooming. Yellow pollen covered their lawn chairs in the backyard, giving everything a sunny hue.

John watched Brandon, who teetered precariously between boy and man. What must he think of him? How could he ever win back his son's respect? Brandon picked up another ball from the ground, sending it airborne. The familiar wooden *crack* filled their backyard. His son was so much like him, maybe too much. When John was his age, he, too, could sit for hours knocking the ball around, losing himself in the game.

Brandon eyed his father behind him. "Hey, Dad." He smacked another ball into the cage.

"Nice shot." John draped his coat over a chair. "Mind if I hit a few?"

"Sure." Brandon stepped away from the cage.

John took a ball from the ground and rolled it around in his hand. It felt good. He always liked the feel of a good baseball. He flung it into the air, quickly loaded the bat, and swung, clipping the side of the ball. "Woulda fouled that one."

"You're just a little rusty. You haven't been in the cage much lately."

"No, I haven't, have I?" John flicked another ball in the air, whipping the bat around in time to send it into the side of the net.

Brandon walked past his father and started picking up the balls in the cage and dropping them into the bucket. John knelt beside him and loaded the bucket as well.

"Brandon...about last night." John worked the ball around in his hand as he sought the right words. "I don't have any excuse or explanation other than the fact that I messed up bad. I've done a lot of dumb things that are catching up to me now, and, well, I was way out of line. I guess what I'm asking is, can you please forgive me, son?"

Picking up the bucket, Brandon walked backward, eyebrow raised. "Don't be silly, Dad. I already have. Do you wanna hit some more?"

His son's free-flowing grace enveloped John, humbling him. Brandon understood clearly what John had fought against for years. Maybe he hadn't been the terrible parent that he felt like now.

"I'd like that. I'd like that a lot." John took the bat and settled into his stance. He lobbed the ball up and *crack*—the ball sailed into the middle of the net.

"You got ahold of that one, Dad."

John's hands trembled as he put the van in park, and Marie saw sweat forming on his brow. His face was pale, and he swallowed hard. She took his hand in hers; it was cold and wet.

"Do you need to take a minute?"

"Yeah, just a second to compose." John closed his eyes and squeezed her hand tight, nearly cutting off her circulation. "I don't know if I can do this, hon. I'm not sure I'm ready."

She stroked his hand. "He's old and frail, John. Even if he wanted to, he's not able to hurt anyone now."

"I'm not afraid of what he might do." John drew in a deep breath. "I'm afraid of what *I* might do. I feel like I'm gonna explode. I need prayer."

Her hand firmly in his, she placed her other around his neck. "Lord Jesus, please be with us today. Bless these two men that they might heal. Let Your peace descend on us."

"Amen," John said, loud and faithful.

"You ready?"

"No…but I don't think I'll ever truly be ready. Let's just get this over with. It's time." He opened the door, and they stepped out into the parking lot of the Riverside Motel.

They had debated several locations to meet. A restaurant was too public, and the park didn't feel right with hordes of children running around. Their house was out of the question. Marie preferred the park, but John insisted on the motel. She conceded. She wasn't about to do anything that would stop this meeting.

They walked hand in hand to room seven. She searched John's eyes before knocking on the door. She needed to see that he was ready. The usually confident man she'd known now looked like a frightened, lost boy. He fidgeted and shuffled his feet as he tucked his shirt in, again. She couldn't imagine what he must be going through. She rapped lightly on the door.

"Come in," Frank called in a low, crackly voice.

Marie opened the door, and the afternoon sun illuminated the shadowy room but could do nothing for the musky smell. Frank balanced on the edge of the bed facing the door, like he'd been sitting there all day waiting for them. His packed bags were on the bed next to him. Both of his hands were parked on top of his cane; his chiseled face drew tight as they entered.

John trailed Marie into the room but stayed close to the door. He wedged a chair into the door, propping it open. "We could use more light in here."

Leaning hard on his cane, Frank rose to his feet. "John, I've waited a long time for this." He hobbled two steps forward and extended his hand.

John didn't reciprocate; he stepped back in a bladed stance, his arms dangling loose, but ready, at his sides.

The vein on the side of John's neck throbbed furiously. "You wanted to see me, so now you see me."

Frank locked his body and met John's glare head-on. "I dreamed of this moment for many years," he said, his voice quivering and hesitant. "I've prayed for this moment more times than I'm able to remember."

"Do you have something to say to me or not?" John said with an impatient jeer.

Marie touched John's rigid arm. "Please let him speak." This wasn't going well. John trembled as he stood in the room, still in his fighting stance. She didn't know if it was from fear or anger or both.

Frank swallowed hard. He appeared shaken but still composed. "I guess I got quite a bit to say." He cleared his throat and started again, as if he'd rehearsed this speech a thousand times, which he probably had. "John, son, I know I've hurt you—"

"Let's get something perfectly clear." John pointed right at Frank's face. "I'm not your son. You lost the right to call me that a long time ago. I'm the son of John Russell, my true father. So don't ever call me that again."

Marie moved toward John, then thought better of it and stepped back again. Although it pained her to watch John vent on Frank, she wanted to stay out of it as much as possible. Somehow, someway, they had to work this out themselves. She prayed quietly for God to intervene.

Frank swiped his hand across his face and nodded. Leaning harder on his cane, he spread his feet a little farther apart for better balance, like a tripod. "John, I have hurt you. We both know that. I can't take back the things I done. Lord knows I wish I could."

"You murdered Mom and beat me every day like a piñata, and the best you can say is 'I've hurt you'? That's the understatement of the year." His hands balled into fists as he marched toward Frank, standing nose to nose with him. Marie eased to John's side. "You were supposed to protect us, but instead you tortured us. You were supposed to nurture us, but instead you tormented us. You made my childhood a living hell. All I ever wanted was to be loved by you, and all I ever got was the bottom of your boot.

"I was just a child. How could you be so sick that you'd murder your own wife and abuse your son? Somehow I don't think 'I've hurt you' does justice to the truth. You *are* evil. That's the truth, and you can't even acknowledge it."

John turned toward Marie. "I don't even know what we're doing here."

"John, let him finish...please," Marie said in the calmest

voice she could manage, not wanting to fuel his rage more. As she fought to look calm and composed, her heart pounded so loud she was sure everyone in the room could hear it. She didn't know what she'd do if John lost it. His eyes were wild, looking at the door to Frank then back at the door again. It wasn't going well at all.

She skimmed her hand down John's arm and gently wrapped it around his clenched fist. He instinctively opened his hand and took hers. Marie pulled him back slightly, and John retreated two steps, giving Frank some space. The tension lightened…a little.

Weary from the barrage, Frank looked at the bed for a moment but remained standing.

Marie's spirit was divided. She wanted to take John away so he'd never have to embrace the feelings gushing from him like a geyser. But she also pitied the sincere, broken old man before her.

"You have something to say?" John said, his eyes closed and his head tipped back slightly.

Frank cleared his throat and took his position again. "I planned what to say for many, many years now." He shook his head, frustration and disappointment showing on his face. "The words just don't seem to work right. All I can say is that since I come to know the Savior, making things right with you has been the desire of my heart. Before I leave this earth, I want to heal what I done. I seek your forgiveness. John, I'm sorry for everything, how I hurt you, how I…killed your mama. I can't change nothing I done. All I have is my sorrow and guilt." Tears filled the creases on his face.

"You want my forgiveness? You want me to forgive you for *everything* you've done to me, Mom, and everyone on the planet?"

"Yes." Frank stood firm, though the tears flowed more freely. "More than you could ever know."

"I only have one question for you." John held up his index finger. "Just one. After you slaughtered Mom, what would you have done if you found me under the bed? Would we even be having this conversation? I think not, because I'd be dead. You would have shot me like you shot Mom, right? Tell me I'm wrong."

Frank swayed, then his knees gave way. He crumbled onto the bed, rolled his eyes toward heaven, and let out a painful gasp.

"John, stop." It was all Marie could think to say. She'd made a terrible mistake. John wasn't ready. He was still too angry, too hurt. She should have seen it coming, should have seen the signs John was giving.

"I want an answer," John said, his voice rising. "After thirty-three years, I think I deserve at least that."

"I don't know what I woulda done." Frank looked at the floor. "Anything's possible. In those days, Satan had ahold of me real bad."

"The devil-made-me-do-it defense isn't going to play well with me. I want an answer."

"I'd...I'd, you know what I woulda done."

"Speak it! I want you to admit it."

"God forgive me, I woulda shot you too, John. Lord help me." Sobs overflowed the room and into the parking lot. "I woulda killed my own son. I can't take it anymore. Jesus, please forgive me, heal me from this pain. Make it go away once and for all. Please, Lord above, make this pain stop."

"I just can't stand the sight of him anymore." John stormed out of the room into the parking lot. "I need some air."

Marie scurried to catch up to him. John lapped up the fresh

air, as if he'd been holding his breath the entire time in the room. He rubbed his face with both hands and held them there for several moments.

"Do you feel better?" Marie asked.

After a short pause, John said, "No, I don't." He wouldn't turn to look at her. He seemed to be speaking to the river.

"Haven't you been cruel enough for one day? I hope so, because it doesn't become you. I hope this isn't the new look for my husband."

John's head hung low as Frank's wailing cut through the stuffy midday air. "I still hate him, Marie. I thought I could just forgive and move on, but I look into his eyes, and all the beatings and horrific memories come flooding back. I have only contempt for him; I can't do this."

"I wonder how much you really wanted to. I love you, hon, but I think you've enjoyed hating him. It's your control, your way of getting back at him. It's your *vengeance*."

John looked at her as if he was going to respond but stayed mute. Leaning against their van, he crossed his arms. Her assessment hit its target like a cruise missile.

"What can I do, Marie? I don't know if I can change. There's been so much pain. I don't know if it's possible."

"There's only one way to find out." She laid her hands on his shoulders, which were like marble. She massaged him, hoping to loosen him up. "You owe this to yourself, to your mother, and, yes, to Frank. It's not as hard as it sounds. Just let it go. Don't use this to get back at him."

John's shoulders softened and lowered as several moments passed. "Let's go try once more."

They walked back to the room, where Frank took a tissue off the counter and blew his nose. He swung his head toward them.

"Are…are you okay?" John asked.

"I'll make it," Frank grumbled and caned his way in front of the bed. "I suppose I deserved that."

John wedged his hands into his pockets. Both men kept their distance, as if stepping any closer would send them plunging deep into the abyss. Marie prayed silently. She could see the change in John's demeanor. He was trying. That was all she could ask.

"Marie says you're sick." John remained stoic, distant.

"Ain't we all sick?" Frank wiped his nose with his hand. "Some just know it a little more than others."

John closed his eyes. "You had something you wanted to say to me?"

"Yes. Yes, I do." He regained his composure and cleared his throat. "Words can never replace what I done, what I took from you. But I want you to know my heart. Ever since I met the Lord, you have been on my heart and mind. I prayed for you every day, *every day*, that what I done could somehow be undone."

Frank's body was restless, and he couldn't hold the passion in anymore. His already dry voice cracked as he spoke. "I'm sorry for all the hurt and torment I put you through. I was never any kinda father to you. I done you wrong in every way imaginable. Even though I don't deserve it, I humbly ask for your forgiveness." Frank pressed his chin forward, ready for whatever would come his way. He'd finally been able to say what he had yearned to say for over a quarter of a century.

John appeared to be fighting to hold back the words. He didn't look angry or sad but more ambivalent, slightly bewildered. "I…I forgive you," he said, as if it had snuck out before he knew he'd said it.

"Praise God." Frank clasped his hands in front of his face.

"Praise God Almighty, the God of miracles." He dropped his cane and clambered toward John with his arms opened wide.

John pushed his hand out as fast as a punch, almost into Frank's midsection, stopping him cold.

Frank froze, his arms outstretched—waiting. He looked down at John's hand and shook it dramatically with both of his. "Thank you so much. I wanted this for so long, it's hard to believe it has happened."

Marie eyed John, not knowing what to think. He'd gone from one extreme to the other. Now he wasn't showing any emotion at all, completely detached from the situation. Something didn't seem right.

"So what do you do now?" John asked.

"I got a bus ticket to the VA in Tampa. They got a bed waiting for me. I leave this afternoon. I wasn't sure if you were gonna show or not."

"We can give you a lift if you need one," John said.

Frank nodded. "That would be nice...I suppose."

John picked up both bags and headed out the door. Marie offered Frank her arm and escorted him to their van, opened the passenger door, and helped him in while John loaded the bags in the back.

The ride to the bus station was spookily quiet. Frank would glance at John, then lower his head. A few seconds later he'd look over again, waiting for John to say something.

"Maybe we can stop somewhere and get a cup of coffee?" Marie said.

"I don't think there's enough time," John countered, focusing all of his attention on the road.

"Suppose there isn't," Frank said, a twang of disappointment in his tone.

The bus terminal was directly across from Melbourne

International Airport, which was little more than a commuter stop for small prop planes. The airport and bus station shared the same parking area.

After whipping the van into a spot, John jerked Frank's bags out of the van and hurried to the ticket window. Frank and Marie lagged behind. She asked him if he had all his medications and what room he'd be in. She wasn't sure what help the information would be, but it was better than the prolonged silence.

After Frank was all checked in, John glanced at his watch and looked at Marie. "Well, Frank...good luck." John extended his hand once more, and they shook. Frank remained somber, appearing to be at a lack for words. John took Marie's hand, and they power walked to the van.

Within minutes, John pulled out of the parking lot and drove toward home. The rush-hour traffic was extremely heavy. The crushing silence in the van made the trip to the bus station seem like an out-of-control rock concert. The van squeaked to a stop at a traffic light.

"'Good luck'?" Marie said.

John refused to look her way.

"'Good *luck*'?"

John hissed like a punctured tire and his head fell onto the steering wheel. "What do you want from me, Marie?"

"Peace. Healing. Completeness. I want it all *for* you, more than you could ever know. I want you to be able to sleep one night without screaming. I want you to truly forgive like you've been forgiven. Or have you forgotten that you were forgiven and delivered once, too? I pray that God's forgiveness bears no likeness to yours, or we're all in trouble."

"I did the best I could."

"You did lip service." Marie crossed her arms and scowled at him. "You said the right words, but nothing in your heart has changed. He's your father, John. God brought you a remarkable chance to heal, and now that chance is on a bus headed for Tampa. Because of your stubborn pride, you are never, ever going to have this opportunity again. This pain and regret will always be in the pit of your soul until you deal with it."

The light turned green, but their van didn't move; John's head was still planted on the steering wheel. Cars behind them honked.

Lord, I'm trying, he prayed while something inexplicable stirred in his soul. He pushed aside his fear and pride for a moment. *But I need help. I can't do this on my own. If this is Your will, Lord, open my hard heart. I'm tired of fighting.* His own son's unconditional mercy from the day before flashed through his mind.

"What are you gonna do, John Russell?"

42

The lobby of the bus station was vast and open like a hangar and mostly uninhabited. Frank rested on a bench along the wall, taking in the corridor that was as immense and hollow as the hole in his heart.

A picking sound echoed throughout the still depot as the young woman at the checkout counter clipped her fingernails, punishing them for the dreadful crime they must've committed. Her short blond hair was gelled up in different directions, which couldn't have been her intent. But it was the large diamond-studded nose piercing that mesmerized him.

He didn't want to look, but he had to. The world had changed a lot in thirty-three years. Maybe too much for him. He just didn't fit, and after his short journey through this new world, he didn't want to fit. But it didn't matter anymore; he wouldn't be in the world much longer.

He rubbed both hands up and down his face. For the first time since his release, he yearned to be back in his cell again. He'd heard of that happening to ex-cons, the sense of not belonging, but he never imagined feeling that way himself. At least in prison, he knew who he was, and he had a goal and the hope that it might be attained. But his purpose, like his body, was all used up now—and it definitely wasn't what he dreamed it would be.

His soul ached. He'd been ready to die for a long, long time now. He accepted his fate and was prepared to be with the Lord. But for the first time, he really wanted to die. Maybe then he'd know some relief. Maybe then his wrecked life wouldn't hound his every waking thought like a menacing, unrelenting shadow he could never outrun. Only then could he truly experience the full grace and peace of the Lord— something he yearned for daily. But peace eluded him. He prayed that his son would find that peace. It was the one prayer he had left.

Frank didn't believe in coincidence. He'd been released from prison for a reason; the circumstances were too odd for any other conclusion. He'd hoped that part of the reason would be for his healing as well. That wasn't an option now.

He prayed quietly for his son, that someday John would truly forgive him. If that happened after his death, he'd be just as happy. After meeting with Marie, learning about their family and John, Frank knew it could be worse. He'd at least been given time to see where his son's life had led—it was a good life. For that much, his prayers had been answered.

A bus rolled into the circular driveway outside the station. Even from outside the glass doors, the squealing brakes reverberated throughout the hall. Frank checked the bus number against his ticket. They matched. He collected his bag, which held two changes of clothes, an assortment of medications, his Bible, and just enough money to get him to the VA hospital.

He hobbled toward the door. The older black driver hopped from the bus and helped passengers down the steep steps one by one. Frank was the only person getting on at this stop. The driver stowed Frank's bag in a compartment along the side of the bus and assisted him up the steps.

Steadying himself by grabbing the tops of the seats, Frank shuffled to a seat in the middle of the bus. He chose a seat with no one next to him, so he could stretch out. With stops and all, the ride would take about five hours. He was going to need some space to adjust his position, or it would be a very uncomfortable ride. Frank squirmed and wiggled in his seat until he found a position that caused him the least amount of pain.

The driver jogged back onto the bus. "Well, everyone, get comfortable. Our next stop is Orlando. Then we're off to Tampa." He dropped into his chair, and the bus hissed as he let off on the air brakes. They rolled forward.

"This is a van, John, not a police car." Marie dug her fingernails into the dashboard. "It's not meant to take corners like that."

"Sorry, hon," he said, fiercely focusing on the road.

"The light's red." She cringed and closed her eyes. "It's red!"

John barreled through the intersection, stopping four lanes of traffic. Several drivers jammed on their horns.

"We're almost there." John's eyes never left the road. "Hold on!"

He skipped over a speed bump, bouncing Marie up and down, and drove into the Do Not Enter section of the bus station's circular driveway. John skidded the van in front of the bus as it was easing forward, jerking it to a halt.

Leaping from the van, John sprinted toward the bus door. He held up one finger. "Can you please open the door?"

The driver shook his head vigorously. John pulled his wallet from his pocket and flashed his badge, hoping to convince the driver he wasn't a deranged person intent on harming anyone.

The driver leaned forward and studied the badge, then opened the door. "What's the problem, Officer?"

"There's been a mistake." John skipped up the steps with Marie behind him. "A huge mistake. Frank," John called out and walked down the aisle searching the faces of the perplexed passengers. "Frank."

He rose from his seat, confusion creased his brow. "I'm here."

With two quick steps, John stopped in front of him. He paused and raised his trembling hands. "Frank...D-Dad." John's body shook as he spoke the word—the soul-freeing word. "I'm sorry. So sorry. I was so stupid." John seized him by the shoulders and embraced him. "I forgive you. I forgive everything...Father."

Frank's cane fell to the floor as he squeezed John with all the strength he had left. "Praise God," he said, his voice muffled from having his face buried in John's chest. "Praise God, the Giver of dreams, my son." Frank's knees went limp, and his body convulsed in John's arms as they wept together. John held the full weight of his father.

Marie hugged John from behind as the bus erupted into cheers.

"I don't want you to go." John pulled back and wiped the tears from his eyes. "We want you to stay with us. We'll take care of you. We're your family."

Marie brimmed with a wide smile. "We have plenty of room. We'd be honored to have you in our home."

A smile formed on Frank's creased face. "I'd like that very much."

John slid his arm underneath Frank's, and he and Marie escorted his father from the bus.

43

Terri Bennett sat on the bench again at Veterans Park, the same place she'd taken the leap of faith just two days prior. After her meeting with John Russell, she'd hoped the sense of apprehension and fear would leave her, but it hadn't. The danger of losing her son to state custody was real and palpable. Why had God so clearly told her six years ago to rescue her son from his pit only to have him in danger of going back now?

Ryan had blossomed in their family in a way that belied the circumstance of his early years, in a way that only God could have blessed him with. He had an internal light, goodness, and sensitivity to the things of the Spirit that amazed her daily. If he was ripped from their home, she feared that could be extinguished. It didn't make sense. But God had led her this far. His promise that "in all things God works for the good of those who love Him" flashed in her mind, easing her spirit some. Although she didn't understand, she would believe.

The lunchtime crowd passed back and forth along the

walkways, but Terri didn't pay any attention. The Tormentor approached her up the sidewalk at a quick pace.

Wearing blue jeans and a tan shirt, Janet Parks appeared a bit frazzled and rushed.

"You're early, Terri. How's your son? What's his name now, Ryan?"

"We've been fine for years now," she hissed. "Until you showed back up."

"Did you bring what I asked for?"

"I did." Anger seethed inside Terri like stoked coals in a furnace. She kept control, though. This was too important. "But I'll give it to you on one condition."

"What's that, little Susie homemaker?" Janet said.

"I don't ever want to see or hear from you again. This is the last payment."

"Watch that little temper of yours." Janet pointed a loaded finger at her. "All it takes is one phone call, and that beloved son of yours is back in state custody, and you will never, ever see him again."

"He's our son now, even if your *adoption* wasn't legal and proper. My husband and I have paid and paid and paid, and we're tired of being harassed and threatened time and time again. No more. We want to know that in another two or three years you won't demand more."

"This is the last time you'll hear from me," Janet said. "I just need a little vacation money. Now does that make you feel better?"

"Not really." Terri reluctantly handed her an envelope. "Just remember, what you meant for evil, God has worked for good."

"Still spouting that God stuff, huh?" Janet opened the envelope and counted the cash. "I thought you'd be over that by now. Looks like everything's here."

"It is. I'm good to my word."

"This should just about cover everything I need," Janet said. "Well, you can go back now to your quaint little life."

"Do not contact me again."

"Or what?" Janet's arms fell to her sides, and she glared at Terri. "What will you do if I come back?"

Terri gritted her teeth and battled the overwhelming urge to pounce on the woman right here. But she stayed silent and composed.

"That's what I thought." Janet walked toward the parking lot. "See you later." Oblivious to all else around her, Janet obtained a more detailed count of the cash as she approached her car in the parking lot.

"Well, well, well, John, look what the cat dragged in," Tim said, an enormous smile pasted on his face. "Hello, Ms. Parks. It's so nice to see you. And might I say you look lovely today."

"What are you two doing here, stalking me or something?" she said, attempting to hide the envelope behind her leg. "It appears I'll have to call my attorney again. This harassment is going to stop."

"No need for that, ma'am," Tim said. "Your attorney is waiting for you at the station."

"What?" Janet's condescension drained from her face.

"He's been with us all morning," John said, "spilling his guts about the illegal adoption of Dylan Jacobs to Terri and Glenn Bennett and bilking state monies for his care. You know, how you and Jesse Lee Morgan are cousins and worked this whole scheme out together. Any of that sound familiar? Seems your faithful attorney wants to cut a deal. Evidently, lawyers don't do well in prison, so he's singing like Celine Dion."

Robbie pulled up next to them in a van. "That was absolutely fantastic video and audio, John." Robbie held up the camera. "It was like watching a soap opera. Terri did a great job, don't you think? I believe she's a natural, and she'll be a fantastic witness."

Terri stood just behind them. She pulled the microphone from underneath her shirt and dangled it for Janet to see.

Relief swept over Terri as the specter of fear that had haunted and controlled her for years evaporated under the cleansing light of truth. The woman who had plagued her peace for so long suddenly seemed very small.

Tim twirled handcuffs around his finger. "We've been doing some detecting. And ma'am, it gives me pleasure beyond words to inform you that you're under arrest."

The tiny shrew of a woman clenched her teeth.

Robbie pulled up a palm-sized digital camera. "Say cheese." She snapped a photo of John and Tim cuffing Janet. "This will make a great screensaver."

Janet growled.

"Take as much time as you need," Alan said as he and John left his office. "Let us know if there's anything we can do. The Jacobs case is cleaned up nicely, the governor and everyone else up the chain is happy, so we're all caught up here."

Alan slapped John on the back. "I have to tell you, I never really thought we'd find that kid alive. Good things do happen every once in a while. So don't worry about anything here. Just go home and take care of family business. That's most important."

"Thanks, Alan. A few weeks should be enough time."

The back door slammed shut, and Tim and Robbie escorted a handcuffed prisoner down the hallway. The prisoner's shirt was torn, his hair was a mess, and pieces of grass covered his hair and face like garland clinging to his sweaty, grimy skin.

"John...John!" Tim called as he skipped toward him. "You should have seen it." He dragged the prisoner over to where John and Alan stood. "We have warrants on Jackrabbit here, we check him out, and he takes off running. Now tell 'em, Robbie. Tell 'em what happened next."

"You made me tell everyone at the scene, in the parking lot, and on the way up here." She rolled her eyes and sighed. "I'm surprised you didn't make me announce it over the radio."

"Hush that." Tim waved at her. "Just tell 'em what happened next. Jackrabbit here takes off running and I..."

"Porter ran him down," Robbie said in her most monotone voice, looking at Alan and John for sympathy.

"Like a dog." Tim smiled infectiously. "You forgot that part. I ran him down like a dog. Two blocks and I had him. Tackled him in some old woman's front yard. Like a dog on a bone." Tim's eyes twinkled with the brilliance of a rookie cop making his first arrest. "Been jogging every day. I've dropped twelve pounds." He slapped his noticeably shrinking belly. "I'm gettin' back in shape. Yep. Tim Porter's back, baby. And it feels great."

"Well, it's nice to have you back," Alan said, his hands on his hips. "But why don't you two get him *back* into booking, so we can process him. We should be on the news in ten minutes." He checked his watch. "Make that eight."

"Robbie," Tim said, "can you take him to booking? I'll be there in a minute. I need to talk with John."

"Sure. Besides, if I have to listen to that story one more time, it could be considered cruel and unusual punishment." She walked Grassyhead down the hallway.

"You look great, John," Tim said, still basking in the afterglow.

"Thanks. I'm a little tired, but I feel a lot better. When I get a chance, I'll fill you in on the details." John fumbled with his keys. "I also wanna thank you for helping me get my head straight. You're a good friend."

"Don't be ridiculous, Russell. That's what partners do. We look out for each other. Just let me know if there's anything else I can do. Remember, 24/7. I'm available."

"I appreciate it." John grabbed several files from his desk to take home.

"By the way," Tim winked, "it's good to have you back, too."

John smiled and sat at his desk for a moment, making sure he'd taken everything he'd need for his time off.

"All right, people." Alan turned on the TV in the center of the cubicles. "It's showtime." Robbie joined them, her prisoner securely in a cell. The news anchorman read the top story of the night:

"Dylan Jacobs has been found—alive. To protect his identity, authorities won't say where he's living at this time, but they did say that Dylan's in good health and has been living with an adopted family for the past six years. The governor said that he's ecstatic Dylan is safe, and he will be issuing a formal statement at the end of the day.

"In a related story, former Department of Family Services worker Janet Parks has been arrested today on fraud, child endangerment, extortion, and human trafficking charges. She will be arraigned tomorrow in a Fort Lauderdale courtroom. Her attorney, Keith Wilson, has been picked up as well and is said to be cooperating with authorities.

"Our sources tell us that by the time the investigation is finished, at least two more people already in custody will face additional charges."

The image on the screen showed Robbie and Tim escorting Janet in handcuffs from their car into the county jail.

"I love my job." Tim danced in a circle. "I never liked that woman, and I truly love my job."

Alan turned off the TV. "Good work, people. That should keep the bigwigs upstairs off our backs…at least until the next case."

The crowd dispersed, and Tim sauntered to his desk and sat down, a smile etched across his face. He picked up the picture of his daughter, studying it for several moments. He glanced over at John at his desk. Tim closed his eyes and exhaled loudly. After he reopened them, he picked up the telephone. Quickly pecking the number, he held the phone to his ear.

"Hello, Ruby?" Tim paused and ran his fingers across her picture. "It's Dad." Several seconds of silence passed. He leaned back in his chair. "Oh, don't do that. Don't cry, baby. I've missed you, too."

44

John dabbed the perspiration from Frank's forehead with a damp towel as he lay in his bed. In the week and a half since his father moved in with them, Frank's condition deteriorated to the point he could hardly stand under his own power. John bought a wheelchair for him, and the boys were good about pushing him to and fro through the house.

Although physically Frank was worsening, his mind remained acute. He fought for every second with his son. He and John spent hours upon hours reliving their lives. Catching up on thirty-three years proved to be an exhausting but rewarding process.

John savored these moments and let Frank ramble on as long as his strength would carry him. He learned of Frank's service in Korea, some of the battles he participated in. And Frank shared how Jesus had entered his life during the darkest days, freeing him from the worst prison he'd ever known—his own sins.

Frank told of those he ministered to in prison. At first many were skeptical of his conversion and other prisoners still wanted to fight him as a badge of honor, but no matter how much he was taunted, he refused to fight. He would not bring shame onto his God. Slowly, Frank developed into the unofficial pastor for Union. Some still mocked him, but many came to him in confidence. He often prayed with other inmates and even some of the guards. The Lord used him in ways Frank never imagined.

"Son," Frank said. "I praise God for what He's done with you and your family...in spite of me."

"Don't talk like that, Pop." John took his hand. "This has all been dealt with. The past is behind us. The Lord has healed us from that."

"I know." Frank cleared his throat. "But I can't tell you how I feared you might turn out like me with the drinking and the violence—just like I did with my dad. He was a hard, mean man, much meaner when he drank. I grew up to be just like him, maybe worse, even though I didn't want to."

Frank motioned to John for the glass of water on the table next to the bed. John passed it to him, and Frank took several sips. "When I was serving my time, many a night I prayed that the Lord would take hold of you and guide you and keep you from the sins of our family. I cried out to Him to keep that awful legacy far from you. The Lord is good. "

"He is good indeed." John pulled his chair closer to his father's bed. John was thankful for the prayers of his father, knowing full well that his life could have turned out radically different. A picture of Frank emerged that John never knew. His father's complexities were laid bare before John, clearing his hazy image of Frank, finally making sense. Not an excuse for his sins, but a simple understanding of the man.

Frank clasped John's hand with both of his. "I'm proud of you, and I love you, son."

John's heart tingled with unexpected feelings for the man he'd sworn to hate. Just not hating him anymore would have been enough, but John's spirit swelled with a love for his father that he hadn't thought possible. The grace and mercy of God was the only reasonable explanation.

"I love you, too, Pop." John squeezed his hands. "Now what can I do for you? There must be something that you want, something we can do while we have time."

"Not much time." Frank grunted in his hoarse voice. He glanced at John with a mischievous glint in his eye. "But there is something."

He took his father's hand. "Tell me and we'll do it."

"I feel bad that I never took you nowhere." Frank coughed into a tissue. "I always wished I woulda took you fishing with me."

"Fishing?"

"You got a pond out back. I wanna go fishing with you and my grandsons."

"Dad, I don't know." John pulled back. "I don't think you're up to it."

"Of course I'm not up to it," he wheezed. "I'm dying. So do me this thing. Let's go fishing…right now."

Frank peeled off the sheets and struggled to sit up. Leaning forward, he groaned as he transferred himself into the wheelchair by the bed.

John shook his head. "You're stubborn, Pop, but I guess we're going fishing." John situated Frank in the chair, folded several quilts on his lap, and tucked them around his legs. Even though it was summer, Frank complained of the bitter cold of the room. He didn't have any cushion left on his bones to keep him warm.

"Brandon. Joshua. We're heading to the pond. Get the

fishing gear." He wheeled his father into the hallway and through the kitchen. The boys followed behind.

Marie took a break from washing the dishes to watch the spectacle.

"John, do you think that's such a good idea?"

"Don't worry, missy. I'll make sure they don't get in no trouble." Frank grinned at her. His head bobbled as the wheelchair rolled over the tracks of the sliding-glass door and onto the patio.

John rocked the chair back, lifting the front wheels off the ground, and forced the wheelchair through the soggy grass of the backyard about a hundred yards to the pond. Frank jiggled with each bump they hit, but his smile remained plastered on his face.

Affectionately named Lake Russell by the boys, the pond was small, more like a giant puddle; John was barely able to keep fish stocked in it. Sometimes during the extremely dry years, it was little more than a glorified hole in the ground. But this year the waterline was high, and the pond bubbled with minnows, speckled perch, and bream. Cattails lined the perimeter of the pond like a fence, except for the area they used to fish or to skip rocks. John parked Frank at the water's edge and locked the wheels in place.

Brandon and Joshua sprinted from the house with the tackle box and poles. John set up Frank's pole, complete with bobber and a morsel of cheese fashioned onto the hook as bait. He then helped Joshua get his pole ready; Brandon could take care of his own.

Frank beamed as he concentrated on his line, his hand poised to reel in his catch. His bobber dipped once, then again, concentric circles racing toward the shore. Frank barked out a laugh as he set the hook, and his rod bowed and wiggled as he did battle with the tiny bream. "I got one. I think I got one."

Joshua kicked off his shoes and tiptoed into the water, following the line out to their trophy. He pulled the fish from the water and held it high. "Good catch, Grandpa," Joshua said, the fish flipping around in the air.

Frank hacked several times until he spat into his handkerchief. His face changed from exhilaration to panic as he labored for air.

"Okay, everyone, we need to get Grandpa back inside. I think we've caught our limit." John feared that they'd pushed too hard. The discomforting knot of the inevitable writhed in his stomach as he watched his father battle to breathe.

Frank waved dismissively at John, then motioned for him to come closer. "You said you was gonna be a preacher, didn't you?" Frank said in little more than a wheeze. He gazed at the body of water before him, his eyes fixed on the brilliant pool.

John knelt to talk to Frank face-to-face. "Yeah, Pop, I was ordained. Why do you ask?"

"I been serving the Lord for twenty-seven years now." He rubbed his bristly chin, giving the impression of sandpaper. "And I never been baptized. They wouldn't let us have a baptismal at the prison. Maybe they figured we might drown each other in it." He coughed out a laugh.

John cocked his head. "You can't be serious? Here? In this pond? It's barely waist deep, and I don't think it would be a good idea. You're not strong enough."

"I know I ain't strong enough." Frank spit on the ground and wiped his chin with his handkerchief. "That's the whole point." He squeezed John's forearm. "I don't have much life left. This is the one thing on this earth left for me to do. And I want you, my son, to baptize me right here in this pond." He pointed his crooked finger toward the now placid waters of Lake Russell.

"I'll help you, Dad." Brandon slid both shoes off with his feet. "We can do this."

"Me, too! Me, too!" Joshua jumped up and down, already soaked.

John glanced behind him and shook his head. He pulled his wallet from his back pocket and tossed it behind the wheelchair. "Joshua, go get your mother. She should see this. Brandon, I am gonna need your help."

Joshua sprinted toward the house, kicking droplets of mud behind his flurried feet.

Removing the quilt from Frank's lap, John draped it over the back of the chair. He bent down and slid one hand underneath Frank's legs; the other he wrapped around his back. "Hold my neck."

Frank hung his feeble arms around John's neck. John lifted him from the wheelchair and took a second to steady himself. Frank's legs dangled like two broken twigs in the wind. "Here we go." John carried his father into the water, which was warm and inviting. Frank's face was serious and purposeful as he clung to his son. Brandon followed his father, keeping his hand on John's back, supporting him.

John waded in about fifteen feet, the water tickling his waist. Brandon trudged through the chest-high water and positioned himself next to his father.

With Joshua leading her by the hand, Marie arrived at the water's edge and locked eyes with John. As he held the full weight of his father in his arms, he mouthed to her, *Thank you.*

She nodded, smiled, and wrapped her arm around Joshua as they watched in amazement from the shore.

"Pop, I'm gonna ease you down now." Frank's already wispy body stayed buoyant as John lowered him into the water. His soaked T-shirt went transparent, exposing Frank's gaunt skeleton.

"Put one arm under his legs, then the other up here on his back," John said to Brandon. John waited until he was in place.

"Ready, Dad?" The emotion reverberated in John's voice. All the classes he'd taken in seminary couldn't have prepared him for this moment. He fought to stay composed as he held his father. "Do you think you can go all the way under?"

"There ain't no going halfway." He scrunched his face tight, preparing for immersion. "I been ready for this for a long, long time."

"Frank Moore...my father, I baptize you in the name of the Father, the Son, and the Holy Ghost." John carefully submerged Frank and quickly pulled him back up, raining heavenly drops of freedom upon the three of them.

Frank gasped. Wiping his face, he looked at John, then Brandon. "Praise God! Praise God, my son." He raised a hand skyward. "That was great. Better than I ever imagined. Thank You, Lord Jesus."

Frank pulled Brandon and John tight, his body trembled. "Thank you so much. This was just perfect."

Marie jogged ahead of the damp crew and hurried in the patio door. She grabbed a load of fresh towels from the closet and headed to the back porch. As she passed through the kitchen, she could see John, Frank, and the boys making their way through the yard toward the house.

John pushed Frank in the wheelchair, with the boys flanked on either side. Frank had a blanket wrapped around him, and his smile could be seen from the kitchen. They were all drenched and giggling about it.

As she struggled to keep her composure, Marie quietly thanked the Lord for nothing less than a miracle. Wielding violence and dysfunction as his weapons, Satan had destroyed the Moore family in a way that seemed impossible to rebuild. Jesus had gently applied the balm to their wounds that allowed them to live again—as a family, if only for a short time.

The waterlogged gaggle broke the threshold of the back door as boisterous retellings of Frank's baptism filled the kitchen. Marie handed towels to the boys, and she and John wheeled Frank to his room and helped him dry off. John lifted Frank from the chair again and eased him into bed. He wheezed in delight.

As she returned to the kitchen to get dinner started, John snuck up behind her and kissed the nape of her neck, causing her to arch back. Sliding his hand across her stomach, he pulled her close and kissed her again. The goose bumps fluttered along her skin as she inhaled and rose to her tiptoes. Too much time had passed since he'd held her like that, since she felt his intimate embrace. She missed it. She missed John.

Twisting to face him, she threw her arms around his neck. "Hey, you better watch that."

"Watch what?" Their lips greeted each other again.

"Dad, Grandpa needs some help." Brandon rounded the corner into the kitchen just in time to see them kiss again. Rolling his eyes and shaking his head, he pivoted on one foot and headed back down the hall. "He'll be there in a minute, Grandpa. They're…busy."

45

Frank moaned and tossed his head from side to side, as if in a fitful dream, then settled down again. He had been unconscious for almost a day and a half. The hospice organization had helped John get the equipment to set up the room. An IV dripped the pain medications he needed. A nurse spent most of the days with him. At night, she was on call and could arrive at a moment's notice if necessary.

John and Marie did everything they could to make Frank's last days as comfortable as possible. A normal man would have already succumbed to the unavoidable, but Frank was a fighter. He was hanging on for every last moment with John and the family. Part of him understood. After so many years in prison, estranged from anything resembling familial love, Frank soaked up every bit of affection and attention that John, Marie, and the boys had to offer. But it pained him to see his father suffer.

John was unshaven and dressed only in shorts and a T-shirt. He collapsed onto the chair next to Frank's bed, waiting. Closing his eyes, John recited the Twenty-Third Psalm aloud. In one of their late-night talks, Frank told him he would often meditate on that chapter in his darkest days in prison. John felt it appropriate now.

As John prayed for his father, his thoughts drifted back to his mother and that awful night. Something in his spirit had shifted. He was now able to remember her fully. Not just her horrific death, but small memories flooded his mind, things he thought long forgotten—the smell of her hair, the feel of her hand in his, her soft voice when she called his name...*Frankie.*

He immersed himself in memories of her without the rage and anguish that had kept them at bay. There was pain, to be sure. But the Lord had given him the gift of time with her again.

John scooted his chair closer to the bed and took Frank's cold and limp hand. "Pop, I know you're fighting. I know you want to stay as long as you can. But it's okay. You can let go. We'll be together again, my father. I give you my word that we'll catch up on everything later, in a place without pain, without misery or despair. In a place that's calling your name, Pop." John choked as he spoke it. "You need to rest now and wait for all of us. Everything is going to be okay here."

Marie and Brandon walked in.

"Y'all are up early." John rubbed the tears from his eyes with his free hand, still holding Frank's in the other.

"I couldn't sleep much," Marie said.

"Dad, you look tired. Why don't you get some sleep, and Mom and I will watch Grandpa for a while?"

Frank's breathing was labored, exaggerated. Marie felt his forehead. "Hmm...cold and clammy. How long has he been like this?"

"Most of the evening. It's been a really tough night."

Marie took John by the hand. Dread blanketed her face. "I think we need to get the hospice nurse here. It could be any time."

Brandon put his arm around John's neck and pulled him close. The three held each other.

Pastor Kevin stood in front of the small graveside crowd with Cheri at his side. The flag-draped coffin was covered by a canvas canopy. It threw just enough shade to shield Kevin and Cheri from the afternoon sun.

John, Marie, and the boys were all dressed in black and sat in metal folding chairs facing the grave. They were flanked by Alan, Robbie, and Tim. Gloria sat behind them and was crying before the service even started. Several other people from church filled the dozen chairs lined up.

It was cooler than usual for a summer afternoon. Dark, swollen clouds obscured the sun, which peeked out for several moments only to be covered again by the gloomy, foreboding armada of thunder clouds sailing toward them from the coast.

Kevin cleared his throat, opened his Bible, and read of the prodigal son's return and how his father greeted him with open arms, celebrating his homecoming. Kevin turned to the crowd, "Frank Moore probably understood better than any of us the depth and breadth of the Lord's forgiveness and healing power. He fought the good fight and ran the race to the end. As Frank could have told you, it's not how you start the race that matters, but instead, it's how you finish. Frank finished strong and is walking with our Lord now."

As Kevin spoke his brief words of comfort, John bowed his head. *Thank You, Jesus, for the time with my father and reconciling us. May I never lose my way again.*

He thought of his father, not the tortured images from his childhood, but rather of the man he'd grown to know and love in such a short amount of time. While John suffered from the sting of loss, something else was at work in him. The hole in his heart, which had been there for as long as he could remember, had been filled with reconciliation and healing.

John wept more than he thought possible as his father's casket was lowered into the ground. He wept for what he had lost; he wept for what he had found; he wept because all things were made new again.

After the service, Cheri and Kevin stood in line with John, Marie, and the boys and received the hugs and compassion from the small crowd. Tim eased in front of John. "I'm sorry for your loss." They shook hands, and John was surprised when Tim pulled him close and hugged him. "We're all here for you, my friend."

Gloria slobbered over John and then Marie; neither was able to make out her words, but her intent was clear. She hurried to her car, sobbing the entire way.

Alan and Robbie filed by, extending hands and hope to them.

A clap of thunder shook the air like the armaments of war. A thin veil of rain passed across the grave and sprinkled on the canvas, beating a chaotic cadence.

Some of the mourners offered quick condolences and jogged off to waiting cars. Cheri, Kevin, Alan, Robbie, and Tim surrounded the Russells, and everyone rushed to open umbrellas. A brilliant flash was followed by an echoing boom from just behind them.

"Give me the keys, Dad." Small bands of rain trailed down Brandon's face. "I'll open the van door for you."

John placed his hands on the sides of Brandon's head as another round of thunder cracked in the distance. "It's okay, son. It's really okay."

John stepped out from the protection of Marie's umbrella

and spread his arms to the heavens. Rain danced on his face like a thousand angel kisses. John laughed as the next rumble passed by, his hands still skyward, unwavering. His mind remained clear and calm, unfazed by the squall.

Lightning struck again and was followed by a sound like enormous chains snapping and crashing to the ground, freeing him forever from the crippling grip of the past. His heart leaped, not from fear but from joy and exhilaration, forgiveness and thanksgiving.

Marie dropped her umbrella in the mud and held John from behind. The two stood together in the storm. Rain gushed down from heaven, drenching them with the cool, pure, cleansing waters from above.

Dear Reader,

I hope you've enjoyed this story and that it has spoken to you on some level. I first came up with the idea after hearing a radio broadcast in which Dr. Dobson spoke of a man in his forties who was still tormented by the memories of abuse by his father. I was intrigued by how a man close to my age could be held hostage by such distant recollections.

Then I reflected on some of the areas in my life and my walk with Christ. And in a more honest moment, I realized that I, too, held onto many things from years past that should have been dealt with long before—although certainly not as dramatic as what John Russell experienced. I wondered if other Christians like me might be clinging to old wounds and scars a little too tightly, not allowing the Lord to complete His healing in their lives. As I worked through those thoughts and emotions, the story line for *Rolling Thunder* was born.

I added that experience to the countless tragic cases of child abuse and neglect I've investigated through my seventeen years in law enforcement. Crimes against children can bring even the most street-hardened police officers to tears. The suffering of the innocent draws a special ire for those who investigate crime, and I believe Jesus certainly had something to say about people who cause little ones to stumble (Matthew 18:6).

My hope is that you've been moved by this story to pray for and support the many dedicated police officers, family services agencies, and foster-care families who pick up the pieces of the shattered lives in our fallen world, as well as the numerous children who suffer so needlessly.

Thank you for joining me on this trek, and I would love to hear your feedback. Please feel free to contact me at my website: www.copwriter.com.

Sincerely,
Mark Mynheir

DISCUSSION QUESTIONS

1. What do you think of Marie's decision to help Frank in spite of John's wishes? Was she being disloyal and disrespectful to her husband? Why or why not?

2. Frank's parole after initially being sentenced to death row parallels God's pardon for our sins. What do you think of jailhouse or deathbed conversions?

3. Frank chose to pursue John's forgiveness even though John wouldn't give it. How far should we go to right wrongs from the past? What should we do if the person wronged won't accept our apology or offer to heal?

4. During his investigation, John was thrust into several violent confrontations. As a Christian police officer, was he justified in using force if necessary to arrest someone?

5. Being consumed with his own anger and sin, John was unable to see Dylan Jacobs, who was in front of him the entire time. Can our own sins blind us to the obvious, too?

6. The generational sins of the Moore family—violence and alcoholism—were a driving force throughout the story. Is there any such "baggage" you might be carrying around? How has that affected your life or those around you? Have you given God the chance to heal you?

7. As John resisted the Holy Spirit by refusing to forgive his father, other areas of his life began to unravel. Is this true in the Christian life? If a believer is in rebellion to the will of the Father, how can this seep into other areas of his or her life?

8. The theme of adoption is present throughout the story. John was rescued from a violent home, and Dylan, the son of a prostitute, was neglected and sold with malevolent intent. Both were saved from their situations and placed into loving, nurturing homes. How do these adoptions compare with the ultimate adoption God performed on us through His Son, Jesus Christ? (Read John 1:12–13; Galatians 3:26, 29.)

CROSSINGS®
THE BOOK CLUB FOR TODAY'S CHRISTIAN FAMILY

A Letter to Our Readers

Dear Reader:

In order that we might better contribute to your reading enjoyment, we would appreciate your taking a few minutes to respond to the following questions. When completed, please return to the following:

Andrea Doering, Editor-in-Chief
Crossings Book Club
401 Franklin Avenue, Garden City, NY 11530

You can post your review online! Go to www.crossings.com and rate this book.

Title _____ Author _____

1 Did you enjoy reading this book?

❑ Very much. I would like to see more books by this author!

❑ I really liked_____

❑ Moderately. I would have enjoyed it more if_____

2 What influenced your decision to purchase this book? Check all that apply.

        ❑ Cover
        ❑ Title
        ❑ Publicity
        ❑ Catalog description
        ❑ Friends
        ❑ Enjoyed other books by this author
        ❑ Other _____

3 Please check your age range:

      ❑ Under 18   ❑ 18-24
      ❑ 25-34   ❑ 35-45
      ❑ 46-55   ❑ Over 55

4 How many hours per week do you read? _____

5 How would you rate this book, on a scale from 1 (poor) to 5 (superior)?
_____

Name_____

Occupation_____

Address_____

City_____ State_____ Zip_____

Shocking Murder Destroys Deputy's Sense of Justice

Don't miss KATHY HERMAN'S compelling new Seasport Suspense
series, full of thrills and intrigue—and lessons about life and faith.

A Shred of Evidence
by Kathy Herman

"When I get myself out of bed
an hour early in order to
keep reading a book, I
know I'm hooked! But I
also squirmed as this
supense novel probed that
uncomforatble gray zone
between what's 'concern'
and what's 'gossip.'"

—NETA JACKSON
Author of The Yada Yada
Prayer Group series.

Ellen Jones is enjoying a leisurely lunch at Gordy's Crab Shack when she
overhears a private conversation at the next table—and disturbing accusations
about her friend's husband. Reluctant to go to her friend with hearsay, yet
compelled to search for answers, Ellen stumbles onto information that gives her
chills—facts too frightening to keep to herself. Is a child in jeopardy? That
question drives Ellen to delve deeper into a stranger's past. How can she turn a
blind eye when she has information that might prevent a heartbreaking tragedy?
ISBN 1-59052-348-2

Available NOW!

Hotter than the eyes of hell...

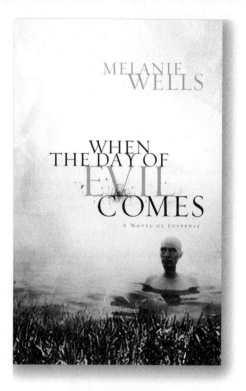

"I saw the first fly alight on the edge of my plate during supper. This was no ordinary fly. It was huge. The size of a small Volkswagen. I could have painted daisies on it and sold rides to small children."

When the Day of Evil Comes by MELANIE WELLS

School is back in session, but for psychology professor Dylan Foster, the promise of a new semester is dying in the heat of the late Texas summer. First, there is the bizarre encounter with a ghastly pale stranger. Then her mother's engagement ring turns up—the same ring that was buried with her mother two years before. Soon, Dylan's carefully ordered world is unraveling, one thread at a time. She is about to get a crash course in spiritual warfare—and a glimpse of her own small but significant role in a vast eternal conflict. But when the dust settles, will anything be left of her life as she knows it?

ISBN 1-59052-426-8

COMING JUNE 2005!

Can Money, Fame, and Power Buy Happiness?

Dark Star: Confessions of a Rock Idol
by CRESTON MAPES

Everett Lester and his band, DeathStroke, ride the crest of a wave that has catapulted them to superstardom. But the longer they're immersed in fame, wealth, and power, the more drugs, alcohol, and loose discontentment threaten to swallow Everett whole. He's headed down a perilous road of no apparent return when he's charged with the murder of his personal psychic. The only hope he can cling to, his only reason for living, comes from Kansas. The compelling letters from a Christian woman cut straight to Everett's empty heart and threaten a fulfillment he's never known. But what if he's found guilty of murder? Will he recognize the spiritual battle that's raging for his soul?
ISBN 1-59052-472-1

COMING JULY 2005!